On the Line

T0351975

On the Line

On the Line

VICTORIA DENAULT

FOREVER
YOURS

New York Boston

Forever Yours
Hachette Book Group
1290 Avenue of the Americas, New York, NY 10104
forever-romance.com
twitter.com/foreverromance

First published as an ebook and as a print on demand: December 2016

Forever Yours is an imprint of Grand Central Publishing. The Forever Yours name and logo are trademarks of Hachette Book Group, Inc.

The publisher is not responsible for websites (or their content) that are not owned by the publisher.

The Hachette Speakers Bureau provides a wide range of authors for speaking events. To find out more, go to www.hachettespeakersbureau.com or call (866) 376-6591.

ISBNs: 978-1-4555-4126-3 (print on demand edition), 978-1-4555-4127-0 (ebook)

E3-20161010-DANF

*For my brother Alan. Thanks for always believing
in me. I believe in you too.*

Acknowledgments

To Jack, Mom, and Dad—thank you for giving me the time, space and support I need to write, even on vacations, which is exactly where I am right now as I write this.

To my amazing agent, Kimberly Brower. I've always wanted to win a lottery and I totally did with you. Thank you for being my trusted navigator on this incredible journey.

Thank you to my editor, Leah Hultenschmidt, for making a crazy schedule easy to conquer and for your keen eye and witty one-liners. To everyone at Forever, thanks for giving me and my Hometown Players a wonderful home.

I'm forever grateful to all the fellow authors, the bloggers and Social Butterfly PR, who have been kind and supportive with all my books. Thanks, Crystal from East Coast Mermaid, for sharing my books and your happy, beach-loving spirit with the world. The universe needs more mermaids like you. Major love to Katherine H. and Bev T., who proudly and passionately promote me and my books, and to my college girls Desiree and Jenn D who are always so eager for the next book. It makes my day!

Prologue

Stephanie

Jessie Caplan and Jordan Garrison finally tied the knot. Their wedding was so amazing I didn't want it to end. The bride was breathtakingly beautiful and her groom looked happier than I had ever seen any man look. Ever.

It was crazy that the calm, confident, beaming guy who got married tonight was the same train wreck playboy I met years ago when he first started playing hockey in Seattle with my brother, Sebastian. The whole night, from the dusk ceremony to the reception under the stars by the lake, had so much love you could feel it in the air.

"Explain to me again why I'm on a canoe in the middle of the lake rehashing the wedding that we just attended?" Avery asks.

I lift my head to level him with a hard stare. "The canoe was your idea," I remind him, and tip my head back to look up at the starry sky. "Being teamless has turned you into a criminal."

He laughs at that. The sound is deep and soothing, but it rocks the rickety canoe we "borrowed" from a dock. I spent a little bit of time with Avery Westwood while we were both in Seattle, and I have never seen him so relaxed. Maybe being a free agent agrees with him.

When he walked into the pre-wedding cocktail party Friday, it was the first time I'd thought of him since he left Seattle and went back to his hometown of New Brunswick for the summer. After congratulating Jordan and Jessie, he walked right over to me, and he hasn't really left my side all weekend. It was probably just because we are two of the only single people here, but I was thrilled because he was different from the typical, distant Avery.

We were walking back to the hotel from the wedding reception, along the edge of the giant lake that sits in the center of Silver Bay, Maine, when Avery spotted the canoe and suggested we take it out. "The stars will be amazing out there and I bet it's cooler," he enticed.

I agreed because I wanted a break from the muggy weather, I wanted to see stars and…I wanted to keep hanging out with Avery. Out of the all Winterhawks players, or hockey players in general, Avery would not be most people's first choice for a fun date. He doesn't exactly have a reputation as being someone who knows what fun is. But tonight, I had a blast.

Even though he was my brother's teammate, I never felt like I knew that much about him; no one really did. I only knew the basics: he was quiet, hardworking and superstitious. Then one day I'd learned he was also uptight, self-centered and a complete puppet to the whims of his father, who was also his business manager. That revelation came when I found out that one of his closest college friends had developed an addiction to painkillers. Avery's biggest concern was how it made him look, so he walked out on his friend to make sure his image wasn't tarnished. That's when my opinion of Avery turned from indifferent to unfavorable. And unlike everyone else in his life, I wasn't afraid to tell him. When I confronted him, surprisingly, he didn't get offended or argue. He agreed he was an ass and then he went out and made things right with his friend, which made me realize he wasn't all bad.

He shifts gently in the canoe and it rocks again, jilting me out of my reverie. He's leaning back against one end of the canoe and I'm against the other. Our feet—mine bare because heels suck, and his in expensive dress shoes covered in sand—are resting next to each other in the center. He reaches up with one arm and points. "See those stars that kind of form a horseshoe? There."

I follow the tip of his finger with my eyes. "Yeah."

"That's the Gemini constellation," he explains.

"That's my zodiac sign!"

He tips his head forward and smiles. "I know. That's why I'm showing you."

He knows my zodiac sign? He laughs at my expression of shock. "You mentioned it on one of our runs."

Right. The running. For the last couple months of the hockey season, Avery had jogged in the park near my apartment, where I always worked out. We would cross each other on the running trail and he would always turn around and run with me.

"I'd point out your constellation, but you barely talked on our runs," I quip with a teasing smile.

"I talked. I asked you questions," he replies.

"Why is that?"

He thinks about it for a minute, his left hand hanging over the side of the canoe, skimming the water with his fingertips. "Sometimes it feels like I talk for a living. I liked listening to you. And besides, if you want to know anything about me, you can probably Google it."

He's right. Sort of. But there's got to be more to him than what he gives away in press interviews. I pretend to dig my phone out of my purse as I say, "Please hold. Googling your astrological sign."

"Aries." He chuckles at me. "Any other questions? Ask away. I'm an open book."

"You are this weekend," I agree, and look back up at the twinkling sky. "It's a pleasant surprise." He was being witty, sarcastic and fun. He had opinions—and he was sharing them in candid, honest ways that I'd never seen him do with anyone else.

I look at him instead of tilting it back to the stars again. "So you're definitely not re-signing with Seattle?"

He's still looking up at the stars, the moonlight cascading down over his perfect skin, making his slight summer tan look more golden. His dark hair glints and his damn lashes are so thick and dark I can see them flutter from across the canoe even in this low light. In his dark summer suit he looks like model in a Ralph Lauren ad right now.

"In forty-eight hours I'll be a free agent. I'll be open to any team, anywhere," he explains, and there's not even a drop of excitement in his tone.

"And where does Avery Free Agent Westwood want to go?" I ask as I realize how much I'm going to dread running now.

"Los Angeles or Manhattan," he answers, again with no joy or excitement

"Shouldn't someone be excited about such a big life change, especially when he is the one choosing it?" I blurt out bluntly as the cool breeze picks up a little. It feels good so I close my eyes, lift my hair and let it wrap around my bare shoulders and neck.

"It's not a personal choice. It's a business decision," I hear him answer. "There's no point having feelings about it."

I open my eyes and give him a bit of a glare.

"What?" he asks.

"That was the first typical Avery answer you've given to me this entire weekend," I explain. "I don't like it."

"Okay." He pauses and takes a deep breath, rubbing the back of his neck for a moment. "I would love to stay in Seattle, but my father explained it wasn't what's best for my brand and, like it or not, if I want to have options after hockey, I need to do what's best for the brand, so I am. Even if it sucks and, yes, it sucks."

"Much better." I smile and close my eyes again, enjoying another breeze. "You sound like a human being again."

"That doesn't come easy for me," he admits, his tone sheepish. "Being human. Unfiltered and honest."

"I like it."

"That's why I'm trying," he replies.

I open my eyes and find him staring at me. Intently. So intently I feel like I should blush, but I don't know why. He shifts a little and shifts again. I grab the sides of the canoe in panic and he grins. "Don't worry, I won't drown you."

"I would pick L.A. if I were Avery Free Agent Westwood," I murmur softly, absently, as the rocking boat slows and I let go of the side of the wooden boat to skim my hands across the glasslike surface of the water. "Palm trees, sunshine, movie stars…Oh! You could date a movie star if you lived there!"

He laughs. "I don't want to date a movie star."

I roll my eyes. "Don't tell me even they aren't good enough for Avery Free Agent Westwood!"

I'm teasing him. I've been doing it a lot tonight. I realize I like it. A lot. And he doesn't seem to mind, since he breaks out in the hottest grin most times, so I don't see why I should stop. He sits up a little.

"When have you ever seen a Hollywood romance that didn't crash and burn in a million ugly, public pieces? No thank you. I'm trying to avoid having my personal life splashed across the Internet, remember?"

"Right. Not good for the image." I nod as I stifle a yawn. The noise from the wedding reception has faded to a murmur, and even the music has stopped. The lights from the houses that speckle the lakeshore are mostly gone. It's late and my flight tomorrow is at seven. "We should head back."

I crawl to the center of the canoe and sit on the centerboard as I reach for the oars. The whole boat shifts drastically to the left and then the right, and I squeak out a panicked sound as I watch him move to sit beside me. I shake my head and put a hand on his chest when he gets close enough. It's like touching a wall it's so flat and smooth and hard. "I'll row. You just sit there and look pretty."

"I am not letting you row me home," he says, like it's the most horrifying idea he's ever encountered.

It makes me laugh. I grab the oar handles and start to move us.

"Seriously, Stephanie. Let me."

"Oh, come on, what's the big deal?" I ask, and keep rowing.

We're not that far from the dock anyway. A couple more good paddles and we'll be there. But he's still kneeling near the center of the boat, frowning at me. He reaches for the oar, his hand landing on mine, and I pull away, which makes the boat kind of start to spin to the left. "You don't have to defend your manhood with me, Avery. I know you're all man. I got the press release on that."

I smile at my own joke, but he doesn't. He tugs the oar again and I let go of the other one to push him back, but he's ready for me this time and pushes into me. He's stronger, of course, so I start to tip back. I let go of both oars and grab his neck and shoulder. Now no one is holding the oars. We're just holding each other. His eyes look like coal as they seem to sweep over my face, and when they land on my lips it makes my tongue dart out and wet them.

"The man I am with you tonight isn't the man from the press releases," he says suddenly in a low, rough voice as his fingers spread out over my lower back.

I take in a deep, sharp breath but I can't seem to let it out. "I know."

"Do you?" he whispers back, and leans closer.

My heart is thumping so hard like it's trying to break through my chest and touch the one thumping just as wildly through the front of his white dress shirt.

I think he's going to kiss me, and suddenly I want nothing more than to kiss him back. The feeling is swift, all-consuming and powerful, like a craving. Like when I would want a pill so bad I could think of nothing else—which makes me panic. I shift abruptly, reaching—almost lunging—for the oar, and the canoe lurches. Avery's big body rights itself too fast, his weight yanking the wooden oar to the left and tossing me that way with it, and then Avery loses his balance, and before I can even scream, we're underwater.

It's not deep at all, so my feet find the bottom, and I'm standing and sputtering in waist-deep water seconds later. Avery is, too, on the other side of the upside-down canoe. We stare at each other over the capsized boat. He doesn't look like he's going to kiss me again, which is a shame because Avery looks even hotter soaking wet. *Ugh. What is wrong with me?*

"We have to get out of here before someone sees me like this," he explains, his voice tight with stress. "Can you imagine the bullshit stories if I'm caught like this?"

Well, that moment's gone. Typical Avery Westwood is back in all his uptight, image-obsessed glory.

Before I can answer, he's pushing the canoe to the dock and climbing up on it. He reaches down and pulls me out of the water like I'm made of cotton candy or something equally airy. I reach for my shoes, which I left on the dock, and when I stand up my brother and his girlfriend, Shayne, are staring at us with amused smiles.

"We had a little bit of a nautical disaster." I shrug.

"I can see that." Shayne smiles.

"Avery, you know the whole point to skinny-dipping is that you're naked, right?" Sebastian jokes, and slaps his captain on his wet shoulder.

"Ha-ha." Avery rolls his eyes. "You really want to give me tips on skinny-dipping? With *your* sister?"

My brother's shoulders get rigid and his smile disappears.

I laugh. "Don't worry, Seb. You know it's not like that with me and Avery." I can feel Avery's eyes on me but I don't look over. "He was my running buddy and now he's my canoeing buddy...except he needs a little work on his paddling skills."

Shayne and Seb laugh at that, but I don't hear Avery join in. I think I might have hurt his feelings, but I'm sure he'll get over it. That moment in the canoe was crazy and it needed to end the way it did, because anything else would have been pointless. Okay, maybe incredibly enjoyable, but pointless.

I don't want to have a one-night stand and Avery doesn't actually date. And even if he did, I am not an ideal candidate for a guy obsessed with what people think. Yeah, I may have ruined a perfectly good party dress and taken a small chunk out of his ego, but it had to be done.

Chapter 1

Stephanie

Ten weeks later

"You call me a lot." I smile into the phone. "You need to get a life."

"I have an amazing life, thank you very much," my brother counters. "I'm just making sure you do too."

I put my Kindle down in my lap, stretch out on the porch swing and inhale the cool, salty night air. "Yes, Sebastian, my life is good. Just like it was last week when you called. And the week before that. And the week before that."

Sebastian and I haven't always been close, but we were essentially inseparable when I lived in Seattle. When I decided to transfer to San Diego with the lawyer I worked for, he was supportive but concerned. Even though he's my younger brother, he's always acted like a protective older one, which is why he calls me so much. I know he's just worried about me because I haven't lived away from a support system—from him—since I got out of rehab.

I loved being around Sebastian—he's a friend as much as a sibling—but Seattle was never really my dream home. I'd fantasized about California since I was a kid, so when my lawyer announced he was transferring and offered me the chance to go with him, I decided I had to take it. It was also a chance to stand on my own two feet without the safety net of my brother being just a ten-minute drive away.

"Did you enroll in the design certificate program you were telling me about?"

"Yeah. I'm jumping in with both feet, taking two classes this semester," I explain, and I feel a rush of excitement I haven't felt for any kind of school before.

"You know if you wanted to quit your job and be a full-time student, I would pay your way," Sebastian says casually, like it's no big deal for him to support his adult sibling.

But it is. And I can't let him do it again. He already supported me while I got my GED and my first online degree. "I know, but I like online classes and doing it in my spare time." Interior design really excites me, and this is something I really want to do for myself.

He seems to accept that answer because he changes the subject. "How's the roommate situation?"

"Good. Even better than I expected, actually," I confess, and I feel relief when I say it.

I've never had a roommate before, so I wasn't sure how this was going to work out. Maddie is a legal secretary at the firm where I work. I met her my first day in the San Diego office. We really hit it off at work and even went to drinks and dinner a couple times in the first two weeks I was here. When I told her I still hadn't found a place to live and that I wanted to be as close to the beach as possible, she mentioned that she lived in a two-bedroom place by the beach on Coronado Island and that her roommate had just moved to San Francisco. She invited me over to check the place out and I fell instantly in love. It was an old semidetached cottage that had somehow escaped being torn down by a developer. She said the owner didn't want it turned into condos but, unfortunately, he also didn't want to spend a lot of money maintaining it. It was drafty and out of date but it was only half a mile from the beach, and when it got quiet late at night you could hear the waves. I loved it. "She's out on a date tonight. With Ty."

"Really?" Sebastian sounds shocked, which I expected. Ty Parsons is a hockey friend of his who plays for the San Diego Saints.

Last month when I moved, Ty came over to see if I needed anything. Turns out he lives just around the corner—in an oceanfront million-dollar condo. He met Maddie that night, and I could tell he was attracted to her. She was cheerful and sweet, with long ash blond hair, wide brown eyes, sun-kissed freckles and giant boobs. He asked her for her number that night, and now they were on a dinner date.

"Yeah. He better not wreck her," I mutter, and Sebastian laughs. "What? I like her. I don't want her hurt, and I don't want her blaming me because I introduced them."

"Maybe he's got noble motives," Seb counters.

"Didn't you say he used to be your wingman at the Olympics?" I say, rocking the porch swing as I reach for the blanket I brought out earlier and pull it up over my legs. I swear I could sleep out here, it's so peaceful.

"Not all hockey players just want to get in a girl's pants." He chuckles. "And speaking of hockey players not interested in sex, have you seen the news?"

"No. I've been happily out of the loop today. Why?"

He pauses. "Westwood signed with the Saints."

I sit up, the swing rocking violently under me thanks to my abrupt movement. I almost fall off of it. "What? The Saints? As in San Diego?"

"Yeah. He's moving to San Diego," Sebastian confirms. "It's all over the news, but I had to call him myself to confirm it, because it's like the last team I thought he would sign with. They suck."

"He's moving here?" I repeat, and stare out at my quiet little street. "He confirmed that?"

"Yeah, he did. I have no fucking idea what he's thinking."

"He said it was between Los Angeles and Manhattan. He said that the whole point of a new team was to be in a larger market with more access to endorsement deals." It's exactly what Avery told me in Maine last June. "He never mentioned San Diego."

"Yeah, we're all pretty stunned," Sebastian says, and sighs. "You know Westwood, though. He doesn't exactly like to share his thoughts. But he said it's what he wanted."

My heart feels like it's been replaced with a hummingbird. Am I having a panic attack? No. I'm not panicked. I'm just…startled? Yeah, I'm startled. And I'm…excited? I don't want to be excited. Being excited over Avery is not a good idea. Besides, it's not like I'll see him just because he's here in the same city as me.

"I gave him your number," Sebastian announces.

"Why?" The question flies out of my mouth too loud and too blunt.

"What? Is that a big deal?" my brother asks, confused. "You guys were friends here. I mean you got along when we all hung out, right? And he doesn't have any friends in San Diego yet."

"He's going to have a whole team of friends."

"Are you crazy?" Sebastian scoffs. "He's the best player in the league: everybody hates him. It's going to take a while to bond with them. I didn't want him all alone."

Something hits me and I say, "Alex is here, isn't he? And they got along when they both played in Seattle, right? He can be Avery's friend."

Sebastian's deep rumble of a laugh fills my ear. "Larue? Yeah he'll be an ally in the locker room, but what about the rest of the time? Avery's not exactly going to go pick up chicks with Rue, which is Alex's only hobby."

Alex Larue has bounced around from team to team every couple of years. He is a grinder on the ice, gets the job done, but there is nothing flashy or pretty or particularly skilled about it. He likes to say his claim to fame is he leads the league in sleepovers.

"Right. Avery doesn't date," I remind myself as much as my brother.

"Actually, he did date someone this summer," Sebastian tells me.

It's another jolt of surprise. I feel like my brother is a human defibrillator and he just keeps zapping me with one shocking announcement after another.

"He has a girlfriend?" *Why is my voice so unsteady?*

"Apparently. I heard a rumor anyway, but when I asked him about it, he said it was over." He pauses. "So anyway, is it a problem? Can you hang out with him?"

"No. Yeah. It's fine. I'm just surprised, I guess, that he's coming here at all." The wind picks up, and I'm suddenly chilled, so I grab the blanket and my Kindle and head inside. "When does he get here?"

"Well, training camps start next week, so probably like tomorrow or the next day," Sebastian says, like it's not a big deal. But my already racing heart picks up speed. "So be nice if he calls you. Remember, he needs a friend."

"Okay," I promise, and I can only hope that's all he needs.

We talk about the vacation Sebastian just took with his girlfriend, Shayne, and some other mundane stuff, and then he tells me he'll call me on the weekend and hangs up. I fold the blanket over the back of the couch and head upstairs to my room.

Avery is coming to San Diego? Seb was right; that didn't make sense. New York or L.A. would have sold their souls to acquire him. And I knew that's where his overbearing, micromanaging dad/business manager wanted him to go. San Diego is a new team—an expansion team—and has only been in the league for four years. They are fighting to steal some of L.A.'s fan base, and it is a struggle because they haven't been doing all that well. They haven't made the play-offs yet. Why would the best hockey player on the planet sign here?

The truth is I don't want Avery Westwood in San Diego. San Diego is my place to start something new, and Avery is the past. It wouldn't be that big a deal if I'd been able to stop thinking about the last time I saw him, at Jordan and Jessie's wedding. Before that wedding Avery had been a comfortable but distant acquaintance. He lives behind a façade—a fake personality built for the media and sponsorships—and I don't know a single person who could say they were part of his inner circle because he doesn't have one. Even his close friends think he's an island unto himself.

Then that weekend of the wedding he dropped the façade with me. He was funny and sarcastic and opinionated and charming. So damn charming. Seventy-two hours after he showed up for the wedding, I found myself on the verge of kissing him. And even though I haven't seen him since that night, which was almost three months ago, I still feel if he let his guard down like that again, and kept it down, I might develop a hell of a crush on him.

Physically, that makes perfect sense. He is all tall, dark and muscles. Seriously, he is built more like an MMA fighter than a hockey player. He has thick, almost black hair with a bit of a wave to it and incredible copper-brown eyes framed by dark expressive brows and a perfect roman nose. He also has the sexiest, prettiest wide mouth, and sometimes it flashes the most panty-wetting, mischievous smile I have ever seen. Sadly, I've only seen it a couple of times because he isn't much on smiles…or happiness in general. And now I know Avery is charming, too, when he lets himself be.

But letting myself develop a crush on Avery Westwood would be the equivalent of psychological napalm. He is off-limits in so many ways it is almost impossible to count.

Chapter 2

Stephanie

He's sitting on a wooden bench outside the Hotel del Coronado, where he's staying. I can't believe he called me. I never thought he'd risk being seen in public with a lone female—especially if he has a girlfriend, and especially the way the media picks up on any scent of a personal life. But he wants me to help him look at apartments.

He doesn't see me coming, so I can take him in without looking like a gawking weirdo. He's got aviators on and a baseball cap pulled low over his dark hair while he stares at the ocean sipping from a Coffee Bean and Tea Leaf cup.

I don't know why, but it feels like there's a hummingbird trapped inside my stomach. I try to quell the feeling by reminding myself he's the same uptight hockey jock he usually is—hiding from the world under shades and a hat but still sitting upright with perfect posture like a Boy Scout in case someone snaps his picture, and probably sipping an organic tea with free-range milk so his drink doesn't offend anyone.

That thought steadies me, and as I reach him I bend down and pull off his hat. His head snaps up, but he breaks into a smile as soon as he sees me. "Hey! Steph!" He's on his feet and pulling me into a hug before I can blink.

It's startling to be hugged by him. He's never, ever hugged me before. I don't think I've seen him hug anyone except on the ice with his teammates after a win or a big goal. It's like having a brick wall embrace you, except he's warm and smells way more appealing than bricks and mortar.

"You look beautiful," he says, throwing me for another loop. "California agrees with you."

"Thanks. It's the sunshine," I say as awkwardly as possible for some reason, and then make it weirder by stepping back and pointing at the sky, like he doesn't know where sunshine comes from.

He smiles again, unbothered by my weirdness. "It's definitely different from Seattle."

I nod and hold his hat up between us. "And you don't need to hide here, Avery. It's not as rabid a fan base as Seattle. No one will recognize you."

He looks skeptical. And concerned. He's comfortable hiding. It's annoying but also really sad when you think about it. Does anyone really even know this guy? I take the hat and put it on my own head, which must look ridiculous, because I'm in a pretty little sundress and wedge sandals—nothing you would normally pair with a baseball cap.

He shoves his hands deep in his pockets as we walk. His shoulders kind of hunch forward, too, because he's still trying to hide, even without the hat. Oh, God, this boy...

"So where are we headed?" I ask, and he pulls his phone out of his back pocket, looks something up and hands it to me. It's an email with a list of addresses for rental apartments. All of them are located here on Coronado Island, which doesn't surprise me because most of the Saints live here. "Okay. We're right near the third place on the list. Wanna start there?"

"Yeah, sure."

As we veer off the walking path and onto a side street, he asks me "Typical Avery" questions: How was my summer? How's my job going? He even remembers the name of my boss, which I told him once while we ran together in Seattle. He was listening. Wow. My own brother doesn't remember my boss's name, and they've met each other. After his tenth question aimed at me, though, I decide it's time I do the asking.

"So I heard you had a girlfriend this summer," I start casually. I can literally see his body tense. "Will she be joining you here?"

He shakes his head tersely. We pass a group of guys on skateboards, heading toward the ocean. They look up at us but no one stops; no one even blinks. I nudge Avery's shoulder with my own. "See, no one screaming your name. No one asking to take a picture or an autograph or tossing you their bra."

He laughs at that. It's a great sound. It soaks into me, warms me and makes me smile back. "No one ever threw a bra at me. I'm a hockey player, not a rock star."

"Same difference to Canadians, right?"

"Maybe," he replies with a grin. "Still, no bras."

We turn another corner. We're half a block from the beach. I stop and take his phone from him to double-check the address again. I glance up and point. "Your first potential palace, Hockey King."

He rolls his eyes and holds the tiny gate open for me. I haven't been alone with a guy in a long time so I can't remember the last time a guy held a door or gate for me. It feels nice. I lead our way up the tiny path to the town house. It's similar to what I expected to see when looking at places with Avery. Spacious, with state-of-the-art appliances and renovated bathrooms. This place is three bedrooms, two floors, with a decent-sized backyard. I like it, but he seems unimpressed. The rental agent who shows us around really tries to sell him on it, but Avery just smiles politely and says he'll be in touch after he's seen the other options.

As we walk back toward the ocean for the second rental, I ask him again about the girlfriend and if she'll be visiting soon. He almost frowns and then gives me a standard media-friendly Avery answer. "I ended it a couple weeks ago. It wasn't serious."

"That's a lie," I reply flatly, and my bluntness throws him off because he stutter-steps and comes to a stop. I turn and look him in the eye, my appearance glaring back at me in the mirrored lenses of his aviators. I don't look like a total dork with his baseball cap on, which I forgot I was wearing. "You've never let anyone see you in public with a girl or called anyone your girlfriend, but you did with her. That's serious."

He doesn't answer. Instead he points to the high-rise just over my shoulder. "That's the other place, right? I recognize it from the listing picture."

"Nice avoidance tactic, Westwood, but I'm on to your bullshit," I reply as he walks by me toward the condo. "I'm not going to let you treat me like a member of the press."

"I wouldn't be touring potential homes with you if you were a member of the press," he reminds me as he presses the apartment number on the intercom outside the front door.

"Then talk to me with real words—ones you mean, not ones you want me to hear."

The door buzzes and he opens it. As I walk past him into the lobby, he puts a hand on my lower back. It feels intimate, and even though his touch is fleeting and his hand is back at his side by the time we reach the elevator, the warm feeling it creates in me lingers. As the elevator doors close on us and we make our way up to the twenty-fifth floor, he turns to me, pushing his aviators up on his head so his eyes, which are a swirl of colors like caramel sauce on a melting chocolate sundae, bore into me. "I wanted serious. I tried serious. In the end, I didn't feel serious enough about her. Not the way I know I could about someone else, so I ended it."

"So we're back to celibacy?" I can't help but ask, even though it's really none of my business.

"It didn't work out with her," he corrects me. "But I still want a serious relationship."

I almost ask him with who, which is ridiculous. But for some reason it doesn't feel like he's saying it in a general way. It sounds like he has something—someone—specific in mind. Of course he doesn't, but even if he does, it's not my business. The fact that he just gave me a real answer about something personal is a miracle. I need to shut up and be grateful for that.

A hefty, squat man in a badly fitting suit opens the door to the apartment at the end of the hall and smiles brightly. "Mr. Westwood! Wait till you see this place. It's amazing."

He wasn't lying. This is exactly the type of place where I would expect Avery to live. A two-bedroom, two-bath condo with marble counters and hardwood floors and a massive balcony with unobstructed ocean views. If I could afford it, I'd take it in a heartbeat. Avery doesn't, though. He tells this rental agent the same thing he told the last one. As we walk back out into the sunshine, I tell him he's crazy.

"I don't really want to live in a generic box with so many neighbors on top of me. I had a house in Seattle, remember? I like my space. This last one is supposed to be a house." He hands me his phone again so I can see the last place on his list and guide him there. It's super close to my place, only a block away.

We walk in silence for a few minutes until I say, "Tell me something about you no one else knows."

He smiles. "Why, so you can sell it to the tabloids?"

A couple a few years older than us with a baby carriage is passing by so I wave at them. "Hey! Do you guys happen to know when the San Diego Saints' first game of the season is?"

The woman shakes her head immediately. The guy thinks about it for a long second as he glances at me and then at Avery. I feel Avery tense again, and I can't help but subtly reach out and rest my hand on his biceps to try to calm him. Instead it makes my heart race because, damn, his arm feels as solid as an oak tree.

"I think it's in November or something?" the stranger finally says with a shrug. "Like most of San Diego, I'm more of a baseball fan. At least they win."

The couple continues down the street. As soon as they're out of earshot, I laugh. "Burn!"

"Yeah, yeah," Avery replies wryly, but the tiniest hint of a smile plays on his lips. "Was there a point to that little scene other than reminding me I'm going to have to carry a shitty team on my back this season?"

"Yeah. To remind you yet again that no one here knows who you are," I explain as we turn off the oceanfront block and onto the street with his next rental listing. "Selling your secrets would earn me enough money for a Happy Meal, if I'm lucky. So spill it. Tell me something interesting about you, not just the boring stuff you tell the media."

"I'm terrified of skunks."

"Nobody likes skunks."

"No. I am *terrified*," he repeats, and I realize, as his voice drops an octave and his tone turns serious, he feels about skunks the way I feel about spiders or serial killers.

I pull off my sunglasses and stare at him. His cheeks are getting red. Is he blushing?

"I once came face-to-face with one on my driveway in Seattle and I started hyperventilating. I couldn't stop. Had to call the team doctor. He gave me Ativan."

I bite my bottom lip—hard—to keep from smiling or, worse, laughing, which is all I want to do. "Why?"

"Because they're evil," he replies swiftly, still serious. "Have you ever really looked at a picture of one? They've got demonic little faces and they stink. And they'll make you stink for a long freaking time no matter how much tomato you bathe in."

"Have you been sprayed?"

He shakes his head vigorously. "No. My father was once when I was a kid. There was a family of them living in the crawl space under our house, right under my bedroom. I used to hear them clawing and scratching at night. One night I woke up and peeked out my window and the little demon was staring back at me."

He shudders. This tall, muscular, perfect athletic specimen of a man just shuddered like a cheerleader in a slasher movie. Something about his vulnerability is so sexy...but also still a little ridiculous, so I let out the giggle I've been holding in. He looks mortified. "I was seven. It was terrifying."

"Don't worry, sweetie." I pat his shoulder. "I haven't seen a skunk since I moved here."

He wraps an arm around me and squeezes me to his side. Sebastian has done the same friendly, brotherly gesture to me a million times, but it feels different when Avery does it. That damn hummingbird feeling starts in my belly and flutters up into my chest. He stops suddenly and points. "I think this is it."

The house in front of us is tiny, run-down and just plain ugly. It's painted a lime green and the concrete steps up to the door are cracked and crumbling. The screen on the storm door is ripped and hanging.

"The rental company said the key is in a box on the porch. I have a passcode for the box." He marches up to the front door. As he unlocks the box and pulls out the key, he looks over at me and notices my quizzical expression. "Let's give it a shot."

He unlocks the front door and we step into the tiny, cramped, musty-smelling front hall. It has badly scuffed parquet floors and a popcorn ceiling. I can't help but raise my eyebrows. He doesn't seem to notice. He walks into the living room where the parquet floors are covered with horrendous golden yellow shag carpet.

It's a tiny, very shabby two-bedroom, one-bath place that makes my semidetached cottage look pristine, which it's not. When we're done with the tour and he's locking the front door, he says something astounding. "I like this one best of all."

"Are you insane?" I can't help but ask.

He shrugs as we walk down the rickety stairs and back to the sidewalk. The sun is even warmer than it was before our tour of the dump. He squints before pulling his aviators over his eyes again. "I want something simple. I'm willing to renovate a little, too, even though it's a rental. So I don't care what condition it's in. And I'm not ready to buy yet because I want to get to know the area first."

"Well, if you're looking for shabby chic—emphasis on *shabby*—the place next to mine is available."

He stops and stares at me. "Seriously?"

"No. Not seriously," I reply quickly as the light wind picks up and I reach to hold down my sundress to make sure I don't flash him. "I mean it's seriously available, but I'm not seriously offering it to you."

"Why not?" he demands. "I'm a great neighbor. Quiet, clean, hardly ever there, with road trips and everything."

He has a point there. Our last neighbors were just out of college and one of them used to throw parties—all-night raging events—at least once a month, and the other one had a boyfriend and her screaming orgasms used to shake my walls every second night. Wouldn't have to worry about any of that with Avery.

"Besides"—he shrugs and smiles—"we could hang out more if I'm your neighbor."

That part is also appealing, which is scary. He steps a little closer and the wind carries his scent across the short distance to me. He smells delicious, warm and spicy.

"You said you were leaning toward a home with no attached walls," I remind him. "This is semiattached. We'd share a wall."

"I'm okay sharing with you. I can be myself around you. In fact, you don't really give me any other choice, which I kind of like if I'm honest," he says, the deep solemn tone in his voice at odds with the easy smile on his face. "And you could protect me from skunks."

I laugh. He grins and takes my hand, pulling me down the stairs. "Come show me this place."

I don't have keys to the other unit, but I know it's empty, so we stare in the windows and then I show him my place because it's the exact same layout and probably in similar condition. He loves it and of course doesn't even blink at the price, which Maddie and I found a little extravagant. After a quick phone call to my landlord to find out if the place is still available, Avery leaves me to go sign the paperwork.

For the next two hours, as I run errands, I try not to think about him becoming my neighbor. Because when I think about it, I like it. I like the idea that he'll be next door and that I'll probably see him every day. I liked seeing him today. I liked pushing him—his boundaries—and the way he happily let me.

I smile as I leave the grocery store thinking about his silly confession about hating skunks and how freaking cute it was—and how real it made him. And how sexy I found that realness. Ten minutes later I turn onto my street and notice a beautiful, bright bouquet of lilacs on my front porch, leaning up against the door.

"Maddie is going to be so excited," I mumble to myself, figuring Ty left her the flowers. I put down my grocery bag and pick up the bouquet as I dig in my purse for my keys. The card tucked into the front of the pink cellophane wrapper around the bouquet has my name on it.

Stunned and still thinking it must be a mistake, I move to the porch swing and sit as I open the tiny envelope. The handwriting is neat and precise, but I would expect nothing less. He probably had a handwriting coach along with his army of other coaches when he was growing up. The note is simple: *A little thanks for helping me find my new place. I can't wait to be your neighbor. Avery.*

My stomach flips, my heart flutters and my brain screams, *STOP!* But it's too late. I have a crush on Avery Westwood.

Chapter 3

Avery

Two months later

I walk into the locker room and immediately start removing my tie. I'm as close to late as I can be without officially being late. This is becoming a new habit for me. One I need to break. Beau Echolls looks up at me and scowls. "Nice of you to show up, *Captain*."

He hates my guts. There's no other way to say it. The fact is he has a right to hate me. This was his team before I showed up. Beau, at thirty, is a veteran and has been with the Saints since their first game. He is from Maine—the same town as my old teammate Jordan Garrison. He is older than Jordan, but not so much older that Jordan didn't know him. Jordan, and all the Garrison boys, knew and disliked Echolls and his younger brother Chance, who is a sports reporter. I never really knew why, but now that I've been spending time with Beau, I can say he isn't easy to like.

"I'm not late," I reply tersely. He rolls his eyes and continues to lace his skates.

I walk over to my designated locker space between Ty Parsons and Alex Larue, who was traded from the Winterhawks last year. Alex gives me a small nod. Unlike Beau, and most of the rest of the team, he's on my side. So is Ty, thanks to Stephanie, who forced us to socialize with her and her roommate, Maddie, when I first got here two months ago.

Ty, who is giving me a sympathetic smile as he tugs on his jersey over his pads, asks quietly, "Everything okay?"

"Yeah." I nod. "I hit traffic on my way back. It was insane."

"Yeah," Ty says quietly. "The trip from L.A. to San Diego can be an all-day event."

"Yeah." I nod and sigh. "I have to get Don to schedule meetings on days off only. I can't keep doing game-day meetings."

My phone rings—loudly. I thought I turned the ringer off, but clearly I was wrong. I dig it out of my suit pocket and glance at the screen. Lizzie. Again. That's the third time this week. Jesus. I am beginning to regret ever meeting this girl.

"Lizzie?" Alex says because the nosey ass read the call display before I swiped the ignore button. "Is that the ex?"

I nod.

"Is she not so ex anymore?" Ty asks casually as he starts putting on his skates.

"No, she's still very much an ex," I reply, and stand to hang up my jacket and untuck my shirt before I start unbuttoning it. I have to change fast because I really am on the verge of missing warm-up.

He nods. "Okay. So…what now?"

I turn and look at him. "What now?"

"I think he means *who* now?" Alex adds because clearly he was eavesdropping. "Or are you going back to being a monk like you were in Seattle?"

"Really?" I stare at him with a cold, hard look that says *fuck off.*

He smiles. "No disrespect, buddy. You know I love you, but it's true. I was shocked to hear there was a girlfriend to begin with, and now that you've had that blow up in your face, I figure you'll revert back to your celibate ways."

I'm pissed. More so than I should be, because Alex is right. I'd been single the entire time I'd played in Seattle. Not a monk, though, like Alex believes, but single. I wasn't just a player; I was a brand. I made as much in endorsements as I made in salary, as my father constantly reminded me, and I had watched too many other guys screw all that up by getting caught with their pants down, sometimes literally, by the all-too-observant media. Alex Larue is the polar opposite of me. He has what I liked to call ADD—attention-deficit dating. He dates everything and everyone. Well, actually, he fucks everything and everyone, but *attention-deficit fucking* sounds rude.

"I'm not a monk," I snap abruptly, and pull my Under Armour over my head. "Not anymore."

Alex nods, and I can see from the softness in his eyes he's sorry. "Okay. Yeah. Things change."

"They do," I agree curtly, and sit down next to him to pull on my pants. "Otherwise, why would I have dated Lizzie at all?"

Alex and Ty both nod, and Ty says, "You're ready to settle down?"

I catch his eye. "Are you?"

Ty looks caught off guard by that. He shifts a little in his seat and stops tying his skate. His boyish face twitches. "What do you mean?"

"I mean are you settling down? With Maddie? Is this it for you?" When I moved here, Maddie and Ty had just begun dating. It seemed casual, but now it is most definitely exclusive.

He swallows and I watch his Adam's apple bob. And then he gives me this dorky, shy smile. "I mean I'm not proposing or anything. But have you seen me even look at anyone else?"

"I don't see everything," I counter.

He laughs. "Yeah, you fucking do. You're like something out of an Orwell novel. You notice everything on and off the ice."

I chuckle. I've always been overly observant—and he's right; it's on and off the ice. I'm ridiculously good at reading people and situations, and I know he's been the definition of monogamous. And not in that begrudging way a lot of guys are monogamous.

"She's the only one," Parsons tells me honestly as he continues tying his skates. "And I'd be okay if it stayed that way for a very long time."

I smile at him, but it's fleeting. "It wasn't like that with Lizzie. Not ever. It just never felt like I thought it was supposed to feel."

"Then why get exclusive with her at all?" Ty asks me.

I shrug and give him a nonanswer because I am not willing to admit the truth to anyone. "It's a long story."

Alex, who is still listening in on the conversation, stands up and slaps my shoulder. "Well, Westwood, I hope you have changed and you actually keep your skate blade in the dating pool. Do you even know how much premium tail I'd get by being your wingman?"

"I hate to burst your bubble, but I'm not going to run out there and bang every girl who winks at me," I explain, and bend to lace my skates. "I'll date again, but it won't be indiscriminately."

Alex groans his dismay and goes back to getting ready.

Ty smirks at our horny teammate and turns back to me. "So you're not going to sow your wild oats?"

"Nah. Even if I didn't have to keep it clean, I would. It's just who I am," I admit, and reach for my jersey hanging on the hook behind me.

"So if you're not going to date indiscriminately," Ty begins as he levels me with a curious stare that's fringed with a knowing smile, "who are you going to date discriminately?"

"I might have someone in mind," I mutter quietly. Even admitting that gives me a rush of adrenaline.

"Someone I know, I'm guessing."

"Yeah," I reply, and swallow. "If she'd be interested."

Ty doesn't say anything, but he smiles at me, and it's reassuring, so I smile back.

"Are you two done with your hen session or should we leave the two of you to eat chocolate and talk about your periods while we go warm up?" Larue asks with a goofy grin.

"Shut the fuck up, Rue," I bark with a smile. Alex flips me the bird, but he's smiling too.

I hurry to finish dressing and try to keep my mind off Stephanie. When I first met Stephanie, years ago in Seattle, I was instantly attracted to her. She's tall and lithe with amazing blue eyes and a warm, sexy smile. But like every other woman I found attractive, I did nothing about it.

With Steph, though, it was more than just the media and my image keeping me away—it was the fact that she was a teammate's sister. That was a can of worms unto itself, one that was far messier than protecting my image. Seb was overly protective of her too. It was subtle, but I always caught the way he kept an eye on her at team events or parties and how he called her all the time from road trips and insisted she live at his house when he was away. Once Alex had drunkenly hit on her in front of Seb, and Deveau flat out threatened his life.

Ignoring my attraction to her was easy for a long time—until suddenly it wasn't. That started one night when we were all at Jordan and Jessie Garrison's house right before play-offs last year. My college friend Trey had opened a gym and wanted me to give him an endorsement by doing a radio spot. I knew I probably wasn't going to stay in Seattle after my contract expired so I shouldn't give him an endorsement, but I also knew I owed him one because I'd bailed on him in college when he got injured and developed a drug problem.

Stephanie basically forced me into explaining everything to my teammates. And while everyone else was trying to forgive my actions, or at least come to terms with them, Stephanie held me accountable. She didn't care how good I was at hockey or how much money I made or how many advertising deals I had: she told me I was handling things like an ass. It was actually some weird kind of relief to have someone treat me like a normal person, and also the hottest thing any woman had ever done.

After that it was much harder to deny my attraction to her. I found myself going out of my way to spend time with her. Running into her by accident on purpose at coffee shops near her place and jogging in the park near her house because I knew she did that too. But it was stupid and short-lived. We lost in the first round of the play-offs and I went back home to New Brunswick knowing I would never be back in Seattle as a player, and that meant the last time I would see her would be at Jordan and Jessie's wedding. When I saw her at that wedding, my feelings for her were stronger than ever. I was about to tell her—and kiss her—when that damn canoe flipped. The next morning she was gone.

I went home, frustrated and confused, and met Lizzie shortly after at a barbeque in Dieppe, my hometown. I wanted to like her because I was just so desperate to have something with someone, since I couldn't have what I wanted with Steph. And Liz made it easy to like her. She was sweet and kind and very easy on the eyes. I wanted to be over Stephanie. Lizzie was an easy fit, a perfect solution; even my father—the man who had been adamantly against me having a public relationship—seemed okay with her. He never once gave me the "you're a public figure" lecture the whole time I was with her.

Then late one night I was too stressed out about all the contract offers and uncertainty about my career and I couldn't sleep. I found myself calling Sebastian. I told myself I was just catching up with an old teammate and friend, but the second question out of my mouth was "How's Stephanie?" That's when Sebastian told me she had moved to San Diego.

The next day I asked my agent to ask the Saints if they would be interested in making me an offer. By the end of that week I'd signed with San Diego, broken things off with Liz and started packing, all to the sound track of my father screaming that I ruined my career.

Since being here in San Diego, my confidence has wavered more than a balloon in the wind. Stephanie is giving off mixed signals. One minute I'm convinced she wants me the way I want her and then—*boom*—she shuts down, not returning my texts, turning down my offers to hang out. So that's why, two months after I stepped foot in California, we are still just friends—and neighbors. But I haven't given up hope. I tried that once—giving up on her—and tried to date someone else and that didn't work. So I am going to keep trying.

There are so many things about Stephanie that draw me to her in ways I never expected. Stephanie is opinionated, loves sarcasm and speaks the truth to me, whether it is what I want to hear or not. My father had told me, from the minute I hit puberty, that I didn't like women like that. He explained that I needed a woman who was passive and demure and didn't get in the way. And that's what Lizzie was, which is why I knew that wasn't what I wanted.

I loved hanging out with Steph as much as, and in the same way, I liked hanging out with the guys. Except I thought about her naked and, on long road trips, I often satisfied myself to that taboo fantasy. But, honestly, her mixed signals are probably because, even if she is attracted to me, she is too smart to get involved in the façade of a life I have to live.

So the question is, can I find a way to convince Stephanie I am worth it?

Chapter 4

Stephanie

Y ou're kidding, right?" Avery stares at me blankly, just blinking his pretty coffee-colored eyes in what seems to be a mixture of dismay and awe.

"Not kidding. Now put on your big boy pants and hop on," I tell him with an amused smile.

"Where's Ty?" he asks, looking around like his friend and teammate will suddenly appear and save his manhood.

"He's with Maddie. They're already at Hamilton's."

Avery is totally horrified. His reaction's the exact response I've been expecting from any male I would ask to hop on the back of my scooter. I get it, I guess. I mean it is going to look hysterical for me to have a two-hundred-pound tough guy hanging off the back of my candy-apple-red Vespa.

"Avery, you can either man up and hop on or spend hours trying to get a cab on a busy Friday night. You decide."

He sighs loudly and runs a hand through his freshly washed hair, which is still damp at the tips, then takes a defeated step toward my bike. He extends his hand for the extra helmet. I smile triumphantly.

"It'll be okay, honey," I say in a patronizing tone. "I promise you'll still be a big strong hockey player afterward."

He smirks, rolls his eyes and pulls the helmet down on his head. I love riding a scooter in San Diego. You can lane share and beat all the notoriously evil traffic.

"Why wouldn't Ty just drive me?" Avery groans as his long, ridiculously muscular legs straddle the scooter and his muscular butt sits on the back of my seat.

"He said to say 'this will teach you to ignore your check engine light.'" I giggle.

Apparently Avery's Audi has had the check engine light on for more than a week, but he didn't bother to take it in. The car finally died tonight, as he was on his way to meet Maddie, Ty and his team for drinks. Maddie asked me if I would bring him since I was going to join them anyway.

"Hold on tight, Princess," I say in a deep, manlike voice.

Avery groans in my ear but snakes his hands around my waist. Despite the humor of the situation, my insides quiver at the feel of his arms around me.

I drive more carefully than normal, knowing Avery isn't all that comfortable or used to being on the back of a scooter. He keeps his big, strong hands flat against my abdomen and I keep getting tingles in my girl bits because of it. Fifteen minutes later I pull to the curb in front of Hamilton's and Avery hops off very quickly and very ungracefully, almost falling over. I pull off my helmet and give my hair a shake before smiling up at him.

"Don't worry. No one saw you," I whisper with a wink. "And your secret is safe with me."

I lock our helmets to the bike and we walk into the bar together. Ty sees us immediately and grins mischievously. "How'd ya like the bitch seat, Westwood?"

Larue, Echolls and their backup goalie Nikolai Furlov, whom they all call Furry, chuckle at Avery's expense, but he just smiles and shrugs. "Call it whatever you want, but I got to spend fifteen minutes wrapped around this fine woman. I win."

He drapes an arm around my shoulder and grins cockily. Normally I would be slightly miffed at a man making a comment that makes me seem like a piece of meat, but…it's Avery. I'm just shocked he said something so cocky.

"Something tells me that's as close as you'll let yourself get to a woman for another half century," Alex pipes up, and grins at me. "Glad you enjoyed it."

"Shut up." Avery gives Alex a friendly shove and then turns to me. "Beer?"

I shake my head. "Perrier."

Avery heads for the bar and I join Maddie and the boys at the table. Moments later Avery puts the sparkling water over ice on the table as he drops into the empty chair next to me. We talk about the game they played last night because they won—breaking their three-game losing streak—and the guys are hyped up. Despite the losing streak, they're doing better than they have in four seasons. All except Beau Echolls, who is scowling, are pumped up but also nervous about the games to come.

Maddie and I listen supportively. This is all new to Maddie, who didn't grow up watching hockey, but it's normal for me because of Sebastian. Even after I ran away from home when I was sixteen, I still managed to keep track of his games. And then after living in Seattle and socializing with the Winterhawks, I became aware of not just the technicalities of the game, but of the emotional side of it too.

Once the team has a few more drinks in them, the conversation turns to lighter things and the guys start to wander throughout the bar. Echolls and his girlfriend, Kyra, head over to the bar, probably just to get away from Avery. Beau hates him. The single guys, like Alex, saunter away in search of a conquest. Avery doesn't join them.

"Not up for the hunt tonight?" I ask him with a smile. "Not that it's hunting. It's more like shooting high-heeled fish in a barrel."

He chuckles and sips more of his pale ale. "You trying to get rid of me?"

I shake my head. "Hell, no. Although it is entertaining to watch the high-heeled fishes swim around you trying to get your attention."

My gaze lands on two girls talking to Nikolai. The one with the darker hair keeps letting her eyes drift over to our table. I lean my head closer to Avery and lower my voice. "Like that one there…in the nude patent leather pumps. She's just itching for you to leave the table so she can pounce."

I watch his dark eyes shift, and he glances at the brunette through his thick lashes. "I don't know. I think she's angling for a shot at Furry."

"Nah. The other one is going for that. She wants you," I reply, and finish my drink. "I'll bet money on it."

"Okay." Avery turns his head and looks right at me, a twinkle in his eye that makes me light-headed. "How much?"

"What?" I blink.

"You said you'd bet money." Avery smirks and it's delicious. "Put your money where your pretty little mouth is, Miss Deveau."

I swallow and suddenly feel incredibly warm. He's making a bet about picking up another girl; that shouldn't feel like flirting, but it does. *Get your shit together, Deveau, and calm the fuck down, libido!*

"The bar tab for the night," I counter, and smile, hoping it looks sexy and doesn't betray the quiver he's started again in my girly bits. "For the entire team."

"That's a little steep. I was thinking like twenty bucks."

"I'm not going to lose, so don't worry about it," I tell him flatly. "Unless of course *you* don't want to pay that much."

Avery looks at the girl again. She's now leaning in and laughing at something Nikolai said. "I'm not losing this," he tells me.

"I'm not worried." I extend my hand.

He reluctantly shakes it and doesn't let go right away. His eyes land on mine and we stare at each other for a long minute.

"So what now?" he asks, his voice husky and somehow flustered.

I try to take a deep breath, fail miserably and settle for a short one. "You get up and go get me another drink. And let Nude Pumps do her thing."

Avery smiles. I pull my hand back, and he stands and walks away. I watch her watching him as he makes his way through the crowd to the bar. She is nodding at something Nikolai said, but she's no longer listening; I can tell. Alex walks over and plops down beside me in the seat Avery just vacated. I glance at him quickly and smile before returning my eyes to Miss Nude Pumps.

"So you and Westwood…," Alex says, letting his sentence trail off suggestively.

"No. No 'me and Westwood,'" I tell him firmly, and watch as the girl downs the last of her white wine and excuses herself from Nikolai and her friend to get another.

"Reallllly?" Alex draws the word out to emphasize his skepticism and nods. *"T'es sûr?"*

Alex, who is also a French Canadian like me, likes to talk to me in French. I kind of like practicing my mother tongue because I only do it now on the occasional phone call with Sebastian.

"Oui. I'm sure." I answer him quietly as Nude Pumps slides into the small space beside Avery at the bar. It has to be that way, I know it, even if my girl parts don't. I am the worst possible match for a high-profile athlete who makes just as much money off his wholesome image as he does putting pucks in the net. I'm damaged goods. The media would have a field day dragging him through the mud.

"You two have sex every time you look at each other."

Alex's statement finally makes my head spin around to face him. He's grinning over the top of his draft beer pint and his blue eyes are dancing at my reaction. "You're bat-shit crazy."

"No. You and Westwood are bat-shit crazy if you won't touch each other, you know, without clothes," he replies, and sips his beer.

"He's my neighbor and a friend. He just broke up with a girlfriend, the only one he's dared to have in five years," I recount. Nude Pumps starts up a conversation with Avery. "And Sebastian would kill him."

"You're stating facts, but none of them mean you two shouldn't knock boots," Alex replies.

I snort. "Knock boots? Classy, Larue."

"Yeah. And chicks dig it." He smiles triumphantly, then points at the bar. "Some of us need to use whatever charm we can muster. We're not all born with the model good looks of your beloved."

"Beloved?" I laugh out loud at that, but it sounds nervous, which annoys me.

"Honey, you better get off your pretty little ass and intervene or he'll be on someone else's bitch seat on the way home tonight." Alex points to the scene at the bar, where Nude Pumps now has her hand on Avery's arm. She's batting her eyelashes at him, her ruby lips in a pouty smile. Avery is smiling down at her.

My heart clenches. Why the fuck is it doing that? I goaded him into this. I just won the stupid bet. I should be happy, not suddenly moody.

"Shut up, Alex," I say flatly, and stand up and head to the restroom.

Chapter 5

Avery

I glance back at the table, but Steph isn't there anymore. It's just Larue watching me with a stupid grin on his fat face. Don't get me wrong, I like Larue, but he makes it his goal in life to be that friend you want to punch. No two ways about it.

"So have you bought a place in San Diego yet?" Jennifer, or Nude Pumps, as Stephanie dubbed her, asks me. "I know most of the players live down on the beach. Do you have a beach house? I love the beach!"

"I'll be right back," I say, and grab the drinks the bartender put beside me about ten minutes ago. "I have to give this to a friend."

I leave Nude Pumps standing there without another word and walk over to Larue. "Where's Steph?"

"Stephanie? You mean your *buddy* Stephanie?" He says it in a way that makes my jaw clench. It's like he's mocking me, but I can't figure out why. It's annoying. I put her drink down on the table.

"Yeah. Where'd she go?"

"You two have been pretty close since you moved here, huh?" His blue eyes are narrowed and accusatory.

"We're good friends, Rue," I say sharply. "Started last year after you were traded. Back in Seattle when Sebastian started dating my friend Trey's sister."

Alex smiles. Actually, it's more of a smirk. "Nah…I love ya, Westie, but I'm not buying it."

I glare at him, and part of it is about that stupid nickname—only he uses because he knows I hate it. "I don't give a shit what you're buying. Did she leave?"

He ignores my question and continues talking, looking totally smug and so freaking sure of himself. "The only type of friends you two can be are naked friends."

"You think girls and guys can't be friends?" I roll my eyes. "I have a brain in my actual head, not just in my jock."

"Oh, I know some guys and girls can be friends. But you two…" He raises his hand and waves his finger in front of his face. "You two are destined to fuck each other."

"You're an idiot."

"Yeah. She said basically the same thing." Alex laughs. "That's how I know I'm right."

I grab the glass of Perrier and ignore my teammate as I see Stephanie weaving her way back toward us through the crowd. I walk over to meet her halfway. She sees me coming and her bright blue eyes dart to Jennifer. I'm standing like a wall in front of her a second later. Stopping her in her tracks, I hold the drink out to her.

"Here's your drink," I tell her.

She takes it and smiles, her lips parting above the rim as she takes a small sip. "Mmm…it tastes free," she says.

Holy fuck, why is she so damn hot?

"Did I win the bet?" she questions.

I nod.

She grins triumphantly. "Then I'll take another."

I laugh.

She glances over at Jennifer. "So go get 'em, slugger," she says, and gives me a tiny shove.

"What?" Is she talking about Jennifer? She is. "Oh, no. I'm not interested."

"Why, because your daddy has to do a background check before you're allowed in her pants?" Steph quips.

"Wow, that was harsh," I reply, and try to act hurt. But she's not far off. I can't go home with a girl I know nothing about. It's too risky. She could sell the details of her night with Avery Westwood to the tabloids. She could take a selfie with me while I sleep and post it on the Internet. It happens to athletes all the time, so it's not just me being paranoid.

"Don't be so uptight. Fucking is fun. You just broke up with someone. Rebound sex might be just what you need." She smiles again.

"Wow. Potty mouth. Kinda hot."

"I'm sure Nude Pumps knows some dirty words," Stephanie counters, and tucks her soft brown wave of hair behind her ear absently. A simple sapphire stud twinkles from her earlobe.

"You know Alex doesn't think I should go home with Jennifer," I tell Stephanie, and try to stare out at the crowd instead of at her, because I don't think I want to see her reaction. "He thinks I should go home with you."

She doesn't answer. I steal a glance, and she's staring straight ahead with no readable look on her face.

"Larue is a logistical genius. You should go home with me." Now

I openly turn and stare down at her. She smiles. "I mean considering you don't have a car and I *am* your next-door neighbor…going home with me is the practical thing to do."

"He meant—"

"I know what he meant." She cuts me off and finally brings her eyes to mine. "He basically said the same thing to me."

We stare at each other. The air is suddenly thick. I shift from one foot to the other uncomfortably.

"Alex is a pig who would fuck anything," she declares suddenly, and pulls her eyes from me. She stares at her drink and uses the straw to stir it aggressively. "He doesn't get that some people have a type. You have a type and it's not me."

"Really?" She sounds so bloody sure of it, so overtly confident, that it's startling. And perplexing. "What's my type?"

She glances up quickly and then back down. "Not me."

"Is this some weird, backhanded way of saying I'm not *your* type?" I clear my throat and shrug. "You don't have to let me down easy. I'm a big boy."

She laughs at that and gives me an incredulous stare. She looks absolutely adorable with her mouth hanging open, and I want to fill that open mouth with my dick. God, that would be hot…

"You're rich, handsome and smart. You're every woman's type, whether they like it or not. You're what ovaries dream of."

I smile. The compliment is an unexpected thrill, but I make the mistake of looking up. Jennifer catches my eye and waves me over. Ugh. I hesitate.

"You can't ignore her. And you shouldn't," Stephanie says to me, pushing her long hair over her shoulder. It looks so silky and soft. I want to touch it. "Just try to keep the noise down. Remember the walls between our bedrooms aren't soundproof. I don't want to hear your headboard banging all night long."

She shoves me toward Jennifer, but I don't move. "You seriously want me to take her home?"

"No. I mean, I don't care either way." She shrugs and runs a hand through her wavy brown hair, tucking it behind her ear on one side before taking another sip of her fresh drink. "But she's interested."

"I'm not," I reply swiftly.

"Why not?"

"Hey, Avery." Jennifer is right beside me now, her hand on my forearm. "Will you take a picture with me? My brother is a huge hockey fan. He'll never believe I met you unless I have proof."

"Uh, yeah, sure. Let's get a group together." I smile and walk over and grab Alex out of his chair because that's what I was taught to do when a single woman wants a photo. Group shots don't insinuate anything. She waves her friends over, too, and I watch helplessly as Stephanie walks away.

I pose for a photo with Jennifer and her friends and Alex, which they need to do four times before they get the angle right. By the time I finally get the chance to politely excuse myself from them, Stephanie is nowhere to be found. I walk over to Ty and Maddie at the bar. "Have you seen Steph?"

"She went home," Ty tells me with a flicker of sympathy across his face. "But don't worry, we'll give you a ride back."

I nod tersely and head back to the table. Alex is there with a brunette, working his magic. He looks up for a second from her cleavage and starts to open his mouth, but I raise my hand. "Not a fucking word."

He smirks. Asshole.

Chapter 6

Stephanie

An hour and a half after leaving the bar, I'm lying in bed, by myself, wide awake and in a crappy mood. The last I saw of Avery he was being Mr. Congeniality and posing for photos with Nude Pumps and her friends. About ten minutes ago I heard a bunch of voices out front on the porch—his voice, Ty's and Maddie's. I know it's not his style, but I find myself wondering if he brought Pumps home with him. Why does the idea bug me so much?

I don't like Avery. I mean I like him as a friend and I'm attracted to him, because who wouldn't be? The boy is built for sexual satisfaction. Not mine, of course. He's too much for me to handle, and I'm not the right fit for him. Knowing that as certainly as I do and then indulging anything more than friendship with him would be purposefully traumatic. I have learned from all my recovery programs that self-destructive behavior is the root of all evil.

Avery needs a girl who not only can uphold his image but one who mirrors it. I was a teenage runaway and recovering drug addict who got her GED and a paralegal certificate through an online school. I am not even using my degree. I am just a legal secretary for now, waiting for a paralegal job to open up in my firm.

Don Westwood would probably have me killed before he let me date his son. I suppose we could have a random one-night stand. His father would never know about that and it would satisfy the craving I feel for him between my legs. But the problem is I already know I like Avery. Really *like* him. In spite of all his uptight, sometimes even robotic personality traits, deep down he is fun and sweet and kind. And he lets me tell him when he is being a putz without throwing a tantrum, which is insane because I'm fairly sure I'm the only one who has ever gotten away with putting him in his place. There's a hard thump from the other side of the wall I share with Avery, the one that borders the left side of my bed. And then another. And then another.

"Here we go," I mutter, and it instantly puts me in a worse mood. He did it. He actually took her home.

Thump. Thump! THUMP! **THUMP!** *THUMP!*

"He's going to put her through the wall," I mutter to myself.

And then I hear him—through the open window above my headboard. "What's that? I'm a sex god?…Yeah, baby, I get that a lot."

Is he fucking serious?!

Thump. Thump! THUMP!

"Oh, baby! What? You wanna call your friend to join us? How about I just ask my neighbor if she'll join? She's listening right now."

I fling the blankets off, stand on my mattress and push the screen aside to poke my head outside. He's leaning out his own window, his head tilted toward me, a big smile on his full lips and the moonlight twinkling in his mischievous caramel eyes.

"You're a total shithead!" I can't help but burst out laughing.

He laughs back. "You should have seen the look on that pretty face of yours!"

"Jerk! Why didn't you bring Pumps home?"

"Because I knew fooling you would be much more fun!" He laughs again. "Are you sleepy? Have you watched tonight's *Walking Dead* yet?"

"No. And no."

"Come over. Let's watch it," he tells me, and winks.

"Okay." I smile. "But if that girl is really over there and this is a threesome attempt, I will castrate you, Westwood."

I close my window to the sound of his laughter, grab a sweatshirt and pull it on over my tank and pajama bottoms and head downstairs. Leave it to Avery to put me in a good mood. Jerk.

Chapter 7

Avery

We've just finished an offensive drill, which I fucking owned if I do say so myself, and I'm skating across the ice toward the coach when Echolls skates up behind me. "You get off on showing up your teammates?"

"Don't start today, Beau. Seriously."

I'm not in a good mood to begin with. The day started with a phone call from my dad, who apparently has decided to stick his nose in my love life, not just my business life. He was nagging me to take Lizzie back. He was so belligerent about it I hung up on him, which I've never done before. So I'm not in the mood to deal with Beau Echolls's ego.

He swings around in front of me and starts skating backward as he glares at me from behind the visor on his helmet. "FYI, Westwood, these are drills not a fucking play-off game. Stop showing off."

He's pissed because I just beat him on a drill. Deeked the puck around him like he was a pylon and scored on Furry. He's sort of right—I don't need to go all in because not only is this just practice, but it's also optional practice, so the guys who did show up are taking it easy. But I like to work my aggression out on the ice, and I simply don't know how to give less than one hundred and ten percent when it comes to hockey. If Echolls had the same work ethic, maybe he wouldn't have lost the captaincy. But I don't say that. I bite my tongue like I always do and mutter, "I like to give it my all. Always."

"Yeah, well, it's not the fucking Olympics, Golden Boy," he bitches.

"I know. I've made the Olympic team twice and won gold both times," I bark back, skating closer so I'm up in his stupid fucking face. "But, please, tell me about the Olympics. Enlighten me. When were you on the team, exactly?"

He shoves me. Hard, right in the chest. Then suddenly Alex Larue is between us, his back to me and his fists curled into Echolls's jersey. "Back the fuck down, Beau. Not fucking kidding."

"Let him fight his own battles, Rue. Stop being his bitch!"

Alex shakes him roughly. "He's my captain. His battle *is* my battle, and if you knew how to play the fucking game, you'd fight his battles, too, instead of being one, *bitch*."

Beau flings his gloves to the ground. Then Coach Meisner's whistle blares and the goalie coach and the assistant coach both step in and pull Beau and Alex away from each other. "Save it for the games, kids," Meisner shouts. "And your actual opponents. Got it?"

Both of my teammates nod gruffly, and I do too. Coach looks at me and then at Echolls, but he points at Larue. "Rue is right, Echolls. Get on board with your team and your captain. I'm not going to tell you again."

He turns and motions me over to him as he announces the end of practice. Everyone skates for the tunnel and the locker room. He waits until the last player is off the ice and then levels me with a serious stare. "Can you sort this out?"

"I've been trying," I reply.

He gives me a curt nod. "So can you keep trying, or should I step in? Because if I step in, this won't end well for Echolls."

I know that. I know I literally have the power to get that stupid jackass kicked off the team. They'll either trade him or throw him back down to the minors. Probably the latter, because I honestly don't see any other team having a lot of interest in him. Beau is a mediocre defenseman who was given an inflated salary when he was made captain, a position he failed at. So, yeah, he'll be dropped to the minors because no one will pick up his salary, and he'll probably stay there permanently. I have that power. "Nah. Give me a little more time. I'll work it out."

Coach has skepticism all over his gruff face, but he just nods and lets me skate off the ice.

I feel as skeptical as he looked, but I know this team is divided. A lot of the guys still think I'm an asshole for waltzing in here, taking the C and a shit-ton of money they could have earned. The Saints dumped four players to make room in their budget for my salary. Some of the guys up for contract negotiations this summer won't be getting the salaries they want if they stay.

Sure, we've been winning more since I got here, and most of my teammates smile and nod and take my orders on the ice, but deep down there are more than a few who feel like Echolls. He's just the only one stupid enough to voice it. If he gets sent to minors or traded, every single guy will know it was on my orders, whether I admit it or not. And they'll all hate me even more. I don't want that. Even if it would be fucking awesome to get rid of Echolls.

I walk into the locker room and hurl my gloves into the equipment bin at the door. I march over to my locker and shove my helmet on the top shelf before dropping with a thud onto the bench to untie my skates. Some of the guys still undressing glance up at me and give me sympathetic smiles. Others pretend they're too busy undressing to notice me. They're most likely the Echolls sympathizers.

Alex is walking back from the showers as I grab my towel to head toward them. As I pass him, he says, "Is Echolls going to evaporate?" I shake my head and Alex rolls his eyes. "You know Saints is just the name of the team, not a lifestyle you have to live. Man, you are too fucking nice for your own good."

"I'm a saint now? I thought I was a monk?" I quip back.

"Both. You're an overachiever, as usual." He grins at me as I raise my middle finger in his general direction and keep walking into the showers.

When I get out of the shower, Ty and Alex are the only two left in the locker room. Ty is just slipping on a Saints baseball cap. "I'm having a barbeque tomorrow night. On the beach in front of my place. Five o'clock. Bring booze and meat."

"I can't," I say without even actually thinking about it.

Ty rolls his eyes and glances over at Alex, who says, "I told you."

"Told him what?" I question as I drop my towel and reach for my underwear.

"That you would say no automatically, without hesitation," Alex explains. "The way most people say yes."

"We have four days in a row without a game, Westwood," Ty reminds me. "What the fuck else are you going to be doing?"

"I have to go to L.A. for business meetings, and I have a concept meeting for my new line of workout wear, and—"

"The barbeque is tomorrow. Is your meeting tomorrow? On a Saturday?" Alex asks as he puts some gel in his hands and runs it through his hair.

"No, but—"

"Maddie and Steph are coming," Ty says. "It's a shame you won't be there."

Without another word, he and Alex walk out of the locker room. As they walk down the concrete hall, I hear Alex's voice bounce back to me. "Stephanie's single, right?"

My stomach knots uncomfortably. Then suddenly my phone is ringing. I'm grateful for the distraction until I read the call display and realize it's my father. He's honestly the last person I want to talk to, but I know if I don't answer it'll only make things worse. "Hi, Don."

I haven't called him dad since I was sixteen. Because he's my manager, he feels it's more professional if I call him by his first name. "Avery. Have you finished throwing your tantrum?"

Funnily enough, his rule of me addressing him like an adult doesn't mean he has to treat me like one. I ignore the dig and answer with a question of my own. "Are you done trying to dictate my love life?"

"Of course not," he replies without even a second of hesitation or remorse. "And I'm not dictating, simply advising. I know what you need better than you do, because I'm unbiased and not thinking with my dick."

"Do not talk about my dick," I warn. I can't help the sour expression that I know has contorted my face. "Please."

"Avery." He sighs. "I'm a man too. I get that you have needs, especially at your age, and that I've asked you to be overly discreet for too long. But I don't understand why, when I finally tell you to get serious with someone, you don't want to do it."

I pause to pull my shirt over my head and then press the phone to my ear again. "Because the person you're telling me to get serious with isn't the person I want to get serious with."

"Who is?"

Loaded question. One that more than anything else in the world I do not want to answer. I cram my feet into my shoes like a rushed ten-year-old and start out of the locker room. "Not Elizabeth."

"Yeah, because she's perfect, so of course that's not good enough." I can practically hear my father rolling his eyes in exasperation.

"On paper, yeah. But I'm not paper, Don," I explain for probably the hundredth time since I was signed to the NHL. "Sometimes what's good for my brand isn't what's good for me."

"That's where you're wrong," he counters firmly, his already deep, loud voice booming with confidence. "I would hate for you to find that out the hard way."

That tone used to intimidate the hell out of me. It used to make me bend like wax in the sun on everything he wanted me to for way longer than I'm comfortable admitting. But not in the last year or so. Now I'm able to see it as it really is—a bullying tactic.

"I appreciate that you've protected me from a lot of potential pitfalls," I tell him, and I'm being totally honest. He's been a good guide and a brilliant confidant on a lot of my professional choices. "But this is a personal matter, not a business one, so I'm going to handle it personally."

He sighs so loudly that it sounds like wind coming through the phone. I walk across the parking lot; the sun is shining and the saltwater air is warm. I really do love San Diego. I could see myself here long after my career is over. "Do I need to hang up on you again?"

I'm half joking, but only half. My father doesn't see the humor in any of it. I don't remember the last time I heard him laugh at anything, actually. "Don't forget you have that meeting in Los Angeles and the—"

"Concept meeting for the workout gear. I know. I'm on it."

"Call me after the business meeting and before the concept meeting," he orders. "I am sending you some sketches I had drawn up to better explain your vision."

I nod, even though he can't see me. "Yeah. I will. I always do."

Of course, when he says "my vision" he means his vision of my vision. But whatever, the sketches might be good.

I hang up as I climb into my car, which is brand-new because it turns out I wrecked the engine on the last one when I ignored the check engine light. I went for a top-of-the-line Audi Q5 hybrid. I sit there staring at my phone for a few minutes and then finally break down and text her.

Hey Steph, are you going to Ty's BBQ?

It doesn't even take a full minute to get a response.

Yeah. I hope you are too.

I smile.

See you there.

Chapter 8

Stephanie

Everyone is drunk. Silly, stupid, fun drunk. All twenty of the guests at Ty's impromptu barbeque. I take another sip of my mojito and dig my bare toes deeper into the warm sand. I lean back in my beach chair and realize I'm slightly dizzy, which means I've had way too much to drink. So I subtly, and even a little regretfully, poor the rest of my drink into the sand under my chair and quickly cover it up.

"Are you going to eat that?" Avery drops to his knees in the sand behind my beach chair and wraps one of his long arms around to reach for the half-eaten hamburger on my plate.

I whack at his hand, grab the burger and take a giant bite, turning my head so he can see the ketchup and mayo smeared on my lower lip.

"Classy, Steph. Remind me to take you to a five-star restaurant sometime soon." He winks at me. His brown eyes are sparkling in the late afternoon sun and he has a nice light golden glow to his sun-kissed skin.

He laughs and uses his thumb to wipe the condiments off my chin.

It's a thing a mom or dad would do to a kid but somehow, when Avery does it, I feel a sexual rush. He smiles deviously and then sticks his thumb in his mouth to lick it off. Holy fuck, my ovaries just did backflips. To lighten the tension building—in my body, if nowhere else—I take the remaining chunk of hamburger and shove it into his smiling face.

He laughs and grabs it, finishing it in two big bites that were much more elegant than the one I took. Maddie laughs, too, as she walks by carrying a plate of burgers fresh off Ty's grill. "You know we've got enough to go around; you two don't have to fight over food."

"It's a mating dance, Mads," Alex interjects from his spot lying flat on his back on a towel a few feet away. "Don't interrupt them. Maybe they'll actually finally get to the good stuff this time."

Avery and I flip him the middle finger at the exact same time, and he lets out a belly laugh. Avery gets to his feet. "I'm grabbing another burger."

He wanders toward where Maddie has put the plate on a camping table we've brought down to the beach in front of Ty's place. Maddie shoots me a smirky little smile and I roll my eyes. She's joined Larue on the Stephanie-and-Avery-Should-Hook-Up bandwagon.

She came into my room last night with the silliest little grin on her face and said, "So Ty tells me Alex thinks you should hook up with our neighbor."

I nodded and shrugged. "Larue also probably thinks I should bang the entire team."

"He thinks every girl should bang the entire team. And they should all start with him," Maddie snarked, and sat on the edge of my bed while I brushed my teeth in the master bathroom.

I nodded and kept brushing until she said, "But why not you and Avery?"

Then I choked on my toothpaste. "Avery? No. We're just friends."

"Why?"

I stared at her. "Because we are."

"But why?" I sighed and Maddie laughed. "You don't have a valid answer."

I walked back into the bedroom, tying my hair in a bun as I went. "I don't know, Mads. We're just friends."

Maddie thought about that a second as I took off my earrings and placed them on the dresser. When I turned to face her, she was smiling again. "I don't know, Steph," Maddie said quietly. "Ty told me that Avery Westwood could have gone to a bunch of different teams. It was totally his call. The Saints weren't even the highest offer. So if it wasn't money that made him come here...maybe it was you."

As I pulled back my blankets and slid into bed, I couldn't help laughing at that last point. "Avery would never make a business decision based on anything other than business."

Maddie barely bothered to consider my words before she turned back into Cupid's little helper. "I still say it seems like you are something special to him," she said. "So is he special to you?"

I panicked and blurted out too quickly and with too much gusto, "As a *friend*."

Maddie stood up, the expression on her face screaming, "Bullshit!"

I punched my pillow and got comfortable. "My brother would honestly kill him if he ever slept with me, and I am *so* not what his father would consider brand-friendly."

"Don't want to mess with the 'brand.'" She did air quotes and didn't sound convinced. She doesn't look convinced now.

To avoid her and Alex, and to keep my eyes from lingering on Avery's ass in his swim shorts as he stands at the camping table squeezing ketchup onto his hamburger bun, I get up and walk to the edge of the water. Nikolai and Beau are playing Frisbee there, and I run in between them and grab the Frisbee as Nik tries to chuck it to Beau. I smile triumphantly and hurl it to him myself.

"Nice arm!" Beau praises. "Are you good with a stick too? You can replace Westie."

I roll my eyes. God, that kid is nothing but venom all the time. His girlfriend, Kyra, gives me an apologetic smile from where she sits nearby. I continue to the water until my toes are immersed. It's a little cold but feels good with the sun being so hot. It's above ninety degrees today.

I stare out at the beautiful rolling ocean. Today is one of those days where I am glad I made the decision to leave Seattle. There are a lot of days like this, thankfully, but today—with the sun and surf and friends and laughter—I feel particularly positive about the decision.

Maddie walks over and hands me a fresh mojito. I don't want to drink it. Well, actually, I do, but I'll make bad decisions. So I walk over and hand it to Kyra. "Here. You have to try these, they're amazing."

She smiles and takes the drink. "Thanks!"

Out of the corner of my eye I see Avery, Ty and Alex walking toward us. Ty and Avery have taken off their shirts and they're just in their swim shorts. It's really hard to force my eyes to Avery's face. I want to stare at his huge wall of muscles he calls a chest and the ripples of muscle he calls a stomach, but when I finally manage to pull my eyes higher I see a goofy, almost lopsided smile on his face. He's up to something. I walk back over to Maddie, who is ankle deep in the ocean, staring lustfully at her shirtless boyfriend, and doesn't seem to see an issue.

Maybe I'm overreacting to that look on his face. Alex smiles. It's definitely undeniably devious. Now I'm really wondering what's going on.

"Hey, Deveau," Avery says to me. "Can I borrow your phone?"

"Sure. I left it up by the chairs," I explain, and his grin grows, as does my uneasiness.

"Good."

"Wha…AHHH!" My question turns into a wail as Avery charges me. I see Ty do the same thing to Maddie and she screams too. The next thing I know I'm falling backward and being engulfed by a giant wave. I come up sputtering. Avery pops up right in front of me. "You asshole! It's freezing!"

"I saw the way you were staring at me, and I thought you needed to cool off," Avery explains, grinning his stupid, goofy, sexy grin.

I splash him. "Egomaniac!"

He grabs me around the waist. I feel suddenly warm despite the cold water.

"Admit it. You were checking me out," he whispers roughly. His hands tighten on my hips and he lifts me easily and once again hurls me backward. A wave rushes over me and pushes me forward and I hit his chest with my own. He grabs my waist again, this time to hold me steady. I put my hands on his biceps.

"I was checking you out," I admit, pushing my damp hair back off my face. "I'd check out any half-naked guy. By the way, Ty has better arms."

He laughs and glances a few feet away, where Ty and Maddie are making out in the ocean. "I'm bigger in other areas," Avery retorts cockily.

"You did not just go there."

"I can prove it." He wiggles his eyebrows. "Want me to prove it?"

Yes! I want you to prove it. My body is screaming, *Prove it until my eyes roll back in my head and I can't walk properly.* "Sure. I dare you to prove it on this very public, very crowded beach," I shoot back instead. "I mean you'll be fine when your junk is on the Internet and no one wants you to endorse anything except condoms, right?"

His sly smile falters. I turn and head for the shore. He's right behind me; seconds later his hands are on my shoulders as we make our way out of the surf. My beach cover-up, a short white gauzy cotton dress, is sticking to me everywhere and completely see-through. I start to tug it off, making sure my bathing suit doesn't go with it.

When I glance up at Avery, he's staring down at my body, and his light brown eyes have darkened to the color of espresso. I feel a rush of heat ripple through my veins again. "You're looking at me like I'm a meal," I whisper.

"I bet you're delicious."

Holy shit.

I swallow and try to clear my head, because it suddenly feels very foggy as I search for a reason he's coming on to me—one that I can live with. "You're drunk."

"So are you," he replies, and takes a step toward me so he's right on top of me now. Our wet, nearly naked bodies are almost touching.

I'm not drunk, but he doesn't need to know that. For some reason it feels safer if I let him think I am.

He dips his head closer to my ear, the water from his hair dripping

onto my shoulder as he asks, "Wanna make horny, drunk, crazy decisions together?"

"Avery! Hey!"

The greeting is like a cattle prod to me. I take a quick step back
from Avery, and his head snaps up. His flirty, happy demeanor and
smiling face morph into a look of frustration. He swears. "What the
fuck?!"

I shield my eyes from the sun and glance down the beach. A few
feet away are two girls. One blonde and one redhead. I don't recognize either. "Fans?"

Avery sighs and runs a hand through his hair, sending salty water
droplets everywhere. "No. Jesus Christ…that's Liz."

His ex-girlfriend?! Is he serious?

He storms off in the opposite direction of the main group,
where the two girls have come to a stop. They're both glaring at
me. When he's close enough, the blonde rips her death stare from
me, morphs her expression into a smile and plasters herself to
Avery in a hug.

I wrench my eyes away and make my way back up to the party.
When I get there, I grab my towel off the chair from earlier and dry
off.

Alex is doing the same. He grins. "Did you drown Avery? Beau
will be thrilled."

I glance over my shoulder to where he's still talking to the blonde
and the redhead. "He's over there. With his ex-girlfriend."

"What? But she lives in New Brunswick!"

I appreciate his total lack of understanding over the situation, because that's how I feel too. When he looks at me, stunned, I just
shrug.

"Which one is she?" he asks.

"I think the blonde, but I don't know."

"Well, I'm going to find out."

Alex drops his towel and starts down the beach toward the trio. I do the opposite, wrapping my towel around myself and marching off the beach toward Ty's place. After I've located my beach bag and pulled a clean T-shirt on over my bikini, I head back outside, but the group has disappeared, Alex included.

An hour later, I'm trying my best to forget about Avery and enjoy the party, but people are talking. Alex, especially, is talking. He'd come back a few minutes ago to report that Liz and her friend had decided to come here on vacation. Apparently Liz had thought it would be fun, and she was actually going to surprise Avery tomorrow with a visit, but running into him on the beach was a perfect coincidence. I didn't ask where they were now and he didn't volunteer the information.

Finally, at around ten, when only a handful of us remained around the dying fire, I curled up in a chair and watched the embers. I woke up to someone giving me a small shake. "Come on, Steph. Let's get you home."

The fire was gone and I was cold—and somehow still tipsy. I'd had a couple more mojitos. I have to remember to rein it in. No more booze for me. I need to get back on track. Alcohol has never been my trigger and it was never my problem—as a teenager I had popped my first pill before I even tasted a beer—but I trusted recovery specialists when they said it could be a slippery slope.

I look up at Alex Larue's big, round, smiling face. He gently grabs my arms near my elbows and lifts me to my feet.

"Where is everyone?" I ask, and notice two other people wandering up the path to Ty's place. I think it's Nikolai and the girl he brought named Nadya.

"Some went home. Some are crashing at Ty's, and he's crashing at your place," Alex explains.

I grab my shoes and start to wander down the beach in the direction of my house.

Alex follows. "Where's Westwood? Shouldn't he be taking you home?"

"Haven't seen him since the ex showed up," I mumble, and run a hand through my hair, which is tangled from the foray into the ocean earlier.

I ignore the slight pang I feel at my own statement. It really is cold. I rub my arms again and suddenly am blanketed in something warm and fuzzy. It's Alex's Saints zip-up hoodie, which he had been wearing.

"I'm not cold, so just shut up," he orders before I can protest.

"You're always such a charmer, Rue," I say in French, but smile gratefully and shove my arms through the sleeves. They're way too long and my hands don't emerge at the ends.

"He's not with Liz. I mean *pas comme ça*," Alex tells me. *Not like that.*

"How do you know?" I ask, and then stop and add, "It doesn't matter if he is anyway."

"Yeah, it matters." He laughs and squeezes my shoulder. "You want to bang him."

"So classy!" I snap back.

"Tell me I'm wrong."

I turn and look at the dark rolling waves without saying another word. He lets out a trademark Larue belly laugh. "I also want to bang Zac Efron and George Clooney. So what? It's not going to happen."

"Sweetie, you don't know those two. And you don't live next door to them." He wraps an arm around my shoulders and pulls me closer. "Currently, George and Zac don't want to bang you. But Avery does."

"Shut up with your theories already, Alex," I snap. This time, I'm actually almost mad. "Seriously. Just let it be."

Alex ignores my request completely as we turn off the beach and head down my street. "I know Westie's got more self-control than a robot, but his little misadventure with that Liz girl proves he's a man and not a eunuch. And you're completely irresistible, but he still can't close the deal. He's a fucking rookie. It's infuriating."

"If he wanted it, he would come and get it," I say, and I regret the words as soon as they leave my mouth. Why am I talking to Larue about this, of all people? Oh, well, too late to stop now. "It's probably better we don't have sex because it could never be anything more. I'm not meant to be with someone like Avery."

"Yeah, that sounds…what's the expression I'm looking for?" He grins, and I see a flash of that charisma that women seem to love. "Really fucking dumb."

"Seriously," I say firmly as we get to my place and I make my way up the porch. I notice the light is on next door. "That Liz girl is from his hometown and she's probably a nurse or something noble. Something great for his image."

"A kindergarten teacher," Alex corrects. "At a Montessori school, whatever that is. Her redhead friend is too. I was chatting her up, trying to see if…you know…"

He grins and a cold slap of reality hits me in the face. We may have some decent sexual chemistry, but Avery needs much more than that.

Liz can give him that squeaky-clean milk-and-cookies image he requires. He's probably figured that out—finally—tonight. I climb my porch steps and dig my key out of the pocket of my shorts.

"He really wasn't happy to see her, if that makes you feel any better," Alex says calmly, and follows me up the stairs. I unlock the door, and inside I hear giggling coming from the kitchen. Maddie's giggles. And then Ty swears in a deep, lust-filled voice.

Alex and I exchange glances.

"Parsons…," Alex calls out hesitantly. "Are you doing some naked cooking in there? Because ready or not, here we come!"

Alex takes my hand and leads me down the hall into the kitchen. I have the urge to cover my eyes. I do not want to see Maddie and Ty naked.

Alex stops short in the kitchen entry. Maddie is sitting on the counter in nothing but Ty's T-shirt. Her legs are parted and a half-naked Ty Parsons is occupying the space between them. He's in a pair of boxer briefs. Boxer briefs that my roommate has her hands in the back of. Ty is holding a Ben and Jerry's container in one hand and a spoon with melting ice cream in the other.

"Food sex! Love it. Carry on!" Alex sits down at the kitchen table and smiles. Maddie rolls her eyes and Ty puts the ice cream and spoon down on the counter.

"Show's over," Maddie announces. She moves her eyes from Larue to me. "Hey! I thought you were already asleep."

"I was. At the beach. Alex woke me up and walked me home," I explain.

"Have you guys seen Westwood?" Alex asks.

"Seen him? No. Heard him? Yes," Ty responds. He's still wedged between my roommate's legs with his back to us, but he's turned his head toward us as he talks. "He and the stalker ex have been scream-ing at each other for about an hour."

"That's what woke us up," Maddie adds.

"See. I told you. He's not *with* her," Alex says to me. "He's just screaming at her."

I ignore him.

"They've been quiet for almost half an hour. I wonder if she left."

"I'm wondering if they're finally having breakup sex," Maddie an-nounces, and glances at me for my reaction. I keep my face emotion-less.

"He's not going to touch her. Breakup sex is sloppy. Avery's not sloppy," Ty says quietly, his back still to us.

"Turn around already, buddy," Alex says to Ty.

"Umm…I need a few more minutes," Ty replies sheepishly, and I can see his eyes glance down. "Or a pair of pants. Loose pants."

I burst out laughing and cover my mouth in horror at the same time. Ty's got a boner. Of course he has a boner! He was just dry-humping Maddie and feeding her ice cream. I turn redder than he is. Alex groans.

"I'm going to bed!" I announce, and start out of the kitchen. "I'll leave you two to your ice cream sex."

"I'm too drunk and too tired to drive. Crashing here," Alex de-clares, and jumps up and follows me. "Ty, wake me in the a.m. and drive me to practice with you."

We get upstairs and I grab the extra blankets while Alex pulls out the couch on the cramped, drafty sun porch. I leave Larue alone and then head into my own room. Too tired and still drunk, I don't even bother to change. I just slide under the covers. I find myself straining to hear any sign of Avery having sex with Liz. I can hear some thumping, like footsteps, and I think I even hear a door close, but that's it. I don't want to hear them having sex, but yet I'm listening for it. I'm fucking insane.

A few minutes later I hear someone walking up the stairs. It's probably Ty. Or Maddie. Or Ty and Maddie. And then my bedroom door opens and there's a tall shadow in the door.

"Rue?" I say quietly, and prop myself up on my elbows. "Is that you?"

"Larue?" It's Avery's voice. And he sounds startled and very, very pissed off.

Chapter 9

Avery

W hy the hell would Larue be in your bedroom?" I bark in a low voice. When she said his name, I felt like I was at the top of a roller coaster going down a huge drop. And I wanted to barf.

She flips on the light beside her bed and blinks. "Avery?"

"Why the fuck would Larue be in your bedroom?" I question, and then I see the Saints hoodie she's wrapped up in with the number twenty-five on the chest. Now I'm going over the edge of a roller coaster and the lap harness has given way. I'm free-falling. "Why are you in his clothes? What the fuck, Stephanie?"

She smiles and almost laughs. "I'm only wearing his hoodie because I was cold at the beach. I thought you were him because he's crashing on the pullout."

"Alex is here?" I'm still startled. And I still don't like the idea of him spending the night in this house. Or Stephanie spending it in his sweatshirt.

"How did you even get in?" she asks.

"Ty let me in. I think he and Maddie are having sex in your kitchen."

"Yeah. Probably."

"Why is Larue here?"

"Avery, why are *you* here?"

I take a deep breath and swallow hard. Her pretty blue eyes stare up at me, waiting patiently for me to explain myself.

"I don't know. I just…" I stop. Here goes nothing. "Liz and her friend are sleeping in my guest room. For some reason I thought you should know."

I shove my hands into the kangaroo pocket in the front of my hoodie and stare down at my bare feet on her hardwood floor.

"Do you want to talk about it?" She sits up, pushing her pillows against the wrought-iron headboard.

"Do you want to hear it?" I counter.

She doesn't answer right away, and when I look at her I can see the hesitation on her sun-kissed features. "Yeah. Some sick part of me does want to know why your ex is spending her vacation hunting you down. So sit down and tell me."

So I open my mouth and word-vomit everything. "Liz came all this way to try and win me back. She didn't even try and hide it. Of course, she was drunk. She and her friend had been drinking Bloody Marys or something, trying to get up the liquid courage to come see me, and then she ran into me on the beach. She says that's fate's way of telling us we need to give it another try."

"So you spent the afternoon with her?" she prompts, lifting her knees up under the blanket and wrapping her arms around them. "Giving it another try?"

"No. But I didn't want her to join the barbeque and everyone, so I took her and her friend here. I was worried she'd make a scene at the beach." Steph frowns. I know what she's thinking, so I say it aloud. "I was worried about how it would look. How very Avery of me. Gotta protect the image. God, even I fucking hate me right now."

I watch her expression soften and then she pats the space beside her on the bed. "Come here. Sit down and relax. I'm not judging you, Avery."

I stare at her hand on the side of the bed. I've sat on her bed before. Tons of times. In fact, just last week, I stretched out on it and told her about our recent road trip while she put on makeup in the bathroom and got ready to go to the movies with me. But I can't sit there now. Not with the way everything is currently raging inside my body.

"I can't sit there. On that bed. With you," I tell her in a low, warning rumble that makes her eyebrows shoot up in surprise. "Lizzie's been hitting on me all night, even though I've made it clear we're not getting back together. She tried to kiss me anyway. I didn't let her, but it made me realize it's been a long time since I kissed someone, Steph."

I stop and take a breath, but she doesn't say anything. She doesn't do anything. She's as still as a statue and so I panic and keep blabbering. "I have to go on long bouts of celibacy because I can't just fuck around and have fun like the other guys. I don't know who to trust, so I play it safe and trust hardly anyone. The guys think I have willpower or control or whatever, but the truth is I'm always so fucking horny I could explode. And my ex is in my place right now, drunk and offering me sex."

"And you...want sex..."

Somewhere in the back of my drunken brain I realize that this is what verbal diarrhea is, yet I don't stop talking. "Yes. I want sex. But not with Lizzie. I want sex with you and only you. So, no, I can't go near that bed with you in it because I will crawl on top of you and tear Rue's fucking sweatshirt and all your other clothes from your body and fuck you like you have never been fucked before in your life."

"You wouldn't." She almost gasps it.

"Yeah, I would." I've never been so sure of anything in my life. "And I wouldn't regret it for a second."

We stare at each other. I try to take a deep breath, but it catches in my throat.

"Still want me on that bed?" I whisper. My whole body is wound so tight waiting for her response.

"Yes."

Chapter 10

Stephanie

The doorbell rings.

I blink, breaking the eye contact with Avery, and glance at my closed bedroom door. He looks over his shoulder too. "Who the fuck?"

I hear footsteps on the creaky wood floorboards in the hall downstairs. Ty swears, and then I hear him stomping up the stairs. My bedroom door swings open, and he's standing there in his underwear with his hand over his eyes. "Sorry if I'm interrupting. Liz is at the door!" he says in a loud whisper.

"Dude, uncover your eyes," Avery says, and looks down. "And put on some pants."

I follow Avery's eyes to the half-hard bulge in the front of Ty's boxer briefs, and then I cover my eyes and groan. Ty laughs sheepishly. "Well, thanks to all this late-night drama, I'm going to get blue balls. Fucking unbelievable."

He storms out. I uncover my eyes and get out of bed. Avery and I stare at each other again but that intense, suffocating sexual tension is gone. "You should go down there and deal with her."

"Fuck her."

"Please don't," I whisper as I grab his hand and lead him into the hall. I stop near the top of the stairs and see her standing in our doorway. She's short, busty, and on the verge of tears. Maddie glances up at me while she guides Liz toward the kitchen, and I hear Liz say, "He said he needed to talk to one of you and he would be right back. But that was half an hour ago."

"Oh my God, why is my life a nightmare?" Avery whispers.

I tug him quietly down the stairs. We reach the front hall. I can hear Liz and Maddie talking in the kitchen. Liz apologizes for showing up so late. Maddie tells her it's okay. I push him toward the kitchen. "Go."

"Kiss me good-bye," he demands, and as I stare up at his beautiful face and his sexy lips it takes everything in me not to do it. But I can't. Not right now.

"If I kiss you, it's not going to be good-bye," I reply, and shove him down the hall.

"What's going on?" I hear Alex's voice from the top of the stairs.

"Is that Avery?" Liz's hopeful voice filters out from the kitchen and I hear a chair push back on the tile floor. Oh, man, I do not want to meet this girl. I want to retreat upstairs before she finds Avery and never ever meet her.

I start up the stairs toward Alex. "Nothing. Go back to bed."

"Who was at the door?" Alex starts down the stairs.

I give him a glare, shooing him back up the stairs. "Shut up and go to sleep."

But it's too late. Liz is standing there, with Ty and Maddie behind her, staring at me. I falter as our eyes connect. She looks from me to Avery and back again. "You're the girl from the beach. The one he was in the water with."

I nod. "I'm his neighbor, Stephanie. Hi."

She glares but shifts the venomous stare to Avery. "You left me alone to come here and see her?"

Liz looks up to glare at me again, but then her watery eyes land on something behind me and she looks startled. I turn my head and see Alex standing behind me in nothing but his shorts. His naked, tanned, and much more toned than expected chest is on display. He lands on the step above me and drops a possessive hand over my shoulders, grinning jovially at Liz. "Hey, Lizzie. Nice seeing you again."

"Uh…hey, Alex." She's clearly confused, but I can almost see her brain putting together the ridiculous puzzle pieces Alex is trying to create, by making it look like he's with me. Like I was upstairs in bed with him. Gross.

"Liz, you can't just wake up my neighbors," Avery grumbles. "Let's go."

"I'm sorry. You said you'd be right back and Tara passed out and I…"

"Later, kids." Alex waves as Avery opens the front door and ushers Liz out. He glances up at me one last time as I peel out of Alex's mock embrace.

"Just go," I urge, and, with a look of frustration on his pretty face, he steps out onto the porch, closing the door behind him.

I look up at Alex. "She thinks you and I…"

He smiles. "Would you rather she know you just kicked her ex out of your bedroom?"

I snap my mouth closed. He chuckles, then bends and kisses the top of my head before sauntering back upstairs. Ty and Maddie disappear into the kitchen, so I walk down the stairs, lock the door and rest my back against it. Wow. What a fucking mess of a night.

Chapter 11

Avery

I just gotta get dressed," I call to Larue, who showed up first thing this morning, as soon as I managed to get Lizzie and her friend out, and is now downstairs eating his weight in cereal.

I step out of my bathroom, a towel wrapped around my waist, and walk across my room to my dresser. We've got ten minutes to get in the car and head to practice, and I can't be late. I drop my towel and grab a pair of jeans out of my drawer, and that's when I hear the gasp. I spin around and find Steph in the doorway of my bedroom, a hand to her mouth and her bright blue eyes bugging out of her head.

"Shit!" I blurt, and use the pants in my hand to cover my junk.

She turns the darkest shade of red I have ever seen anyone turn and spins around to face the other way so quickly she almost falls down. "I'm so sorry! Alex told me to just come up."

"Of course he did." I pull on my jeans.

"I didn't know you were naked. Your bedroom door was open. Who walks around naked with the door open?" she asks, her face still turned toward the wall.

"Someone who lives alone and thinks the only other person in the house is his teammate who has seen him naked before and doesn't care. You can turn around now," I tell her. She hesitantly peeks over her shoulder, her eyes going straight to my crotch. I smile and stop buttoning my jeans. "Want another look?"

I pretend to undo my pants.

"No!" she nearly screams and then giggles, embarrassed again.

"You have seen one before, right?" I tease. "In daylight? 'Cause you're acting like you haven't."

"Shut up," she says, and finally turns around to face me. "I just wanted to see how you were doing."

I grab my T-shirt and pull it on over my head. "Liz is gone. For good. It took all night of relentless discussion, but I made it clear that we are not getting back together."

"I can't believe she came all the way out here," Stephanie says. She sounds awed, in a slightly horrified way. "Who does that?"

"Girls I date, apparently," I reply, embarrassed. "I guess she ran into my father back home and he told her that it wouldn't be a bad idea."

"Are you kidding?"

"Not kidding," I reply tersely. "He's been against me having a girl-friend my entire career and now he's trying to get this one to stalk me. I have no idea why."

"Maybe stalkers help sell a brand?"

She's grinning, and it makes me grin. I appreciate her trying to keep things light, especially after that drunk, hormonal gong show last night. She starts toward the hall to go back downstairs, but I grab her arm, circling her wrist with my hand. "I feel like I should say something to make things normal between us, but I don't know what that is."

She glances at my hand around her wrist and back up at my face, biting her lip for a second before admitting, "Yeah, I came here hoping I'd think of something to say to make it less weird too."

I turn her around and walk her into the hallway. Alex is staring up at us from the bottom of the stairs, grinning. Nosy little shit. "Larue, go get Parsons outta Maddie's bed and meet me at the garage."

"Sure thing!" he calls back. "Feel free to have sex while I'm gone!"

There is no playing dumb about last night now. I threatened to sleep with Steph, and she threatened to let me. The front door opens and then closes.

She clears her throat. "Well, that didn't help the situation."

A smile tugs at my face and then at hers. And then we're both grinning. Our smiles get bigger and bigger until she starts to laugh, and that makes me laugh. Suddenly we're both almost hysterical. She has tears running down her face and my stomach hurts.

"I don't know why this is so funny," she admits through giggles. "But I can't stop laughing."

"I'm going to try not to take it personally," I manage to gasp between laughs. "That the mention of sex with me makes you giggle uncontrollably."

We both laugh harder, and even though it's insane, it's exactly what we need. Last night was ridiculously out of control and I said some things that normal, in-control Avery would never have even let himself think. Who threatens to climb into bed with a woman and have sex with her? Not me. Not Avery Westwood, the poster boy for milk and Wheaties and Gatorade and the UNICEF ambassador and…Jesus, what is it about this woman that makes me forget the rules? That makes me cross all the lines of proper behavior? I really need to sort out my feelings for Stephanie and figure out how to go for this—for her—without losing my mind.

"Westwood, let's go!" Ty yells from outside.

Steph smiles and starts down the stairs.

I follow her. In the downstairs hall, I grab my keys off the hook by the door, and she opens the front door. Ty and Alex are standing on the sidewalk. I toss my keys to Ty. "Go to the car. Be there in a sec."

He nods, and they disappear around the side of the house toward the garage.

"So…I was stupid drunk last night," I tell her out of nowhere, because now that the tension spilled out with our laughing fit, I feel like I need to address that whole disaster in her bedroom.

"I know," she replies, and tucks her hair, damp from a shower, I'm guessing, behind her ears. We don't say anything else as I watch her sit on the railing that divides our porches and swing her legs over to stand on the other side. Our eyes lock.

"I totally would have jumped you if you'd let me."

She smiles. "I totally would have let you."

"You're bluffing."

Her grin widens. "Really? Because I think you're the one who's bluffing. You wouldn't go through with it. You've trained yourself not to be that guy."

"I would have."

She simply shrugs. "Too bad the moment's gone and we'll never know."

She disappears inside her house before I can say anything else.

The whole ride to the rink Alex talks nonstop about Stephanie—first he was grilling me on what happened when she came upstairs but when I refused to give him any information, he then decided to just contemplate Stephanie herself—her looks, her personality and how completely "bangable" she was. I almost leaned over, opened the passenger door and pushed him out onto the free-way.

Now in the locker room I'm stripping out of my street clothes, getting into my practice gear when Larue brings up Steph—*again*. "So how naked were you when she walked in? More naked than you are now?"

I decide to give him something because clearly if I don't, he won't shut up. "Yep."

I pull off my shirt and reach for my pads. He points. "More naked than now?"

Ty laughs beside me. "It sounds like you're pretty obsessed with naked Avery. Anything you want to tell us, Rue?"

Larue rolls his eyes. I smile at him sympathetically. "It's okay, buddy. Remember, we're an inclusive sport. We don't care what hole you put your dick in, as long as you put the puck in the back of the net."

"Fuck off. I'm just wondering how she saw you naked and didn't bang you," Alex explains, and Ty bursts out laughing.

"Do you want to bang Westwood when you see him naked?" Parsons wants to know, and a few more guys in the room chuckle. "Is that a daily struggle for you, Rue?"

Alex makes a face and flips off Ty. "I watch chicks drop their panties at the sight of him clothed, so how does Stephanie see him naked and not let him stick it to her?"

"Larue, you are a hillbilly dirtbag," Parsons announces, and shakes his head before turning his eyes to me. "But seriously, dude. You were in her bedroom last night, too, and you were fully clothed. I thought for sure I'd see nothing but your naked ass when I opened that door."

"You guys think highly of me, huh?"

"We think highly of Stephanie's hotness," Larue retorts, and grins. "Which is why this is so disappointing. Nothing's happening!"

I chuckle, "Oh, something's going to happen. I know that now." And I do. I knew that after our conversation last night. Any doubt I had this morning, with the sobriety of a new day, disappeared with our conversation this morning.

"So what are you waiting for?" Larue asks before he tugs his jersey over his fat head. Before I can answer, Larue rolls his eyes. "You're really going to let this go because you're too uptight and obsessed with your career? Really?"

"I didn't say that," I reply, but he's not listening.

He laces his skates and announces, "Well, your loss is going to be someone else's gain. Maybe mine."

"That's not your typical Rue victim," Nikolai pipes up as he tugs on his skate laces. "She's got a career that doesn't involve tips. She's a natural beauty. She has real tits. She's bright. She's not going to fall for your usual sleazy bullshit."

"Thanks, Furry. Asshole," Alex replies.

Everyone laughs. The guys start to wander out of the room toward the ice. I have the unfortunate luck of ending up next to Beau as we make our way down the tunnel. He fiddles with his gloves and glances up at me. "Sebastian Deveau lives to punch people. He doesn't even need a reason, but banging his sister would be a damn good reason."

"Seb's my friend. And I'm not banging his sister." Yet.

He shrugs. "Not my business…"

He steps onto the ice and skates away. He's right; it's not his business. But the fact that our little exchange just now didn't involve any major insults felt like maybe we were making progress.

After practice Ty is asking what everyone is doing tonight. He's talking about getting a group together for drinks. He's doing a roll call. Larue, Furlov and our rookie defenseman Drew Abbott are all in. Echolls mumbles a maybe.

"I'm out," I add. "I'm going to be on a date."

"Your dad in town? Your sister?"

"Shut up, Rue."

I've been stagnant long enough when it comes to what I want. It's time to go after Stephanie. She's a normal girl and she deserves to be wooed by a normal guy—or at least in a normal way by a not so normal guy. So I'm going to ask her on a date and I'm going to take her out in public, even if it means taking grief from my team or getting photographed by media or pissing off dear old Don.

Besides, Steph isn't some puck bunny. She's not a risk to me or my brand. I've known her for a few years now. She's the sister of a player, so she knows what my life is about. She doesn't need to fuck me for perks.

But God, it's nice to know she wants to fuck me.

Chapter 12

Stephanie

When Avery texted and asked if I had plans for dinner, I didn't know he meant this. In the last couple months since he moved here, we've gotten dinner a lot—everything from takeout Thai to sushi to Taco Bell.

But never a five-star restaurant. Until now.

I met him on the front porch in boyfriend jeans, a T-shirt and flip-flops and knew right away that I needed to change, because he was in dark, expensive denim and a fitted, button-down shirt. I smiled sheepishly. "This isn't a Taco Bell run, is it?"

He laughed. "Not exactly."

I ran upstairs and threw on something more appropriate, along with a little more makeup, and twisted my hair up into something I hoped was sexy since I didn't have time to curl it.

Now here we are sharing a strawberry shortcake over candlelight. And the scariest part is how quickly the evening has passed and how much I loved every second of it. The atmosphere is intimate and expensive, which when we first walked in made me panic a little. This felt like a date. An actual, real date, not just two friends who flirt grabbing a bite. I haven't been on a real date in almost three years and that last date was a disaster. Not something I am looking at repeating. Especially not with Avery.

But if this is a date, it isn't a disaster. Avery is acting like Avery, talking easily about his team, making jokes about my brother and our mutual friends and being his usual charming self with the rare but stunning smiles and that damn twinkle in his caramel eyes.

"I shouldn't be eating this," he murmurs as he takes a forkful of decadent whipped cream, luscious strawberry and airy pastry and lifts it to his open mouth.

"Dessert is the most important meal of the day," I tell him, and smile, scooping up my own piece of heaven and closing my eyes in delight as my lips cover the fork. "Mmm…"

When I open my eyes, he's staring at me, his eyelids low, his tongue skating across his bottom lip. Jesus, he's doing that thing where it feels like he's about to devour me. "Why are you single?"

The tone of the question—a low whisper, almost a growl—shocks me as much as the words themselves. I drop my fork to the plate quietly and pull my hands back, holding my wineglass as an anchor. "I just moved to a new state, working in a brand-new office, with a new roommate. I guess I just decided to focus on that for a while, you know?"

"Oh, I know all about focusing on a career." He shakes his head. "And I don't recommend it."

"Is that why you started dating Liz this summer?" I probably shouldn't bring her up, because ex talk isn't exactly good first date etiquette, if this is a first date.

"Yeah, I guess I just got tired of being alone," he admits, and lifts his napkin from his lap, dropping it on the table between his hands. "But being with someone for the sake of being with someone is just as bad as not being with anyone."

I blink. "She didn't seem like just anyone. I mean she seemed like the right type of girl."

"Is that so?" His dark eyebrow cocks and he tilts his head curiously. The candlelight brings out the amber in his eyes. "What type is that?"

"Pretty, sweet, kindergarten teacher, probably volunteers with the homeless."

"At a food bank," he corrects, and I smile.

"See? That type. Oh! And a hometown girl. Hockey boys love their hometown girls."

He leans forward and takes my fork off the plate, scooping up the last strawberry and dredging it through the dollop of whipped cream on the edge of the plate. He lets the fork hover in front of my lips. I open them and wrap them around the fork.

"You're from my hometown," he says as the fork slips out of my mouth.

I almost choke on the strawberry as I swallow it down. He's right, technically. I was born in Dieppe, New Brunswick, just like him. "I haven't been back since I was a kid."

"I'd have to check the rulebook, but I don't think frequent visits are a requirement," he responds, his voice abnormally low. Like turning the dial on a thermostat, he's cranking the heat higher and higher with every syllable.

He gently puts the fork back on the plate and lets his hand drop onto the table, resting on top of mine. My eyes are riveted to his face and I am deeply aware of how good it feels to have his skin, even just his hand, against mine. Then a shadow falls across the table and we both startle, looking up to see a middle-aged man in a pristine white chef's outfit standing beside our table.

"Mr. Westwood, I'm Chef Ned Felder. I am a huge fan of the Saints, so I wanted to come out personally and make sure your meal was enjoyable."

Avery's hand slips away from mine and he stands, shaking the chef's hand and complimenting him on the meal. I nod and thank him as well before excusing myself to use the restroom. They're still chatting as I slip away from the table and make my way to the ladies' room at the back.

My brain is spinning the whole time. I have somehow accidentally fallen ass-backward into a first date with Avery Westwood and I am now officially in the deep end of my feelings for him. The more time we spent together, the deeper the deep end seems to get, but the fact is, all the reasons why I shouldn't get romantically involved with him aren't disappearing. They are as solid as ever. I am still not the right girl for him. In all honesty I'm not even sure if I am the right girl for anyone. I have a truly dismal history with relationships.

I went out with Mike for almost four years, from sixteen to twenty. He's the one who first gave me Oxy that he'd stolen from his mom. We ran away together. He was emotionally abusive. When that ended because he ran off to Colorado with some girl, I found myself with Joel, who turned out to be physically abusive. That ended six months later when he broke my arm and I went to the emergency room higher than a kite. They called the police, who had a missing persons report on me from years before, and called my mom and Sebastian. I got clean shortly after, thanks to a pricey rehab in Washington that Seb paid for, and then settled in Seattle. Sebastian was completely nonjudgmental and incredibly supportive.

Once I was sober and building my life back, I dated Marty. We'd met at a mixer for Seattle locals enrolled in my online university. He was in the paralegal program too. He seemed funny and sweet, but, thankfully, I found out on the second date he was a married sleazeball with a wife and a kid.

That's when I swore off relationships and focused on just keeping my life on track. I may be clean and have done a fairly good job of keeping myself that way, but when it comes to picking men I am still a mess. In a way, Avery isn't an exception to that rule, because we have bigger hurdles than a wife and kid to get around: we have public Avery. The person the world believes he is—and that person wouldn't date a recovering pill popper.

But when I'm with Avery and he's looking at me the way I look at strawberry shortcake, he makes me want to forget all that stuff. He makes me…crazy. Crazy isn't good for me. I know this. The off-kilter, out-of-control feelings Avery brings out in me are unfamiliar and addictive. Honestly, no man has made me feel like that. With Mike and Joel, I was addicted to the way the narcotics they gave me made me feel, not how they made me feel. With Marty it was short and never once did it feel as amazing as it does when Avery simply smiles at me.

I feel light-headed and giddy, like I'm drunk. But I've only had one glass of wine, which is why when I hear my name called as I make my way back to the table, I think I'm hearing things. But then I glance to my left and see Daniel, a junior lawyer from our firm, standing up at a table a few feet away and smiling at me. My feet stumble to a halt in my high-heeled booties as he comes around the table and I glance at the men in expensive suits that he's with. None is a client, at least not one I recognize. Possibly they're other lawyers, but not from our firm, or I would know them.

"Hey! What are you doing here?" I say with a smile and let him hug me.

"Dinner out with the guys," he tells me. "The wives are doing a girls' weekend in Vegas. When the cat's away…"

He laughs at his own joke, and I force another smile. Daniel is from San Diego and was hired new to the firm when we opened this office; he wasn't transferred like my boss and me. At first he seemed friendly but professional and the consummate family man. He talked about his wife and kids a lot at the office. But the longer I work with him, the more I realize that's an act. He's become more…sleazy. Not with me but in general, with some of the things he's been doing, like leering at me in the elevator and ogling Maddie's ass the other day while she was at the photocopier. "What about you?"

"Dinner with someone," I say vaguely, because I just want the conversation to stop so I can get back to Avery and out of this place.

"Stephanie, these are my friends Phil and Ben," he introduces the two at the table, who both stand and shake my hand. "They're senior partners at Staal and the entertainment law firm around the block from us."

"Nice to meet you both," I say quickly, and turn back to Daniel. "I should be going."

"No. Stay for a drink. Just one."

"I'm here with a friend…," I reiterate politely, and glance toward the front of the room.

"Is it Maddie? She's your roommate, right?"

I try not to gag at how needy he sounds when he talks about her. That's not good. At all. Why did he have to turn into such a sleazeball? He glances at his buddies and chuckles. "Boy, if our legal secretaries are eating here, we must be paying these girls too much."

The men chuckle, as they would. Because they're dicks.

"Hey! Steph!"

I turn and see Avery coming toward us. Suddenly I panic. I have no idea why. I take a small step away from Daniel and give Avery the "one-minute" sign with my hand, but he keeps on walking right toward us. "I have to go…"

But Daniel is no longer looking at me. He's looking at Avery. The next thing I know, Avery is standing on my left and Daniel is on my right. I'm sandwiched between the two of them. Avery is smiling down at Daniel, but it's guarded. Daniel is looking up at Avery like he's trying to figure out why he recognizes him.

Avery glances at me quickly before turning his gaze to Daniel and extending his hand. "Avery Westwood. Hi."

"Hi. I'm Daniel Jackson. A lawyer at Steph's firm."

One of the guys at the table—the one I think he said was Phil—perks up. "Avery Westwood! Man, I'm a huge fan! I was so psyched when the Saints landed you."

Avery slips into that Colgate smile he has for fans and media and milk commercials. "Thank you very much. I'm happy to be here. It's a great city and a great team."

"We weren't great last year. You've really turned the team around!"

Before Avery can answer, the other guy is introducing himself and shaking Avery's hand.

"Should we get going?" I finally find my voice and look up to see Avery's face. He's smiling down at me. Smirking, actually. It's hot but disconcerting at the same time.

"Yeah. Ty and Maddie are at Alibi with some friends. Thought we'd join them?" Avery says, and I nod.

"Yep. Sure." I turn to Daniel. "Nice seeing you, Daniel. Have a good night!"

I smile at the trio, give them a quick wave good-bye, and head back to my table. Avery takes an extra second to shake their hands again and follows me. At the table I reach for the bill. Avery's hands land on my hips and send a ripple of heat to the spot between my legs.

"I took care of it," he tells me.

"How much do I owe you?"

"Nothing. Unless you want to pay me in something other than money."

I turn in the small space between the back of my chair and his body. I let my eyes take their time as they crawl up his chest, clad in a soft, slightly clingy black and gray striped dress shirt, strong neck to his biteable full bottom lip, to his kissable top lip, to his perfect nose to his warm eyes. "I can't. You shouldn't pay."

"I asked you here, didn't I?" When I nod, he continues. "In case I didn't make it clear earlier, I'm telling you now—it's a date."

Okay, now we've officially changed the trajectory of our relationship. Officially. Oh, God. Those crazy, out-of-control feelings are filling me up again. I feel like a helium balloon getting lighter and lighter. And that's completely terrifying.

Avery dips his head, his eyes still glued to mine. "Don't look so uneasy. I'm the one who doesn't do this, the monk as your brother and everyone else nicknamed me, so I should be the terrified one."

"Yes, well, I'm accidentally on a date with God's gift to hockey and women," I snark, and try hard to smile and start toward the door.

"It's not accidental," he whispers back, his face still incredibly close to mine. "It's on purpose."

The walk to the bar where Ty and Maddie are is short—about half a block. We walk in silence for a few feet until Avery looks over his shoulder and back at me. "I bet he shows up at Alibi."

"Who?"

"Daniel."

"What? No. Why would he do that?" I ask.

"Because he heard me mention it and he knows you're going to be there and he checked out your ass when you walked away." He's leaned down to say this in my ear, and his breath tickles the back of my neck. I'm suddenly thrilled I wore my hair up tonight.

I quicken my step to pull away from him a little bit—it's either that or turn around and start to rip his clothes off. "Daniel is not going to follow me to the bar."

Avery takes one step with his long muscular legs and is back in step beside me. "He's going to show up."

"Nope."

"Wanna bet?"

We're a few feet from the bar. I stop and turn to face him. Avery smiles down at me, his caramel eyes mischievous and his lips curled into a smile that I want to kiss right off.

"You're on," I say, and extend my hand. Avery wraps his hand around mine and holds it more than shakes it. His grip is solid and warm and it makes me feel tingly.

"What's the wager?" I ask.

"If I'm right…" He stops talking and we stare at each other for a long, sexually charged minute that has my panties getting damp and sucks the air from my lungs. "You have to come home with me."

Did he just…? Does he mean…? "I live next to you. I always go home with you."

"I mean into my house, up the stairs and into my bed home with me," he clarifies without blinking, which is fine because I'm blinking enough for the both of us.

"You're really good at clarifying things," I can't help but chirp, which is so silly it makes him smile.

"Years of media training finally comes in handy." He cocks his head and I realize we're still shaking hands. And I just agreed to sleep with him if I lose this bet. When I take my hand back from his, I'm amazed it isn't shaking. "Deal."

I force myself to turn and walk toward the bar. It's like trying to drive a car with the parking brake on. My body does not want to leave him behind. But I have to or else the bet will be off and we'll be naked in an alley. And I mean that, which is why I need to stay away from him until I get myself together. I will sleep with him. I know this without a doubt now, whether Daniel shows up at Alibi or not. I will, because I want to, but I have to somehow keep myself from drowning in him, because drowning in anything is too scary for me.

I slip into the bar and slide past Larue, who is standing near the open door. He winks at me. "Ty said you were joining us but I didn't believe him. *Tu sais que le plusieurs temps que to prends avec nous…*"

"Shut it, Alex," I say before he can finish his sentence that started with *the more time you spend with us*, but he finishes it anyway.

"The less time you spend between the sheets!"

"I said shut it!" and for good measure I repeat it in French. *"Ferme ta gueule."*

I go straight for the bar to order a mojito and find myself praying that, even though it would creep me out, Daniel shows up here tonight.

Chapter 13

Avery

The night's almost over. It's a little before midnight, and I know any second Ty is going to say we should get going—and he would be right. The team flies to Milwaukee early tomorrow for a game the following night.

But that Daniel dude hasn't shown up yet and I really don't want to lose this bet. I glance at Stephanie, who's at the bar with Maddie getting fresh drinks. Ty is standing with me, and he and Larue are making fun of our teammate Drew's latest conquest, Anne, who has gotten sloppy drunk and is trying to talk about "where this is going" with Drew on the other side of the small bar. Drew is giving the guys quick "help me" glances when she's not looking and they're smiling, raising their drinks in his general direction and completely ignoring his requests. I can't keep myself from staring at Steph.

"You know what works better than undressing her with your eyes?" Larue says, nudging me. "Undressing her with your hands."

I smile. "Mind your business, Alex."

"Love is my business," he replies with a grin, and sips his beer.

Maddie and Steph make their way back to us. Steph hands me a new beer. "Trying to get me drunk?" I ask.

She smiles. "Yes. So I can take advantage of you."

"No booze required," I promise, and then I glance at the other drink in her hand. It's the third glass of clear liquid with lime I've seen her drink, and suddenly I'm worried that she's nervous about the bet. Is she trying to drink away her fear of hooking up with me? Oh, God, I don't want her to have to be drunk to sleep with me. I point to the tumbler in her hand. "What about you? Is that liquid courage in case you lose the bet?"

She glances down and swirls the clear liquid in my glass. "Soda water with lime."

I can feel my face get tense, and I nervously lick my lower lip. I can't help but notice that her eyes are following my tongue. I want to think that's a good sign. "So you've stopped drinking? Why?"

She moves her eyes from my mouth, blinks as if trying to bring herself into the moment, and then smiles brightly and coyly says, "I need to be sober so the naked pictures I post of you on Instagram later are in focus."

Those words have been my biggest fear since Instagram—and social media in general—became a thing. I frown, and she bursts out laughing. "Oh, come on, Avery! You *know* I'm kidding."

Of course she's kidding. Stephanie could have already sold a lot of personal information about me to the tabloids. She hasn't and she wouldn't—I know this, but thanks to my father's harping I'm always waiting for people to stab me in the back. Before I can try to blow off my reaction or even apologize for it, Maddie nudges Stephanie.

"Why does Drew keep looking over here like he's about to be stabbed or something?" Maddie asks Ty, and Larue and I chuckle.

"Anne is trying to talk about their relationship," Ty explains.

"Trying to have a meaningful conversation after three martinis?" Stephanie raises an eyebrow. "She's looking for trouble."

"She found trouble when she hooked up with Drew," Maddie adds, and then tugs on Ty's hand. "Let's go save him."

"What? No. We have to let him suffer. It's the bro code." Ty's eyes twinkle with mischief. Maddie rolls her eyes and drags him with her anyway.

Larue puts his glass on the bar and glances at us but his eyes linger on Stephanie. "If you'll excuse me, I need to go to the not-so-little boy's room."

He gives her an exaggerated, comical wink and she looks at him with the best unimpressed face I've ever seen—God bless her. Now, alone with Stephanie again, her gaze shifts to me, and I take in those insanely clear blue eyes and watch as she wraps her lips around the straw in her drink to take a long sip. It feels like foreplay. I'm that hot for her.

"So looks I'm going to win the bet," she tells me when she stops drinking. She licks her lips, then starts to walk over to the corner of the bar where two stools have been vacated. I follow her. She jumps up and sits in one and I sit in the other, but we both turn the stools so we're facing each other. I look down to where our knees are almost touching. She's wearing a short black lace skirt; all night I've been admiring her tanned legs all the way down to her slouchy black high-heeled ankle boots. I've been picturing those boots next to my ears.

"Night's not over yet," I remind her as I send out another silent prayer that this guy lets his dick lead the way and shows up here. I could tell by the way he was looking at Stephanie at the restaurant and the way he asked about Maddie that he wants one—or both—of them. She looks skeptical, like she believes the night is over and she's won. And then I realize I don't know what that means if she does win.

"So let's say this guy turns out to be gay," I joke, and she giggles. "If he doesn't show up tonight, what do you win?"

"What do I win?"

I lean forward and casually put a hand on her bare knee. Her skin is warm and soft and makes my dick start to come alive in my pants. "Yeah. You know if *I* win you have to come home with me. And if *you* win…?"

She looks me square in the eye but says nothing for a long minute. Then she slides off the bar stool and uses her hip to push my legs apart so she can get closer. Standing between my legs, she leans in next to my ear, balancing herself with a hand on my shoulder. I have a brief, strong urge to look around and make sure no one is watching us—or worse, has their cell phone out taking pictures. But I fight the impulse and concentrate on the feel of her wedged so close to me. I even dare to let the fingers on my left hand run gently up and down the outer side of her thigh.

"If I win…then *you* have to go home with *me*."

My heart flips and my dick twitches. I pull back just a fraction of an inch so I can look in her eyes. She's got the same look on her face that she had last night in her bedroom. The dead serious I'm-going-to-let-you-fuck-me look. I move my hand, pressing my palm flat against her lower back and pull her farther into the small space between my legs.

She's still got one hand on my shoulder and the other one curled around the glass she's holding up near her chest. I realize I'm about to kiss her at the same time she realizes I'm about to kiss her. She takes a deep breath and lets it out almost audibly. She dips her chin. I tilt my face.

And then suddenly the sound of the bar fills my ears. The laughter is amplified, the sound of glasses clinking, the conversations—everything. It seems like someone just turned the volume up, and I'm acutely aware of how crowded this place is and how many people could be watching me.

I hate myself for it, but I have to look up and glance around the room. She takes a step away from me so big she bumps the stool she'd been sitting on and it wobbles. She turns to steady it, and I try not to punch myself in the face. I'm so mad at myself for ruining what could have been the kiss I've been fantasizing about since Seattle.

"Stephanie!"

At the sound of her name, her head snaps up so fast some hair tumbles out of her twisty updo. I literally groan and, from across the room, I hear Larue yell, "YOU SUCK, WESTIE!"

Stephanie hears him, too, and simply lifts her arm above her head and gives the finger to his general direction. Then she steps away from the bar to greet the person who called her name: Daniel.

"I figured we'd bring the party here, and I could buy you and Maddie a drink," Daniel says, and runs a hand through his short Supercuts-looking haircut.

"Oh, that would be great, but we're actually on our way out," Steph says with regret dripping from her voice that only I know is fake. "I've got an early day tomorrow."

"Come on. Just one drink?"

"Sorry. And I'm…his ride home." She points to me. "I can't let him drive. He's had a couple beers. He's a total lightweight."

She just threw me under the bus, and I don't even care. In fact, it's kind of cute. I bite my lip to keep from smiling and I nod. Daniel looks confused but nods. "Okay, then. Well, I'll see you at the office next week."

I watch Stephanie nod and smile brightly. Then she gives him a quick hug and reaches back for my hand. She's trying to give him the idea that I'm with her. Like, actually *with* her as her boyfriend or something and, although I get a quick wave of panic like I'm conditioned to with any woman who insinuates anything about me in public, it washes away quickly, replaced by a wave of happiness. I want people to think I'm with her. That's a first. So not only do I let her grab my hand but I also lace my fingers through hers and watch as Daniel notices.

Yeah, that's right, douche, she's taking me home.

Ty and Maddie are also walking toward the door. Larue is smiling at me and giving me the thumbs-up. Drew is too busy dealing with his drunken sort-of girlfriend to notice anything else.

Out on the sidewalk I don't let go of Steph's hand, and she doesn't let go of mine either. We walk for a bit along the water, with Maddie and Ty a couple feet in front of us. Then Ty says he's going to call two Ubers and announces he and Maddie will be staying at his place. He does it like he's declaring his candidacy for president, all loud and definitive. His eyes are on me the whole time. When the Uber cars pull up to the curb, Ty gives me an exaggerated wink as he climbs into the back of his ride.

Despite the large space in the back of the Escalade we're in, I sit right next to Steph and she drops a hand on my thigh. It's just there, not rubbing or grabbing, just resting. It still feels fucking amazing. When I move and rest my hand on top of hers, she smiles softly to herself, her pink lips parting a little as she gazes out the window at the passing scenery. Man, she's beautiful. Not pretty or cute or sexy or…Well, she's all of those things but mostly just plain knock-the-wind-out-of-you beautiful. Fuck, I hope to God she's going to let me have sex with her. This time, there's no one to interrupt us.

The Uber pulls up in front of our places and we get out. I ogle her ass because I can and because it's a mighty fine ass. Her step slows as she reaches the stairs. She turns to face me and suddenly I'm nervous, unsure and awkward. I've never been this way before. Like never. Not even when I was a teenager. Lizzie was my first real adult relationship, and I didn't even feel this way when we got together. Maybe it's because Stephanie's looking at me with this expression I can't read. It might be excitement, but it also might be fear or regret. The bet is on both our minds, I can tell.

"I was just kidding around back there, you know." I find my mouth saying the complete opposite of what my heart and my dick are thinking. "You don't have to…I mean it wasn't a serious bet."

"So you don't want to sleep with me?" she questions, tilting her head and raising an eyebrow. Her arms cross in front of her chest.

I open my mouth and stare at her. I don't know how to answer that. Do I tell her the truth or lie? What's less offensive, wanting to bang her or pretending not to want to?

She smiles at the stupid look I'm sure is on my face. I clear my throat and shove my hands in my pockets. "I don't want to force you to be with me just because you lost a silly bet."

"I don't make bets I don't intend on keeping. Win or lose." She unfolds her arms and puts her hands on her hips. "Do you?"

I shake my head no, because I don't trust my voice to not crack, out of desire. She turns and walks up the stairs to my porch, not hers. Her perfectly round ass swings back and forth under the short, clingy lace skirt. She turns back around, facing me again from the top of the stairs. I look up at her. The moonlight is making the lighter strands of her hair glow a kind of golden color and her tan skin glisten, contrasting the light blue of her eyes.

"I want to kiss you," I admit gruffly.

"I want to let you."

And that's it—the green light, the starter pistol, the rocket launching. I climb the stairs two at a time. When I'm one step below her, I reach out and grab her waist, pulling her in and up at the same time. She wraps her arms around my neck and as I step onto the top step, holding her an inch off the ground in my arms, our lips connect for the first time.

Chapter 14

Stephanie

His lips are *finally* on mine. My heart skips and then starts to race. I almost want to sigh with relief. I knew I wanted him, but I don't think I even realized how much until we finally kissed. His lips are warm and soft and his stubble scrapes my chin.

I've never been attracted to athletic men, even though I've been around them more than any other kind, even lawyers. I always found them so chaotic. They're loud and rough—both in physical appearances and mannerisms—and they're energetic. Nothing is ever peaceful, and after my tumultuous past, I felt like I required orderly, calm, peaceful.

Avery Westwood has a structured life, but even he lacks a sense of calm and peace. Being around him has started to make me crazy and unraveled, and now kissing him intensifies those feelings but somehow fills me with peaceful feelings too. Everything gets frantic: my heart rate, the speed my blood travels through my veins, the way my thoughts ricochet around my brain. And yet it doesn't terrify me. Kissing him is like finally scratching an itch that I haven't been able to reach in months. It's nothing but pure relief to finally end the frustration of not being able to satisfy a need.

Our mouths move together in perfect unison, like they know the steps to a dance Avery and I are unaware of. His lips move seamlessly against mine. I open my mouth even before he does because it's not enough—just lips—and then his tongue readily slides out to meet mine. A tsunami of desire for Avery rolls through me.

My arms squeeze tighter around his neck and my hands dig into his hair. I press my whole body flat against his because I want to—I *need* to—touch as much of him as I possibly can. He's still got me a couple of inches off the ground and he's walking toward the door. And then the door is flat against my back and Avery's mouth is on my jaw by my ear and he's kissing and sucking, and I tug on his hair as fire licks me from the inside.

With the door and his body weight holding me off the ground, he moves his hands from my waist down to my ass and palms it greedily. I let my arms slip from my shoulders and my fingers trace his spine as I lower my hands to *his* ass. Because what a fucking ass it is. I've wondered exactly how perfect it must feel since the first time I ever met him. It was before one of Sebastian's games, in the tunnel outside the dressing rooms in the Seattle arena. Avery was stretching in nothing but black nylon workout shorts. Right leg bent, left leg straight behind him and perfect, round, full ass stretching the seams on his nylon shorts to their limits. And now that it's in my hands I can confirm that I've never felt such a solid, perfectly round mass of muscle in my entire existence.

His fingers skim the hem of my skirt and curl their way underneath as his tongue slides over mine again. I arch my back slightly against the door, pushing my hips toward him, and he pushes back, and then I feel another perfect, hard mass of muscle. This one is rubbing against my thigh.

"Avery," I whisper as his mouth moves to my neck and his tongue traces a path up to my ear. "Open the door."

His right hand leaves my leg and digs his keys out of his pocket. He kisses me again as he slides the key into the lock behind my left elbow, and when he turns the handle we both stumble into the hallway. I'm so off balance that I have to reach out and grab the stair railing behind me to keep from falling. Avery slams the door shut and reaches out to steady me. He pulls me to his chest and I put my hand on his flexed biceps.

Our eyes meet in the darkened hallway, the only light coming from a table lamp he had left on in the living room to my left. He keeps one hand wrapped around my waist and lifts the other one to my hair, where he expertly pulls the clip out and drops it to the floor. My hair tumbles to my shoulders as the metal clip clatters on the hardwood by my feet.

"I have waited way too long to do that," he says, his eyes locked on mine and a sincere smile on his lips, which are stained ruby from my lipstick.

I reach up and cup the side of his face, his stubble tickling my palm, and I run a thumb over his perfect bottom lip. "Show me what else you've been waiting to do."

He kisses me again, which is exactly what I want, because kissing him is incredible. It makes me feel wild. Out of control. Electric. Just like the first time it progresses into a hardcore make-out session almost instantly, and just like last time my body is flooded with wild, uncontrollable desire.

He's filled with the same sensations. I can tell by the way he pushes me, backward toward the stairs. My knees are buckling and so he reaches out with one of those giant arms of his and holds me tightly and eases me down onto the stairs. He lets me unbutton his crisp, tailored shirt, bunch it up in my hands and slip it off his shoulders. Then my hands grab the bottom of my shirt in the back and tug it up, off my body. Because I want him to know I wasn't playing. This is no joke; I want to make good on the little bet. I want him naked and inside me, and I want it now.

I'm so happy I'm wearing my best matching underwear—a white lace demi-cup bra, the kind that has my tits all pushed up on display for him. He cups them as soon as he sees them, then dips his head and gently kisses the right one where it's spilling out of its confines as he runs his thumbs over the delicate white fabric. I can feel my nipples harden because of the delicious sensations he's creating, and it's amazing. It's been so long since a man has touched me, and, oh, God, I've missed someone else's hands on my body.

I run my own hands down his back, around his sides and then up to his chest. I can feel his left hand behind my back, and with a quick flick of his wrist and twist of his fingers, my bra is undone. I smirk at that and can't decide if I'm surprised or impressed. It's honestly both.

"How did a monk become such a pro at removing girls' undergarments?" I ask.

His answer is to kiss that smirk right off my face. His hands tug my bra down my arms and off my body, and then his mouth leaves mine and covers my left nipple. He bites down gently. My back arches and a rush of air leaves my open mouth in a throaty gasp.

I love when men lick and touch my tits. It's my favorite thing in the sexual universe, and maybe it's because it's been so long, but I don't ever remember it feeling as good as it does now with Avery. He uses just the right about of wetness and lips and teeth, and by the time he moves to my right breast I'm panting and tugging so roughly on his hair, which is twisted in my fingers, that I'm surprised he isn't yelping.

But he's doing the exact opposite. He's responding with rougher licks and harder nips, making it even better. I swear I must be leaving a puddle of desire on the stairs under my ass. He starts kissing his way back up my chest to my neck and finally my mouth, and I lower my hands, snaking them from his hair around to his rock-hard stomach. My only goal is to get to his belt and get it undone.

Two of my fingers graze his belly button and then slide through the narrow trail of hair that leads down. I press my hand firmly against the front of his jeans and he groans into my mouth. As I slide down the zipper on his pants, I can't help but gently bite my lower lip in anticipation. My hand slips into his now open pants and…he isn't wearing underwear. *Holy sweet God in heaven.* For some reason that's the hottest thing ever.

Also, he's huge. There was a rumor going around that he was packing. It started from what was supposed to be an innocuous picture in the sports section of the Seattle newspaper of the team getting ready pregame the year they won the Cup. Avery was in the Under Armour players wear under their pads. It's kind of like a skintight spandex T-shirt and spandex tights that end above his knees. The camera caught Avery standing to the side, and there was quite the bulge in the front. The Internet exploded, especially on puck bunny sites. But it didn't end there. Full-on sports news sites were speculating over the size of Avery Carter Westwood's personal hockey stick. No one could verify the rumors at the time but now I can. He wasn't wearing an oversized cup. His personal hockey stick needs its own arena.

"Stephanie." He pants my name and hooks his hands under the back of my knees and firmly pushes them up toward my bare chest and then apart, so he can slide his now exposed cock along my panty-covered core. My delicate lacy skirt is pushed up around my waist. I graze my lips across the vein thumping in his neck, down to his collarbone, and push his jeans down his hips, giving his not-so-little friend more room to play.

His lips brush my ear and he whispers, "God, I've wanted this…fantasized of this…forever."

He grinds into me again, with nothing but my underwear holding us back from what we both want. He hand is moving toward the offending article of clothing, my heartbeat getting harder and louder with every inch his hand gains. I don't know why, but I feel like I need to say something, but all I can manage is his name.

"Avery." I arch my back in anticipation as his hand slides up my inner thigh.

"You want my hand there?" he asks, his voice low and gruff. The tips of his fingers graze the white lace thong I've got on. He's asking in the cocky tone that implies he already knows the answer. He'd bet a year's pay on it. And it's so damn hot. "You want me to touch your pussy, Stephanie?"

"*Oui*," I manage to whisper. Avery is Canadian. He was born in the same town I was and raised among the Acadian French. He's not fluent, but he knows enough. And honestly, he didn't need verbal confirmation. The wet lace against his fingers should be answer enough.

Avery hooks his fingers into the skimpy fabric and slides under it. I push up into his hand and bite down on his earlobe as he slides a finger into me. I moan as my eyes flutter closed, and I don't even care how fucking desperate I must look. I can't be bothered to try to restrain even an ounce of the desire I feel for him tonight.

"Are you sure you've had sex before?" he asks quietly as he pushes his finger deep, uses his thumb to gently slide over my clit. "You're so tight."

"I've had sex," I assure him in a pant and roll my hips, causing more friction between my button and his rough thumb pad. "Just not with everyone and not in a while."

I turn my face, and our eyes connect. I don't need to tell him it's been almost three years. I've been around him almost as much as I've been around my own brother, since they played together, and when Seb was single I was his perpetual plus-one for events and parties. He probably knows, just like I know that other than Lizzie, he's had sex like maybe once in the last three years, and that was with Jessie Garrison's sister. Well, before she was with Jordan's brother Devin.

A lock of his dark brown hair is curling over his forehead. I reach up and brush it away and then hold his face in my hands and pull it down to my lips.

He slips another finger inside me and I roll my hips against his hand. I want so desperately to come. Our tongues battle and I know his fingers are slick with my need, and only getting slicker, as he works them in and out and his calloused thumb keeps rolling over my clit. I'm not just getting wetter; I'm getting warmer. The heat starts between my legs, but it spreads everywhere and I start to tingle. My cheeks are flushed and I'm panting, and then I reach down and wrap my hand around his erection, which is throbbing impatiently. The contact makes me shudder. "I want your dick inside me, Avery."

"And I'll be inside your tight little pussy soon, I promise." He kisses me lightly.

I barely notice because I'm so focused on the flutter I feel between my legs with every curl of his fingers inside me.

"But if you come…it'll be easier."

I shake my head, which makes me an idiot, because he's about to give me an orgasm. Why would I argue against that? I rub his cock again and he groans, which I love.

"I'm a big girl. I can take…*Oh*. Avery…" My argument falls from my lips as he licks one of my nipples again and sucks it into his mouth. And then he's kissing the flat of my stomach, then the edge of my belly button.

He's not stopping there. He's sliding lower between my legs. He bites down on my hip and slides his thick body down a step. I tug on his hair again. Hard. He bites down again. Harder. His fingers are still moving inside me and I'm struggling for breath now. His head dips below my bunched-up skirt.

He kisses my clit, his lips pressing firmly on it, before he opens his mouth and swirls his tongue across it. "Oh, God, Avery. Avery! Oh, Avery."

That's it. That's all it takes. I'm so worked up from his fingers, and it's been so fucking long since someone made me come, and I'm so unbelievably turned on by him that I break halfway through the second pass of his tongue.

Chapter 15

Avery

I'm almost disappointed that she comes so quickly. But listening to her gasp my name, feeling her pussy suck at my fingers and tasting her need on my tongue makes up for it. I don't stop until her hips stop twisting and my name stops falling from her lipstick-smeared lips. Then I pull back, kneeling, and shove my jeans down to my knees and grab a condom out of the back pocket.

It's such a dick move to carry readily accessible condoms, and I fully expect her to call me on it. I can't remember the last time I carried a condom on me, because I can't remember the last time I hoped I would have spontaneous sex.

Lizzie and I had sex—not a lot, at least not as much as I'd have expected to have in a relationship—but it was never spontaneous. It was always in the same place: my bed. At the same time: just before sleep. In the same position: missionary. Don't get me wrong—I don't mind missionary at all, but I like to mix it up. Lizzie, despite having the tight little body of a cheerleader in a porno, wasn't all that adventurous.

Anyway, luckily, Steph doesn't notice. Or if she does, she doesn't comment. Lowering my body over hers again, I grab my cock, cover it, and ready myself to push my way into the promised land.

I hesitate for just a second because she barely looks conscious after that orgasm. Her head is resting against the hardwood of the step, turned to the left, eyes fluttering open and then closed. She's so damn gorgeous with her pink cheeks and her heaving breasts and her dark, thick fluttering eyelashes. I can't help but let my eyes slide lower; because she's not looking I don't even try not to admire her naked lower half. Her skirt is still hiked up around her waist.

As I force my eyes back to her face, she's looking back at me. Well, her eyes are open, but they seem unfocused. I lean over her and brush her hair off her face. I think she might be done for the night. I'd be devastated, but I would never push the issue. If this is all we do tonight, so be it—I'm confident there will be another night. Hopefully a lot of them.

But she reaches up, runs her fingernails over the back of my neck and says in a rough whisper, "I still want you. Inside me."

Her hand leaves the back of my neck and reaches between us. She holds my sheathed cock in her hand and it jerks at her touch. She smiles softly at that. I lay my body down so our torsos are pressed against each other. I move my face so my lips are against the shell of her ear. "I'm ready when you are. Show me the way, baby."

She opens her legs wider on either side of my hips and uses her hand to slide my tip over her opening. "I'm so ready," she whispers back, and as she tilts her hips, I push.

She's unbelievably tight. Seriously. It's almost painful. Almost. Not enough to stop or anything. I push a little more and she sighs and rocks her hips, taking more of me with each swivel. The heat, the pressure, the fact that she's still quivering from the orgasm I gave her with my tongue and fingers is sensation overload. And I swear I don't think I've ever wanted anyone more in my life. She's acting like she feels the same way as she grips my shoulders and arches off the stairs as she hooks her feet behind my ass. "If I wasn't so wet and spent from that orgasm, I don't think I would be able to take all of you. I can barely do it now, but oh, my God, you feel incredible."

There isn't a guy in the world who doesn't want to hear they're hung and they feel incredible. Not one. And I've heard it before, but from her it feels so authentic, like she's talking to herself and not trying to say the right things to some hockey millionaire she's trying to impress. I push into her—hard—and she moans, and my eyes roll back in my head.

"Kiss me," I hear myself beg. She grabs my face in her hands and complies.

As our tongues touch, I keep rocking inside her, my pace picking up speed with every thrust. I'm frantic to get there—and get her there one more time. She grips my shoulders and lets out a soft noise, like a gasp and a moan all at once. I realize she's about to come again. My body starts to hum. My balls start to tingle. I'm not sure she's there yet. I want to make sure she's there but…

"Stephanie. I can't… You're too fucking tight. You feel too good. I can't stop it," I pant apologetically against her lips.

"Oh, God," she moans, and her back arches.

"Fuck!" I push so hard into her the wood under us squeaks and her head bumps the step above it. I struggle to keep from collapsing on top of her and crushing her into the stairs. I can't open my eyes and I feel her lips press to the vein in my neck I know is throbbing and I feel my dick jerk over and over inside her.

When it stills and my pulse starts to regulate, I heave a deep breath. "Holy fuck, Stephanie. I have never come like that in my life."

"Neither have I," she confesses against my ear.

I reach up and run my fingers over the top of her head. "Are you okay? I made you hit your head."

"Mmm…I have no idea. Can't feel anything anywhere."

I laugh. "Sorry. I didn't mean to do this on the stairs. It's not what I'd planned for a perfect first time."

She kisses my cheek. "It wasn't perfect. It was better."

"Yeah. It was." I grin at her because even though it was crazy, it really was perfect. Just like everything else about Stephanie.

Chapter 16

Avery

My alarm screams and I promptly reach across her and slam the snooze button, then immediately hit the off button. I yawn and gently move her arm off my chest. I hate myself for it but I sit up. She pulls at me and lets out a tiny, sexy little groan of protest. It makes me smile despite the fact that I'm exhausted and bitter about having to get up at all.

Last night on the stairs blew my mind. There are no words, which is crazy because I always have words for everything. I can talk about anything and everything. My father hired a public relations coach for me when I was fourteen right after I did an interview with a local paper. When they asked me what I would want to be if I didn't make it as a hockey player, I said firefighter. He was furious that I had an answer for what I would do if I didn't end up playing hockey and that I offered it so quickly. Apparently there was no way I would do anything but professional hockey and I needed not only to say that but also to think it.

The PR coach was a cool, fast-talking thirty-year-old named

Padma. And thanks to two years with her I knew exactly what to say in any situation, whether I was talking about charity work or play-off-ending losses or Stanley Cup–winning games.

But after one night of hot sex on a set of rickety stairs, I was speechless. Words couldn't do sex with Stephanie justice.

And it hadn't been awkward or weird afterward. I was never one for cuddling. Not with Lizzie, not with anyone. In fact, after the few one-night stands I'd given in to while I was in the league—there were four, to be precise—I'd kicked all but one to the curb as soon as the condom came off. And that one rolled away from me as soon as sex was over and fell asleep. There was no touching, let alone cuddling.

It wasn't that I didn't like Lizzie. Honestly, I liked all my hookups. I had to like them enough to trust them. None of them were random strangers, like Alex's always were. And of course I liked Lizzie a lot, but I just…I'd been trained not to express physical intimacy in public and somehow that spilled over and made it hard to express it in private too. The girls never complained; even Lizzie didn't.

But I hadn't felt the need to create distance with Stephanie. When we made it to the bedroom, we'd had sex again. Afterward she collapsed on top of me and I wrapped my arms around her and let her nuzzle into me as we fell asleep. Not only did I let her nuzzle, but I fucking loved it too. Who knew it could feel great and not like I was suffocating.

Now her slender, bare arm reaches out for me from under my duvet. I lean down and kiss her forehead. "I gotta get ready to catch my flight, babe."

She groans her discontent again and curls deeper under the duvet. I smile and sneak off into the bathroom. For the first time in my entire hockey-playing life I kind of wish I didn't have a game. Leaving her is going to suck, especially before we have a conversation on exactly what last night meant. I want to make it clear to her this wasn't some bet to me. It wasn't a one-night thing either. I want this—the sex and everything else—to keep happening.

I open the big glass door and turn on the shower. The first thing I did when I got in this place was get the landlord's permission to update the bathroom. The rest of the house's character is kind of funky and charming with its old built-in shelves and creaky stairs, but the master bath—well, I take my showers very seriously and the crappy old stall with a separate, tiny tub was not going to cut it. I took one whole side of the room and had a contractor make a huge shower with a big bench at one end, a rain head shower and two other showerheads at either end.

My father was irate. He hated that I had decided to rent this "shithole," as he called it, instead of buying one of the multi-million-dollar places on the water with security, like Ty and Alex and other players had. He hated that I then dumped money into the place by renovating the bathroom. Of course he had done nothing but complain over everything since I chose to play for San Diego. He had wanted Manhattan or Los Angeles. In fact, he'd insisted on it. It was only the second time I'd ever ignored his business advice.

I'd lived to regret the first one, which was picking college instead of going straight into the league. I'd regretted it when two of my close friends and college teammates, Cole Garrison and Trey Beckford, suffered career-ending injuries. I realized that the same thing could happen to me and I would never make the NHL. And then in my junior year Trey had become addicted to painkillers, and rumors swirled that the entire team had drug issues. I dropped out and took my place on the Winterhawks. My father loved to remind me how

I wasted three years in school and how if I'd only listened to him, I would have avoided all that and be millions richer, much sooner. He might have been right then, but after last night I knew I would never regret coming to San Diego.

Everything I had hoped for when I came here was asleep in my bed.

I step under the warm spray and close my eyes. Behind my eyelids all I see is her smooth white skin, her bouncy breasts, her round, tight ass. I still have my eyes closed, smiling at the memories, as I lather body wash over my chest, when the glass door opens and I feel a wave of cool air followed by a warm body pressed to my back.

"You always shower with a smile on your face?" her voice, still grainy with sleep, says softly against my wet shoulder.

"I'm pretty sure this is a first," I reply.

"But something tells me this"—her arms snake around my waist and her left hand palms my half-erect cock—"is not a first in the shower."

"No. I've had a lot of hard-ons the shower," I admit as I smile bigger and gently push myself into her palm. "And this isn't even the first one you've caused."

She laughs at that. It's breathy and raspy, and between that and her lips on my shoulder, my cock surges to its full potential. I turn to face her, run my soapy hands over her half-damp hair and tug on it. Her head tilts back, her mouth opens for me, and I press my lips to hers and bury my tongue inside her mouth at the exact same time.

Her grip on my cock gets tighter and she flicks her wrist. She breaks the kiss and smiles up at me. "It may not be the first hard-on I've given you in the shower, but it's the first I'll take care of for you."

She rocks onto her tiptoes, kisses me hard and then disappears. My hands slip from her hair as she drops to her knees and covers as much of my cock as she can. My knees almost buckle at the first touch of her warm, willing mouth. She can only take half of me, but she's doing a fucking perfect job massaging the rest of me with her hand. And the tongue swirls and licks and her lips pull and suck in the most perfect fucking way…

I've been deep throated before and, yeah, there's a thrill to that, but it can't compare to the meticulous work Stephanie is doing. I'm close, and an image of me pumping a hot load into her mouth while she looks up at me with those perfect blue eyes and I tug on her hair almost sends me over the edge, but then I remember the feel of her pussy.

I take a shaky step back and tug her hair, pulling her lips from my shaft with a wet pop. Those blue eyes blink up at me as I let go of her hair and pull her to her feet. I press her against the glass while I kiss her, as my body melds into hers.

"I want you to come in my mouth," she pleads softly.

"Holy fuck, don't talk like that," I hiss back, and nip her jaw. "You're going to make me come."

"That's the point," she responds, and takes a long, slow lick from my collarbone to my ear. "Come…in my mouth."

"Stephanie…" I push my hips into her, spreading her legs with my hands on the back of her thighs.

"Avery, just let me suck you off…I don't think I can…" Her face is freckled with shower water that's bounced off me and sprayed her. Then she looks down at where my tip is pressing into her upper thigh, just left of its target. She meets my eyes again and looks almost embarrassed. "You're bigger than I'm used to and last night…both times…kind of wrecked me…Just let me…"

She tries to slip down the shower wall, to her knees again, but I grab her and hold her in place. She's not trying to flatter me; she's just being honest. I've heard it before but for the first time, I care about who is saying it.

The water continues to pelt at my back and bounce off my shoulders, leaving drops on her pretty face. I hold her head gently on each side and use my thumbs to wipe them from her eyelashes. When I kiss her, it's soft, gentle and promising. "We don't have to do anything."

"You're leaving," she reminds me. "I want to give you a send-off. And honestly, I want you to give me something else to remember you by."

"Something like an earth-shattering orgasm?" I glide my lips along her jaw to her ear and bite down on the lobe. She shudders. "Let me fuck you again, baby. I'll be gentle."

She nods. I leave her there and step out of the shower and fling open the medicine cabinet. I grab a condom from a box on the top shelf and step back into the shower. She's leaning back against the glass shower wall, but only her upper back is against it because the long, tiled bench is behind her, making her body angle off the wall. She leans there and watches me cover my dick with the condom. When I'm done, I toss the wrapper to the floor and run my right hand over her ass, down the back of her thigh, and hook it behind her knee. She lets me lift it, up off the shower floor.

"I won't hurt you. I promise. Do you believe me?" I whisper against her ear, and pull back to look into her eyes. She bites her bottom lip but nods.

"Put your foot on the bench," I tell her. She does, and then I lift her other leg off the ground and hold it against my side, just above my hip. Instinctively she wraps her leg around my waist. I shift my hips and my hard, throbbing cock finds her opening. I look at her and she's looking back at me, expectant, her face a swirl of emotions. The lust, nervousness, and, ultimately, the trust I see there are overwhelming. I bite my bottom lip to keep from saying something stupid, lean my forehead against hers and slowly push up into her.

The tip of my dick separates her pussy lips gently…It's fucking torturous and yet so crushingly erotic. I feel every inch of her inside as I slowly move into her, every delightfully slippery ridge as I push past and find just enough room to keep going. She's rolling her hips slowly, meticulously, her eyes closed and her mouth open as she pants her way through it.

"Are you okay?" I ask in a voice so thick with restraint I don't recognize it.

"OhGodyes," she replies breathlessly, and grips my shoulders tighter.

I keep nudging and she keeps wriggling, until there is no more room to make for me and nowhere farther for me to go. My whole cock is held tight by her perfect little pussy. I open my eyes again and she's looking back at me. She lifts a hand from my shoulder and runs it over my hair, spraying water everywhere, and then she grips my neck. And pulls herself closer, close enough to kiss me.

"Slow."

The word is barely audible, but she didn't even have to say it. My body already knows what she needs. It's instinctual. I move like we're having sex in quicksand. My body feels like a live wire; my nerve endings are sparking with every movement. Everything is so…intense.

I'm always a fast and furious type of guy when it comes to sex. I like it quick and hard. But I'm feeling stuff right now…like the way her pussy walls pulse with every heave of her chest…like the way the space inside her narrows and tightens around my tip...I've never felt that before. Fast, hard sex is great...but this sex is incredible.

Are all women like this? Do they all feel this good when you go slowly? I wonder as I fight to keep the tingle in my balls from erupting into orgasm. Then I realize I honestly don't give a fuck what other women feel like...I just care that Stephanie feels this good.

"Avery...I'm close..."

I keep one arm around her tiny waist but move the other from where I was holding her thigh and snake it between us. I move my hand to where our bodies meet and slip my finger over her clit, giving it a firm rub.

"Avery." She gasps it. And then goes silent except for a soft mew as she comes.

And suddenly, where there was room, there isn't any. Her body tightens around me, the space I was moving in becomes less, painfully less. And the tingle in my balls rumbles up my shaft and I grunt so loudly I swear the glass rattles as I explode inside her.

Chapter 17

Stephanie

He pounds the glass beside me with an open fist and I feel his legs tremble under me. The orgasm is rocking him to the core and all I can think is, *I did that*. I made this hockey God weak-kneed and wobbly. I smile to myself triumphantly as my own body-rocking orgasm subsides. His head is on my shoulder now as he pants and regains his senses. When he finally pulls back to look at me, I can't hide my grin.

"You almost fucking killed me," he pants, and smiles back at me. "And judging by that smirk on your face, you enjoyed it."

"You bet your sweet ass I did," I reply, and we both laugh.

Just as slowly and gently as he's been all morning, Avery pulls out of me. And then he lets my leg down, and as I place my other foot back on the shower floor from the shower bench, he pulls me to his chest in a hug. We stand there under the spray and hold each other for a long, perfect moment.

"I have to get ready," he finally says.

"I know."

We don't move.

"You're going to be late," I say.

"I know."

"Do they hold planes for errant hockey stars?"

"I don't know. Guess I'll find out."

I laugh and finally pull away, giving him a little shove. "Go. Get ready."

He kisses me hard on the lips and then contritely opens the shower door and slips out. I close my eyes and dip my head under the spray. I'm just rinsing shower gel off my body when he comes back into the bathroom ten minutes later, dressed in black pants, a black jacket and a crisp white shirt and a Tiffany blue tie. I turn off the water as he opens the door and hands me a towel.

"You don't have to leave. Stay as long as you want," he tells me.

"I'm just going to dry off and get dressed and then head next door," I reply, and wrap the towel around myself. "Maddie's not going to let me do anything today until I talk to her, so I better get over there and get it done."

"Talk to her about what?"

"What you're like in bed," I reply casually, and his caramel eyes get instantly wide. "What? You thought only guys had locker room talk?"

"No, but..." He's seriously terrified. I feel horrible.

"Don't worry, Avery," I assure him, and smile. "I'm not going to tell her anything intimate. Or post the details of our one night together on puck bunny message boards like the Warren."

"You know about the Warren?" It's a site dedicated to talking about sexual encounters with NHL players. He looks completely floored that I know about it.

"Seb made me get an account so he could read all the stories about himself," I explain. "He thought they'd somehow trace it if he started a fake account himself so he had me do it. Do you know there's like four pages of hookups about him? All before he met Shayne, of course, but he admits they're mostly true. There's even a dick shot on there, but he swears it's not his. I hope to God it's not, because I can't unsee it."

"Who the hell posts dick shots on the Internet? Who the hell takes dick shots?" He looks completely horrified. I know I'm just adding to his already deep paranoia of social media and the Internet in general. "And who the hell's dick is it if it's not his?"

"He says it's Larue's dick from a night the two of them screwed some girls in a hot tub in Vegas after a game." She shrugs. "I hope it really is, because I'd rather see Alex's dick than my own brother's."

"I don't want you to see Alex's dick," he says, and it comes out like a growl. A kind of deep, totally possessive growl. It's fucking hot as hell, but the way he's looking at me is very serious, and I'm suddenly feeling like I need to lighten the mood.

"It's no weirder than me knowing Ty likes his balls squeezed when he's about to come."

"Oh, God, you did NOT just say that!" He clamps his hands over his ears like he's doing a "Hear No Evil" monkey impression. It makes me burst into giggles. "I never ever want to know what Ty is like in bed. Never ever."

"Then get going! Before you miss the team plane and have to fly coach or something," I tell him. But he doesn't move. He's still got that serious, intense look on his face. He shoves his hands in the pockets of his suit pants. I start to feel a nervous flutter in my stomach.

"I really don't want you to see Alex's dick," he repeats, and then gives me a very small, sheepish smile. "I don't want you seeing anyone else's dick anymore."

We're having a talk. The talk. While I stand here in a towel and he's on the verge of missing his flight. I realize I am so not ready for this. I knew it would come—Avery is not one to leave anything up in the air or open to interpretation but…I'm terrified. I want him to say he wants this to be something, but I also know in my heart of hearts that that would be the worst possible thing he could say. We can't be anything—at least not anything serious, because I could ruin everything for him.

"I'm pretty sure you must realize seeing dick isn't really a daily occurrence for me," I mumble back, and pick at the terrycloth of the towel around my chest.

I feel his giant hand under my chin and he tips my head up to look at him. "I want to change that. But just me."

I nod. He smiles. His phone rings in his pocket. He pulls it out, looks at the screen and swears under his breath. "I have to go."

"I know. Go. Win some games," I demand. Then I add, "But let my brother score one or two."

"No way," he replies, and I follow him out into the bedroom, where he grabs his packed bag and heads for the hall. He pauses and glances back at me.

"I'll miss you." His tone is suddenly serious, and it makes me happy and nervous at the same time. He starts down the stairs. I walk into his upstairs hallway and watch him descend the stairs.

"Hey!" I call. He turns around and looks up at me with the cutest hopeful look on his rugged features. "I'll miss you too."

Chapter 18

Avery

We're warming up. The music is blaring through the arena—some Eminem song they've managed to score a swear-free version of—and each team is skating around, making sure not to cross that centerline. It's my first game back in Seattle since the trade. I have no idea what kind of reaction I'm going to get. I've been told that they'll do a tribute during a TV time-out. A montage on the Jumbotron. That might be met by applause or by boos. A lot of people are still grateful I led the team to a Cup a few years ago, but a lot are still resentful I didn't become a franchise player and spend my whole career here. Only time will tell which side is more represented at the game tonight.

I drop down on the edge of the blue line away from where my team is cycling and taking shots on Furry, who will be in net tonight. I lean forward on my gloved hands, my knees splayed on either side as I stretch out my groin. A pair of Seattle skates glide by and stop near my hip, just on the other side of the blue line. Sebastian drops down to stretch beside me.

"How's my sister?"

I blink and stare at him through my visor. He looks over at me. He's decided not to wear a helmet for warm-up so I can see his entire face. I'm glad he can't really see mine, because I'm sure I look stunned and probably guilty.

"How is she?" he asks again. "Is she good?"

I start to blush. Fucking blush! I cough and turn away, staring at ice in front of me, trying to will the heat rising on my cheeks to disappear. He doesn't mean it the way it sounds, I remind myself. He has no idea I just had sex with her so he's not asking that way. It just sounds like he is, which is not only disconcerting but downright perverted.

"I haven't talked to her lately," he goes on. "I haven't been able to get her on the phone for about a week. And she barely returns texts. You live next door to her; you must be seeing her."

I cough again and change my stretch position. "Yeah. I saw her today before I left. She's good. I mean she seems like she's happy and everything."

If I sound as stupid as I feel, Sebastian doesn't mention it. He kneels and twists at his waist, opening up his back. "Okay, good. I don't like it when she disappears. It makes me nervous."

He's a good brother. I've seen it with my own eyes, but I have to say he is a bit overprotective. I have a sister, and I look out for her, too, when I'm home, over the summer mostly, but she's younger and I feel like my parents pay too much attention to my career at the cost of raising her. So I go out of my way to meet her friends—and the boyfriends—but Sebastian is even more protective than that.

When I was playing in Seattle, the first year Seb came up from the minors, I noticed he was constantly calling his sister—like a couple times a day on road trips. He said she lived in Seattle but was vague about the details, and I didn't really care to push him. I was busy getting used to the league and my responsibilities as captain.

And then he invited everyone over to his condo right before the start of the second season we played together, and I finally met Stephanie. She was living in his guest room. He said it was temporary until she found a place, which I thought was totally weird because I thought she'd been living here the year before too. Why she had to leave her last place and was looking for a new one, I didn't know, and once again I didn't ask. I did notice that she was gorgeous, but that was about it. I was too busy trying to get our team to their first Cup in over a decade.

Stephanie started showing up at games, parties and events. She was funny and nice, but when I first met her, she had this Bambi-like quality to her. She seemed...not so much weak but fragile. And kind of easily startled, like a deer in the headlights. But the WAGs, as we called them—wives and girlfriends—all liked her.

Sebastian gets to his feet. "Next time you see her tell her to call me. Tell her I'm not kidding. I mean it."

I nod. He nods back, and then the serious look darkening his light eyes, which are incredibly similar to Steph's, melts away and he's giving me his best Deveau smirk. "I always dreamed about handing you your ass. My chance is finally here."

"You wish," I bark back with a smile, but he's already skating away.

The game goes well. The tribute happens during the first period and it's actually pretty cool with a mix of clips of my on-ice accomplishments and the charity work I did with the local children's hospital while I was here. Luckily, it's fans and not haters who make up most of the audience. I get a standing ovation, and it almost makes me choke up as I stand and wave to the crowd. Even the Seattle players are tapping their sticks on the boards.

We don't win, but we take them all the way to shoot-out, so at least we get a point. That's actually a win with the Saints, who are used to coming in dead last in the league every year. So far this season we're firmly in the middle and actually only two spots out of play-off contention. And tonight I scored once, assisted once and scored in the shoot-out, so I did my job.

Echolls missed in the shoot-out and didn't do much of anything during the game, so he's in a hell of a mood. It was like a dark cloud over his head, so we all just do our best to avoid and ignore him.

I walk to my stall after tossing my gloves into the equipment bin. I yank off my helmet and pull my jersey off so I'm just in my Under Armour on top. I grab my Saints baseball cap and tug it over my sweaty hair. The hat is stiff and new. In Seattle I had been wearing the same cap for postgame interviews since the first game. It was ratty and had permanent sweat stains and it felt…right. This one doesn't—yet. Kind of like the team itself. I walk over to Furry, who is sitting in his stall, his head down and a scowl on his face. I pat his shoulder pads and lean in.

"You did great," I tell him. "This is not on you. We got a point because you held them off in the third."

"Thanks," Nikolai replies gruffly, but he gives me a bit of a smile.

"Saint Westwood," Echolls mutters from two stalls over. "Trying to make the guilty feel innocent."

Is he for fucking real right now? I stand up and glance over at him. "He stopped twenty-eight shots."

"But he didn't stop thirty-one," Echolls barks back. "That's what counts. We're not the fucking Smurfs. This isn't about positivity and rainbows, Westie."

"Okay, then." I turn so my whole body is facing him with my shoulders back and my chest out, arms crossed. "Nikolai let in three shots. You took two shots on their goalie that weren't even close. Then you failed to cover the right guy when they scored the first time and took a stupid penalty that costs us the second goal."

The room is silent. I don't need to look around to know that every set of eyes in the room is on me—or Echolls. I try not to smirk like a pompous ass when I ask, "You prefer that type of leadership, Echolls? Feel better now?"

If Beau Echolls could take a swing at me right now and not cost himself his career, he totally would. I get the impression he's thinking about doing it anyway. I take a deep breath and force the next sentence out of my mouth. "But you stopped that breakaway in the second and you kept Deveau contained most of the game, which is not an easy feat. And I'm telling you that not because the other shit isn't true but because I believe focusing on the progress we're making is better than focusing on the mistakes we're making. And also because I'm not the fucking prick you want me to be."

The room is still deathly silent probably because I swore, which I rarely do out loud, especially seconds before the media…Someone clears their throat. I look behind me and see four reporters huddled in the doorway. Dammit, I hope they didn't hear much of that.

If they did, they don't say anything. Two of the reporters are the regulars from the local Seattle news: Brenda from the TV station and Lloyd from the newspaper. It's good to see them again. One is a guy I don't recognize from a Canadian network and the other is Chance Echolls, Beau's younger brother and a reporter for NBC Sports.

The interviews go well. Even Chance, who I really believe heard all of that rant directed at his brother, only asks me a couple of straight-forward questions about being back and the game and the future of the Saints. Once the reporters have been cleared out, I wrap a towel around my waist and get ready to hit the showers. I pull my phone from my suit hanging in the stall and check my messages. I have a text from Stephanie from about forty minutes ago when the game had just ended.

You were a monster out there! Sorry it wasn't a win.

I smile and text her back with a smiley face emoticon and tell her I'll call when I get back to the hotel. Ty leans in, like he's try-ing to read over my shoulder. I tuck my phone back into the suit jacket.

"Creeper."

He chuckles. "By the look on your face that was a juicy text."

"You've got your own girl. Have her send you juicy texts," I say.

"Ah, so you admit it's a girl putting that stupid look on your face." Ty walks with me toward the showers. "You finally seal the deal with Steph?"

"Yeah. Sort of," I reply, not really wanting to share because we're in public and she's not some bunny to swap stories about in the shower.

"Sort of?" Ty's face twists into a look of horror. "Oh, my God, did you forget how? You couldn't have forgotten how. I mean, Lizzie and you must have been having sex, right? Besides, it's like riding a bike."

"I didn't forget how, asshole." I roll my eyes. "We hooked up. It was great, for her and for me."

"So you say, but I'll take her word for it," he says as he steps under his shower spray. As he turns his back to the water, and I step un-der my own stream, he continues. "She'll tell Maddie how it was and

Maddie will tell me. And then I'll tell you the truth, not some bull-shit ego boost Stephanie told you."

"She wasn't bullshitting, but thanks for your faith in me." I roll my eyes, but he's not looking so he doesn't see it. It'd actually be kind of awkward if he was looking since I'm naked in the shower and every-thing. "I'm more worried about what's next."

Alex, who is under the shower stream on the other side of me, is of course listening. "Wait. You finally nailed Steph?"

"I didn't nail her." God, I hate that term. "I'm not a carpenter."

"No, you're a monk," he replies flatly. "Parsons, get the real scoop from Maddie. If Stephanie is still sexually frustrated, I'll step in like the sexual superhero I am and fix her little red wagon."

My spine stiffens. "Not even funny, Rue."

My voice is hard and deep, and I think that's why he doesn't try to defend his cocky bullshit. Instead he turns off his water and wraps a towel around his waist, running a hand through his hair, shaking out the water. He walks out of the shower room, and I watch his back, covered in that massive, crazy tattoo he got a few years ago, disappear.

"You know he's just being a jackass because he's a jackass," Ty says quietly. "He's been a big supporter of a Westwood–Deveau fornica-tion movement since the beginning."

"Yeah, well, like I said, it's not just about the fornication," I reply, and rinse the soap and shampoo from my body. "I really like her. I see this being something significant. I mean, it already is. Now it's just nakedly significant too."

Ty laughs. It echoes off the tile walls. "Nakedly? That's not really a word, Av."

I smirk at myself. He's right. Something about thinking about this thing with me and Steph makes me tongue-tied and slightly inarticulate. Maybe I need to call that PR coach and get a refresher. I'm sure she could walk me through what I need to say to get Stephanie to be my official girlfriend.

I finish showering and head back into the locker room. Alex is half dressed, standing at his cubicle beside mine. Beau is over at his stall, yanking on his clothes with force, like he's got a personal vendetta against them. He's got his back to us and his wireless headphones on. They sync to his iPod, which he usually keeps in the pocket of his suit. I hope he's listening to an anger management podcast. Dick.

"So, seriously, you and Steph, huh?"

My eyes leave Beau's back and land on Alex, who is buttoning his shirt. I nod. Alex grins at me and it's a rare sight—because it's genuine and not snarky or cocky. "Good for you, Avery. Finally."

I pull on my pants as he buttons the cuffs on his shirt and reaches for his suit jacket hanging on the hook in his stall. "You going to tell Sebastian or you going to let her do it?"

"I'm not sure yet," I admit. "I mean one of us will tell him…when we figure out what we're telling him."

"So there's no plan?" He chuckles.

"Not really. I mean last night there wasn't a lot of talking," I admit. It makes his grin grow so big the dimples in his cheeks look like golf divots.

He laughs again. "Avery without a plan. That's something I never thought I would see."

"Just do me a favor and don't tell him for us, okay," I request seriously because I know that he's going out with Seb and Jordan and a bunch of our old teammates tonight.

"Don't worry, precious." Alex winks at me. "I don't kiss and tell."

"Thanks, asshole." I chuckle as he walks out of the room.

Chance Echolls appears in the doorway. He glances at me but walks over and taps his brother on the shoulder. Beau's reaching for his suit jacket. He sees Chance, yanks off his headphones and shoves them in the man purse he carries everywhere. "Hey. I'm ready. Where to?"

Chance shrugs. "Wherever the Winterhawks won't be. I don't want to run into that ass Garrison and his girl."

I concentrate really hard on buttoning my shirt so I don't react to Chance's comment. Chance is still bitter he failed miserably at trying to get Jessie to be with him instead of Jordan.

Beau slings his jacket over his shoulder, gives me some sort of weird vicious-looking smirk and storms out with his brother. I'm pulling on my suit jacket as Ty finally hauls his ass out of the shower. He's always the last one ready. He takes ridiculously long showers.

"About time, princess," I snark, and he rolls his eyes. He's heard it all before.

"You going out with your old team?" he wants to know.

I shake my head. "Nah. It won't look right."

Ty smiles, but it's rueful. "Fuck how it looks. They're your friends."

He's right, but Don advised that I avoid it. I was supposed to say hello to them before the game, in the hall, and make sure a photographer was there. I did that. Don said going to a bar with them would look like fraternizing or like I was sleeping with the enemy, so I should avoid it. Plus we had to get up early tomorrow morning and fly into Vancouver for another game the next night.

I tell Ty the other reason why I am going straight back to the hotel. "I kind of want to avoid Seb until I know what Steph wants me to say."

Ty seems to find that acceptable, unlike the first reason. I don't really find my first reason acceptable either, but I've learned to pick my battles. I'd pissed Don off a lot lately with choosing the Saints, moving into the cottage instead of a fancy condo or house, dumping Lizzie. So I'll give him this; besides, I kind of want to just go back to my hotel room and call Stephanie.

As soon as I step out of the locker room, I'm assaulted by Sebastian and Jordan. They flank me and both wrap their arms around my shoulders. A few feet away are Alex and Choochinsky, the goalie for the Winterhawks and a good friend.

"Here are your options, Captain," Jordan says in a deep, menacing voice, which sounds ridiculous on him, especially because he's wearing a giant lopsided grin. "You either come out with us willingly, or we overpower you and make you come out with us anyway."

"Very funny." I roll my eyes, but I'm smiling.

"Jessie is waiting in the car in the player lot, engine running," Jordan goes on, his blond eyebrows wiggling deviously. "All we gotta do is carry you to it."

"Shay offered to get the rope she has in her trunk, but I told her I didn't need it," Sebastian goes on, referring to his girlfriend. "I can contain you if I have to."

"You guys are ridiculous. You know I can't. It wouldn't look right," I mutter. I think they can tell this isn't my opinion by the lackluster tone in my voice. And the guys, because I played with them for years, have developed an instinct for deciphering what is Avery's opinion and what Avery has been told should be his opinion.

"Don can suck it," Chooch announces, surprising everyone. He's not usually so bold or outspoken. In fact, last time we were together he was kind of a kicked puppy because he was ending his engagement to his one and only girlfriend. "Besides, Alex is with us too. Consider it a Winterhawks–Saints mixer or meet and greet."

I realize, because Jordan and Seb still have their hands on my shoulders and are shoving me toward the player parking, I do not have a choice in the matter. Honestly, it'll be great to catch up with everyone. But there's no way I can text or call Steph with her brother hanging off me. Dammit. I hope she doesn't mind late-night, after-the-bar, slightly drunk texts.

Chapter 19

Stephanie

The first thing I do when I wake up is check my phone. No texts. No missed calls. Then I start to feel upset. Then I hate myself for it. Ugh. I force myself through the ritual of getting ready for work. Maddie is downstairs already, dressed in her cute black-and-white sleeveless dress and apple-red cardigan. She hands me a latte she's made from the fancy coffee machine Seb gave us as a housewarming gift, and I smile gratefully. But the smile is tight and slightly tense, and Maddie knows it.

"They lost. No one is in the mood to talk," Maddie says quietly.

I nod. "Did Ty call?"

She falters and takes a small sip of her own latte. "Avery isn't Ty," she says as I grab my keys off the hook by the back door.

I yank the door open but stand still at her words. "See you at work."

I try, unsuccessfully, to push Avery and my feelings out of my head as I hop on the scooter. Normally we'd carpool and Maddie would either hop on the back or I'd jump in her car, but I have to run some errands on my lunch break, picking up supplies for a project for my interior design class, so I drive.

Just days after having sex with him, the euphoria has vanished and so has the delusion. Why would I be any different to Avery from anyone else he's slept with? I know he's had a few no-strings flings. They're usually with friends of friends and people he knows he can trust to keep it secret. Is that what I am to him? Because I'm his neighbor? Because I'm his former teammate's sister? Because I'm a friend? Did he just slide me into the "benefits" category and that's all?

I want to feel relief at that, because if I'm just a friend with benefits, then I don't have to tell him about my past. I'm not a risk to him and he won't have to worry about how I affect his image if I'm just a friend he had benefits with. But...the idea that might happen, even if it's an easy out...hurts.

Am I overreacting? Part of me says I am. But I'm so emotionally involved in this, I just can't be rational. My heart is too attached. I've had feelings for Avery since Seattle. At first I thought he was weak and kind of a giant pussy for letting his dad run his life. And I completely wrote him off in my head as a jerk when one night before play-offs last year he talked about how he had ignored his friend Trey in college when he was going through an addiction to painkillers. That hit home because I had the same sort of addiction when I was in high school, and into my twenties.

I ran away from home. I did very, very stupid things and made horrendous decisions, but my brother Sebastian never walked away from me—even when I was running away from him. Even when my mom gave up on me and our father disowned me, Sebastian tried to keep tabs on me. He spent stupid amounts of money on investigators to find me. And when I finally crashed and burned, he was there and he got me the help I needed. So to hear that Avery was good friends with Trey but abandoned him in his time of need made me want to write him off, not just as a friend but also as a human being. Sure, he was very attractive and he was one hell of a hockey player—the best, there was no denying that—but he wasn't a good person, in my opinion.

Avery, for some reason, after that confession and my judgmental reaction, had the exact opposite reaction. He decided to try to become a close friend of mine. He started calling me—which he had never done before—and I ran into him at the coffee shop outside my work a few times. He started jogging with me.

It was impossible to write him off completely because he was charming, and he was candid. He opened up to me, and I realized he wasn't a bad guy; he was just a guy with a lot of pressure who didn't always handle it well. I found myself liking him as a person—really liking him. When he left the Winterhawks and I moved to San Diego, I figured my little crush would eventually evaporate, but then he ended up on the Saints.

I park the scooter in employee parking and smile at our security guard behind the desk in the lobby of our building as I head up to the seventh floor where my office is located. The floor has a loft-like feel to it. All the secretaries' desks are in a large open space at the back of the floor, away from the receptionist, with a wall of windows behind us. The lawyers we're paired with are in offices directly across from us. They have the water view, while we have the city view. Both are gorgeous, though.

I smile at Letitia, our receptionist, and keep my head down as I make my way to my desk. I just don't feel like making small talk with anyone. I sit at my desk, tuck my helmet into the big drawer at the bottom of my desk, and flip on my laptop. I check my emails. Three new ones from clients, one from a paralegal and nothing else. I feel deflated and then I feel stupid again. Avery has my work email, but he's never used it. Why would he start now?

My phone, which I placed on my desk when I got here, starts to ring. I usually silence it as soon as I get to the office because personal calls are frowned upon, but I forgot. Luckily, it's early, and my boss isn't here. I glance at the screen and see Avery's name. A smile bursts across my face.

"Hey."

He groans instead of returning my greeting, like he's in physical pain. "Your brother is the devil."

I laugh. "What happened?"

"He made me go for a drink after the game," Avery explains. "Actually, he made me go for ten drinks after the game."

I laugh again. "You must really miss him to let him convince you to go out at all, let alone get hangover drunk."

He pauses and the groaning stops. "Actually, I think I miss you more, which is why I decided to hang out with him. He reminds me of you."

And just like that I am no longer feeling doubt or panic or anything but a warm swell of bliss in my chest. "You're a charmer when you're hungover."

"I'm a charmer all the time. If you haven't figured that out, I'll have to work harder," he murmurs, and it's sexy as fuck. But then he clears his throat and his tone changes, becoming less intimate and more businesslike. "So I have a message from your brother."

Oh, God, this can't be good. I don't say anything. I just wait for Avery to continue and nervously fidget in my desk chair.

"He says you need to call him. I guess he feels like you've been ignoring him."

I sigh. "Not on purpose. I've just been busy. He's just used to me being in Seattle and talking every day."

"You should call him today so he knows I delivered the message," Avery advises, and adds, "Maybe it'll make him less likely to kill me when he finds out about us."

I swallow and feel another wave of relief because that means he didn't say anything to Seb. I want to be the one to tell him…eventually. And the other thing that has me feeling warm and fuzzy is the use of the word "us." But it also makes me nervous because if there is an "us"—which I think would be kind of amazing—I have to tell him about my past.

"I would have called or texted you last night, but I didn't want him to see and start asking questions," Avery goes on. I hear some noise around him. "And then it was late when I got home and I was so inebriated that I just passed out. I'm sorry."

"It's fine," I say, because now that I know the situation, it *is* fine. "Thanks for not saying anything about our night to Sebastian."

"You know me, I'm excellent at being Fort Knox when it comes to my sex life," he returns. I hear someone call his name. "Listen, I have to go. We're about to board the plane to Vancouver."

"Okay."

"I'll definitely call you after the game tonight," he promises, and then hangs up. I smile that kind of smile that's all-consuming and so big it almost makes your cheeks hurt but you have no control over it.

He likes me. In *that* way. And I like him. In *that* way. A lot.

I take a deep breath and try to calm down. There are still hurdles in our path. Big ones. I can't get too excited. Yet. I decide to call one of our smaller hurdles.

"Finally," is how Seb answers the phone.

"You sound chipper for such an early call after a night of drinking," I can't help but observe.

"Shay made me go to her yoga class at the crack of ass this morning," he explains. "And how do you know I was drinking last night?"

Oops. "I, um…"

There's a slight pause. "Did you talk to Avery already?"

Sometimes I wish my brother was a stereotypical dumb jock. "Yeah. He told me you wanted me to call you."

"I didn't expect him to call you first thing in the morning," Seb laments. "I thought he would just tell you when he ran into you again."

Yeah…about that. He's started running into me naked. Are you okay with that? I think it, but I don't dare say it. I honestly don't know how Sebastian will feel about this thing with Avery. He likes Avery. He's defended him even when I wouldn't have. I know he wants me to find someone. He's made that clear more than once. But all of that doesn't mean he'll be cool with his former captain, teammate and friend dating his sister.

"Yeah, well, he called, so I called," I reply lightly, and lean back in my chair. "Is everything okay?"

"Yeah. Everything is better than okay." I can hear his smile through the phone. "Our team is doing well. Things with Shay are fantastic. Mom came to visit last week, and she's doing great. She asked about you."

Seb will never let this go. I know it, so I try not to get annoyed by his constant attempts to make me and our mother closer than we are.

It's not that we don't get along; it's just that we aren't friends. I don't know why. It's probably a little of her not forgiving me for my past and me not forgiving me for my past.

I made life very hard on her when it was already hard. She was dealing with her divorce and scrounging up money for Sebastian's hockey, and I was off stealing prescriptions and getting high instead of being a good daughter. Of course, when she realized what I was doing, her idea of helping me was to call my absent father in the middle of the night and tell him I was his problem and he was to come and get me. She had to focus on Sebastian. He had a real shot at the NHL and she wasn't going to let me derail it. She was abandoning me. So I abandoned her and ran away.

I don't actually hate her anymore for that because she was right—Sebastian had potential and I didn't…or at least I didn't see it at the time, and I wasn't giving her or anyone else any reason to see it either. She was suffering emotionally and financially from the end of her marriage, and I was more than she could handle. But forgiving her, and myself, for the past doesn't mean I can forget it.

"Tell her I say hi," I reply swiftly, and immediately change the subject. "So you got Avery to go out with you. That's a first."

"We didn't give him much choice," Sebastian admits. "But he actually seemed to enjoy it. The first couple of drinks were forced on him, but the last four or five were all his decision. You know that guy is a lot of fun when he lets himself be."

"Yeah. I know," I can't help but say, and my mind fills with images from the stairs and the shower.

"You hang out with him a lot, huh?"

I swallow. "Yeah."

"I hope you're meeting new people too," Sebastian replies.

"Sure," I say with a smartass twinge to my words. "I met a guy named Ty and a guy named Nikolai and…"

"Steph, you should meet people who aren't hockey players." He laughs. "People who I might not punch for work."

"Ha-ha," I say, and actually laugh afterward. "I've met some people at work. But between the Winterhawks alumni here and Maddie dating Ty, hockey players are an inevitable part of my social life. It's not a bad thing. It's comfortable."

"Speaking of comfortable…" Here it comes. I both dread it and am soothed by it. "You doing okay? Nothing too overwhelming?"

He knows my triggers are feelings of helplessness, like when my parents' marriage fell apart, and also feelings of inadequacy, like when he excelled at hockey and I didn't have a passion or talent in high school.

"Actually, I feel pretty much like I'm on the right path," I reply, and I mean it. "School is going well. I'm really loving my classes."

"Cool. You'll be able to help me on my next big project," he says, and I can tell he's excited. "I'm looking at property all over the place."

Sebastian renovated his home in Seattle and fell instantly in love with the process. He's looking to do it again. I helped him with the design part of it and it became an instant passion, which is why I'm taking some online interior design classes. He's talking more and more about starting a house-flipping company so he can work on projects in his off-season and also when he's done with hockey.

"Cool." I see my boss walking toward me. "I gotta go, Seb. Time to work."

"Okay. But, Steph, don't ignore my calls, okay?" he says sternly. "I need to know you're okay. And if you ever aren't…"

"I'll call. I promise," I say.

"I've got your back. Always."

"I know. And I've got yours," I reply, even though he doesn't need me. Sebastian has always been able to handle himself on and off the ice. I hang up and quickly silence my phone and shove it in a drawer.

My boss, Mr. Archer—or Conrad, as he likes to insist I call him—nods at me as I stand up. "Are we in a latte or an espresso mood today?"

"Latte. Hazelnut. Thank you, Stephanie." He gives me a genuine smile and walks into his office. I grab the corporate credit card out of the locked drawer in my desk and head for the elevators like I do every morning when he gets in. It's been our routine since Seattle.

I appreciate Sebastian's concern and his constant attention, but I really am doing fine. I like my life here—and I like the direction things seem to be going with Avery. I know it's potentially dangerous because, well, anytime you start to give your heart to someone it's dangerous, but I think I was giving him my heart long before the sex happened.

Chapter 20

Avery

The plane was painfully silent. We dropped both games, the one in Vancouver and the one two days later in Calgary. With losing in the shoot-out to Seattle, that meant we only got one point out of the potential six on this road trip and we've dropped in the overall standings. No one was pleased. I didn't know if we could come back. I knew how to battle—I'd done it before with the Winterhawks and so had Alex. But this team, I don't know if they have it in them. Or if I know how to get it out of them. Right now all I am sure of is that we are all exhausted and frustrated.

Coach must feel the same way, because when the plane lands, he stands and blocks the exit before we can get off and clears his throat.

"I want you to go home and burn this off. Go out with your buddies. Play with your kids. Play with your dog. Hell, play with your wife or girlfriend. Or both." There are some snickers at that, and the coach gives us a quick smirk. "Do whatever it takes to get your heads in a better place. Then sleep in. Practice tomorrow at three p.m. And when you show up, I want the exhaustion and the grumbling gone. If you're not careful, your attitudes will knock you straight to the bottom of the league before another team does."

We all file out of the plane and make our way across the tarmac toward the private parking lot. People are starting to talk again. I hear Larue making plans to go out with Nikolai and Drew. Ty falls in step beside me.

"Maddie's meeting me at my place," he says.

"Yeah. So?"

"So Stephanie will be home alone. Thought you might want to know." Ty is trying to sound casual.

"She's not home alone," I reply. "Because she's going to be at my place."

"So you've made plans?"

"Yeah, Dad, I asked her to come over. Texted her when we boarded and she said she'd be there," I inform him, and he smiles guiltily at me. "Now mind your own fucking business. You're a shitty Cupid."

Ty chuckles. Larue wanders over. "What's so funny?"

"Nothing." I blow it off, not wanting Alex in on any conversation about Steph. I'm still a little choked he mentioned that he wanted to bang her back in Seattle.

"Don't suppose either of you two want to join us for a drink? Coach's orders and all," he asks as I stop beside my car and Ty wanders over to the passenger door.

"Nope," Ty replies for both of us. "We're going home to play with our girlfriends. Coach's orders and all."

"Pussies," Larue snarks.

"Exactly," Ty replies with a wink.

Alex lets out a booming laugh and waves as he heads off to hitch a lift with Furry. The fucker never drives himself anywhere if he can help it. I'm not sure if it's because he's so cheap and doesn't want to waste his gas, or because he's lonely and likes the constant company, or because he knows what a shitty driver he is. Maybe it's all three.

As we drive toward Coronado, Ty talks about the losses and how hard it's been already this season.

"This is going to be a grind," Ty mutters as he watches the barren scenery on the side of the freeway fly by.

"I'll make sure we turn it around. I've led Seattle through some rough patches," I remind him.

"Yeah. But you didn't have Echolls," he replies, and rubs his forehead. "You know he's not going to play nice all of a sudden. His attitude might start to get contagious. Like the fucking plague."

I nod begrudgingly. "Yeah. I'll get him to play nice."

"Hope so," Ty replies.

I hope so too.

We're silent for a few minutes. Ty is probably singing along in his head to that annoying Taylor Swift song playing over the stereo. He loves that catchy pop crap.

"So not to play Cupid or anything," he starts suddenly with a guilty smirk on his face. "But so things are going good with you and Steph?"

"What does Maddie say?" I ask pointedly. "I think I've figured out that it's going however she says it's going."

Ty smiles. "She's says you're talking every night."

"We are."

"Cool." Ty smiles and I grin back, but mine is a little more forced than he realizes—or than I want it to be.

Sure, Steph and I have talked a lot. Every night for at least half an hour, and we text about ten times a day. And even though I'm always smiling when I hang up, I wouldn't say that we're getting closer. She's flirty and funny—which I love about her—but when I try to ask her a serious question or move the conversation toward that ever-dreaded but always necessary "so where is this going?" she says something that derails it. Not in a bad way—she usually says something that makes my dick hard, but still.

"I'm thinking tonight we'll really, you know, figure out if this is serious," I admit to Ty.

"You mean have that 'are we a couple or are we a couple of horny friends' conversation?" Ty wiggles his eyebrows as I look at him at a stop sign, and that makes me roll my eyes. "I thought you'd already have done that."

"I tried, but I think it should be done in person."

"So what are you talking about, then, if it's not your relationship?" Ty wants to know, the nosy bastard.

I shrug. "Well, I've told her about my plans for the clothing line. To have the proceeds go to charity, and my dad losing his ever-loving mind over it."

"What does she think?" Ty asks as I ease off the freeway.

"She thinks it's a great idea and that I should tell Don to back off," I explain.

"Smart girl."

"Yeah, I've always appreciated her blunt honesty." At a red light, I let go of the steering wheel and lean back in my seat, reaching up and gripping the headrest with my hands as I try to stretch. My muscles—all of them—are killing me. I wish I had a hot tub at my place. "We talked a little about Dieppe."

"Right. You're both technically from the same place," Ty replies.

"Sort of. She moved when she was young," I explain. "We probably wouldn't have known each other even if she stuck around. I went to that boarding school in upstate New York for a good chunk of high school."

"Yeah. She tell you about that uptight Catholic private school her mom made her go to?" Ty asks. I shake my head, so he elaborates. "She came over with Maddie a while ago, before you moved here, and we were talking about high school once, and she mentioned that her mom stuck her in this school that was super religious and uptight. She had a uniform and no school dances, no pep rallies, just prayer groups. High school would have sucked."

"Yeah, but I bet she looked fucking sexy in the little uniform," I can't help but mention, and Ty grins like it's not the first time he's thought that either.

I'm kind of bummed that I'm hearing this from Ty and not from her. I mean I hadn't asked her about her high school experience—ever—but I have asked her about growing up in Quebec, and she's never really said much or volunteered much personal information.

We hit another red light, and I grab my phone and send her a quick text as a bit of a joke and to let her know we're on our way.

Carpooling home with Ty. He says u went to Catholic school. Would've killed to see you in a schoolgirl uniform. I bet u looked hot.

A few seconds later she responds.

Not as hot as you look in your Under Armour. See you soon.

I pull up in front of Ty's place, and as he gets out of the passenger seat, he looks up and smiles. I glance up too. The only light on is the one in his master bedroom. He smiles from ear to ear at that.

"I love my girlfriend," Ty mutters to himself more than me. "She knows I don't need to talk right now...at least not with clothes on."

I laugh. He winks. "Have fun, Westie. I know I will."

I pull away from the curb and continue the short distance to my place. Driving by the front, I see the light that's on at my place is the living room light. That's a good thing. As much as I fully intend to get Steph naked tonight, I want to have that official talk first.

I drive around the corner and enter the alley and hit the garage door opener. I'm suddenly a little nervous. I'm sure she wants this to be an official relationship. Steph isn't the type of girl to do the bed-buddy thing, and that's not my thing either.

What makes me nervous is how badly I want it. I want it bad. Worse than I've ever wanted anything from a girl.

I wonder, as I get out of the car and walk around and pull my bag from the trunk, if other guys feel this with every new relationship. I wonder why I'm only feeling it with her and never felt it with Lizzie. Am I a late bloomer at this, or is it different with Stephanie because she's the one?

As I inwardly chastise myself for once again being a giant vagina, the door that leads from the garage to the kitchen opens. I glance up and freeze. Stephanie is standing in the doorway. Her shiny golden brown hair is in pigtails with soft blue ribbons. She's wearing what has to be her Catholic high school uniform. Blue-and-gold tartan skirt, crisp white button-down shirt, knee-high blue socks.

"You said you would have killed to see me in my uniform…," she says softly, and bites her bottom lip in a way that I somehow feel in my groin. "I knew I was holding on to this for a reason."

"I'm pretty sure if you wore that to school…like that…you'd have been suspended," I croak, and rake my eyes over her again.

The white shirt is rolled at the sleeves and unbuttoned enough that her cleavage and her white lace bra are showing. And it's not tucked into the skirt but tied just under her boobs. The skirt is rolled at the waist so its hem falls barely below her ass instead of down at her knees where it's supposed to be. The socks are pulled up, the way the nuns intended, but she's wearing patent leather sky-high heels instead of schoolgirl loafers.

"Not suspended. Expelled," she confirms. She hits the button to close the garage door behind me and slowly walks down the three steps into the garage. The open door behind her spills light into the dark garage and illuminates her from behind as she walks toward me.

I've still got my hand in the trunk of my SUV, reaching for my bag, but I'm frozen. She slides her tight little body between the car and me and leans forward, reaching in to pull my bag out. The effort causes the skirt to rise and reveal the round of her ass and the white lacy boy shorts covering it.

"Steph, I am going to fuck you right here in the garage," I groan, feeling defeated because we need to talk, but, oh my God, she's in a schoolgirl uniform!

As she starts to pull the bag out and straighten up, she takes a step back, her ass bumping right into my lap. My bag hits the concrete floor with a thump. She swivels her pretty little head to look back and up at me. Batting her eyelashes at me, which I notice have a thick and sexy but uncharacteristic coat of black mascara on them.

"Steph…I…" *Think we should talk* is the rest of the sentence that never makes it out of my mouth before she turns to face me and her lips cover mine.

I fucking love kissing her. It's as amazing as I remember. Despite the schoolgirl Lolita thing happening on the outside, the kiss is just as gentle, almost timid, as I remember, and that makes me hornier than the mascara and the outfit.

"Steph…let's talk for a second," I pant out, to the dismay of my throbbing cock rubbing up again her thigh.

Her icy blue eyes flutter open and seem dark. I would think it was lust, but for a second her eyebrows knit together, indicating something less positive. I open my mouth to say something but she turns away from me. "Sure. Let's talk inside. I just have to get your bag…"

She bends from the waist again and that perfect round ass with the virginal white lace undies is on full display. She arches her back a little and her ass bumps my hard cock and my brain and willpower implode. I grab her hips and pull her back as I push forward. She lets out a squeak that is more triumph than shock. I grunt and reach forward with my right arm around her tiny torso, my hand cups her left breast and I pull her to standing again and turn us both. In one quick motion we're facing the open tailgate of my SUV and my left hand has moved from her hip, under that tiny skirt and into those lace boy shorts. I bite down on her neck while I push two fingers into her.

"Avery," she sobs out my name, and braces herself on the car.

"You're so fucking hot," I grunt, and push my palm into the front of her pussy, making sure to rub her clit as I move my fingers in and out. "You must have had every boy in that fucking school jerking off before first period."

She sobs out another breath.

"Were you wet like this in high school, knowing you got boys hot?" I murmur, and suck on her neck.

"Only you make me this wet," she whispers back, and I feel a rush that goes straight to my dick. "God…I'm going to…come."

"Not like this." I pull my fingers from her.

She lets out a whimper and I spin her and grab her waist, lifting her up and throwing her back into the open trunk. Her skirt flies up and I grab a hold of her pretty white panties with one hand and yank them down her legs, which are dangling out of the trunk. I undo my belt with the other hand.

"You said you wanted to talk…," Stephanie says softly as her hand wanders over her stomach, down her plaid skirt and through the downy short trail of hair…She's touching herself…looking right at me and playing with herself. Fuck, I couldn't form a sentence at this point if my life depended on it. I shove my pants and underwear down in one push and yank her toward me until her ass is dangling on the edge of the trunk bed. She stops playing with herself and reaches into her bra, pulling out a condom. "But I thought you might change your mind…"

I grab the condom from her hand and slide it on as she slowly slides her legs apart so I can step between them. I bite back a groan as I grab my cock in my hand and line it up with her opening. As soon as the tip disappears into her warmth, so does any self-restraint. I grab her hips and bury myself balls deep.

Chapter 21

Stephanie

If you'd told me two months ago—hell, two weeks ago—that I would be in my high school uniform lying in the trunk of Avery's—hell, anyone's—SUV having sex, I would have told you that you were insane. Of course, if you told me my options were to have sex with Avery in the trunk of his car or to tell him about my past addiction, I wouldn't be so surprised with my current situation. I tend to do anything to avoid talking about my past with anyone, let alone someone I don't want to lose.

Avery's eyes are open but hooded with lust as he stares at my chest as it jiggles from the impact of his dick pumping in and out of me. I arch my back to make sure the view is perfect.

"Fuck...," he growls, and grits his teeth. I arch my back again. "Touch yourself again."

I do what he asks. Normally, touching myself in front of someone would make me too self-conscious to climax, but seeing Avery so riled up—knowing he's so turned on he is about to lose it and that I did that to him—has taken away my inhibition. His lips curl into a sexy smile and he pumps harder. The new angle and the speed it causes has his tip tapping a part of me no one has touched, and stars explode in front of my eyes. What is that? Is that my G-spot? Holy God…

It's minute after minute after minute of ecstasy, and I fight the orgasm pushing down on me because I don't want this bliss to end. He's fighting it too; I can tell by the strained look on his face, the way he's biting his lip and the thump of the blood making the vein in his neck throb. I gasp for breath and pant out. *"Baise-moi."*

He knows what that means. He knows I just said *Fuck me.* "Come for me. Come all over my dick."

I hear the whimper escape his lips and turn into a moan as my body tenses and releases with a mind-blowing orgasm. A minute later I hear Avery make a similar sound and shudder between my legs. Then his torso lands on top of me like a warm, heavy blanket. He turns his face to my neck; his breath dances softly across my skin. "Are you okay?" he mumbles into my neck.

"Mmm…" I assure him softly.

He presses his lips to my jaw and then slowly pulls out and stands up, discarding the condom in the garbage can in the corner of the garage before grabbing his pants from his ankles and pulling them up. I pull my skirt down modestly and he grins. "Oh, now you're shy?"

I laugh self-consciously and feel my face flush, which makes his smile deepen. When he smiles so deeply he almost has a dimple—almost—on his left cheek. I've seen it before—rarely—because deep, organic smiles like this aren't in Avery's daily life. I have to say, I adore his almost-dimple. I adore everything about this man, which is why this is so scary. He takes my hands and pulls me to a sitting position and then carefully reaches up and pulls my hair out of their pigtails. I shake my hair out, hoping it doesn't look stupid. "Were the pigtails too much?"

"Hell no," he replies, his eyes twinkling. He leans close and tilts my face and kisses me. It's soft and long and his tongue is tender and languid as it passes over mine. "But my dick will never go soft again if we don't get you out of this outfit."

I smile, feeling victorious.

"Let's get you inside and into some sweats or something," he urges.

"Too bad you don't eat more carbs. Then maybe you'd have a potato sack I could wear," I joke, and jump off the trunk bed.

"Let's not go crazy...," he says, and as I climb the stairs to the kitchen his hands go under the back of my skirt and he palms my ass.

I squeal and run through the house, with Avery chasing me. I make it to the living room before I feel his big hands on my waist and he tosses me onto the soft leather couch and crawls on top of me. We lie like that staring at each other for a while. His hands are in my hair, brushing lazily through it every couple of minutes. I have my arms around his neck, my thumb tracing his hairline.

"So...did you talk to Seb?"

I nod. "Yeah. He's good and he knows I'm good."

"Did you tell him? About this?"

I shake my head. "I wasn't sure what to say."

He blinks and runs his hand through my hair again before locking his eyes with mine. "Tell him the truth."

I bite my lip for a second and then grin. "Hey, Seb, your friend and ex-captain, the guy you think is a monk, had his dick in me the other night and I'm kind of hoping it happens again."

He laughs, shaking his body and mine, before shaking his head. "I didn't mean that."

"But that's the truth," I argue back, still smiling but kind of embarrassed.

He pauses to kiss me softly on the mouth. No tongue, but it still creates heat that ripples through my body and pools between my legs. "I didn't mean you should tell him the whole truth. Just the dumbed-down PG-thirteen version."

I pretend to think really hard about it. "Hey, Seb, Avery and I have kind of become more than friends?"

"That's a start." He smiles and drops his head a little so our faces are closer. His lips are near my cheek. "Hey, Seb, I think I want to date your amazing friend Avery."

"Amazing, huh?" I laugh, and he pulls back to catch my eye again.

"I'm not amazing?" He rolls his hips, creating a perfectly delicious friction against the front of my underwear.

"Oh you're amazing…" I sigh and roll my hips back.

"So are you going to tell him?" He rolls his hips again. Oh, God, that feels good.

"Can we not talk about my brother while you dry-hump me?"

I grab his ass and give it a squeeze, which causes him to hump me again, and then I start to tug his pants down, which he never bothered to button. "Okay, how about you just tell me then?"

I open my eyes, which had fluttered closed, and look up into his caramel ones. His dark brows are set in a serious line, but he's trying to force a lighthearted smile onto his full, perfect lips. He swallows, and his Adam's apple bobs. His hips have stilled. "Do you want to date me?"

I feel a flutter of fear, or maybe it's dread, roll through my chest and into my belly like a bowling ball down a lane. That question is like a giant can of worms. My answer will determine if he opens it. If

I tell the truth, he'll rip the lid right off that can. If I lie, the can stays sealed forever, and Avery's life will remain smooth and perfect without any of my worms in it.

He pushes himself up on his elbows, moving away from me because of the long uncomfortable pause I've created. "I want to date you, Stephanie. In case that's not clear. I've wanted it for a while. Longer than I am willing to admit because it makes me an asshole. But if you don't want to…"

He's about to climb off me and off the couch. I reach up and clasp the back of his neck. I pull him down so our foreheads touch and blurt out the truth. "I want to date you."

His mouth crashes down on mine. I know we have more to say. I know that proverbial can of worms is lying open on the floor, and I need to have a serious talk with him, but right now Avery's lifting my skirt and kissing his way lower and lower on my body and the only thing I want to do right now is see if I can make it past two licks this time.

Chapter 22

Avery

I sneak down my oak stairs, painfully aware of all the creaks and groans coming from the old wood as I walk. I don't want to wake Steph yet. We'd both woken up at six a.m. when her phone alarm had chirped it was time for her to get ready for work. But instead of getting out of bed, she let me pull her closer and then crawl on top of her. After some mind-blowing barely awake sex, she called in sick to work. After another round we fell back asleep. Now it's almost ten-thirty and I'm awake, so I leave her perfect naked body tangled in my sheets to venture out for some bagels and coffee. I can't expect her to start her first day as my girlfriend without food and caffeine, can I?

I quietly slip out the front door and make my way toward Western Bagel and Starbucks, just a few blocks away. There's what Californians call a "marine layer" hanging low in the air this morning, which creates a dense fog everywhere and makes it impossible to see the beach, but the sun is already starting to burn it off.

One big plus to coming to San Diego was definitely the weather.

And now, officially, I can say Stephanie is a big plus to playing in California.

But win or lose this season, I will spend the off-season back in Dieppe, New Brunswick, at the Atlantic beach house I call home. Steph might have been born in Dieppe, but she wasn't really raised there and as far as I know hasn't been back in about a decade. Her family isn't there anymore and even if they were, she has a life and a job here.

I could do long distance for a few summers. I could and I would—for her. But I'd hate every second.

I know I am jumping the gun thinking about something that hasn't happened already, but that's what I do. I think ahead and plan and assess and predict. The fact is, I expect her to still be around, like this, all naked and in my bed, in the off-season. I can't stay here once the season is over. I have a camp for underprivileged youth I donate time and money to in New Brunswick and a bunch of events and promotions I will have to deal with that will have me hopping around from New York to L.A. And I truly like my place in Dieppe and reconnecting with my childhood friends and just relaxing. Maybe Steph will come visit me there and she'll like it as much as I do and consider making it her second home too.

Okay, I'm getting way ahead of myself. I shake my head and take a deep breath. *Relax, Westwood.*

I stop at Western Bagel first and get six everything bagels and a tub of cream cheese. The bagels are still warm and make my stomach grumble in anticipation. I head back out into the foggy morning to go next door to Starbucks. I know that Steph loves vanilla lattes, so I get in line to order her one and grab one for myself. My phone buzzes in my pocket.

I try not to sound annoyed as I answer it. "Hey, Don."

"Avery," he barks, and I know he's pissed about something. "You wanna tell me why I'm looking at a photo of you and two Winter-hawks holding beers?"

"Because you're surfing some sketchy website probably run by a puck bunny," I say, and instantly regret it.

He huffs. "You watch your words, buddy."

"Sorry," I reply gruffly. "Alex was there, too, and it was just a couple of beers with old friends. I hang out with Sebastian and Jordan in the off-season, too, you know. Seb will probably be on the Olympic team with me next year."

"You know where this photo is? The San Diego Sports Zone," he announces angrily. "They're not exactly thrilled with your little reunion since you lost to the Hawks and then went on to lose every other game on this swing."

"It's a team sport," I mutter. "I'm not the only one out there not winning."

"You're the only one who matters."

My father honestly thinks I'm the only one who matters on every team I'm on, maybe even the only one who matters to the league. His ego over my achievements is his most annoying quality.

It's my turn at the counter, so I cover the phone with my palm and whisper my order of two grande vanilla lattes. He's got ears like a damn wolf and manages to catch it. "Where are you? Who are you talking to?"

"I'm grabbing breakfast," I tell him.

"That kitchen in your shitty rental not working?"

"Don, did you call to tell me something or just to chat?" I clench my jaw in frustration.

"I sent you some new sketches of the clothing line. They want to add women's clothes, but I don't know…I showed your sister the designs and she made a face," Don explains, and sighs.

"Okay. I'll look at it as soon as I get home," I promise. "How's Kate doing?"

"She's fine, I guess. Busy with your social media and school," Don explains. "You could call her sometime. Find out for yourself."

"I will. I kind of want to do some of my own social anyway and give her a bit of a break," I say as my lattes are placed on the counter by a perky blond barista who is smiling and blushing, so I know she knows who I am.

"Thank you, Casey," I say, reading her name tag.

"You're so welcome!" She shoves a coupon at me. "And sorry for the wait. Here's a coupon for a free drink next time."

I want to argue with her, because I didn't wait longer than anyone else and I hate when people give me free stuff just for being me, but my father will hear and he always tells me not to argue when people want to give me things. So I just smile at her and tell her she's a sweetheart and hightail it out of the place before she, or anyone else, can ask for an autograph.

Stephanie might be awake by now, and I don't want her to think I ditched her.

"Avery, Kate is taking courses in social media marketing just so she can manage this side of your brand," Don reminds me. "And you're paying her to do it."

"Yeah, but I want to be more involved," I explain, and I mean it.

"You don't have the time," he tells me. "Have you talked to Lizzie lately?"

"What?" That's a weird change of topic. "No. Why would I? It's over."

"Not permanently," Don replies.

"Yes. Permanently." I feel so many things and none of them are good. "Don, she's not my girlfriend anymore."

"But she might be your girlfriend again," he says, like he knows more on the subject than I do. "She would be willing to talk to you and try again. Even after the way you treated her when she visited."

"She didn't visit, she stalked, and I'm not getting back together with her," I tell him firmly, and pause at the bottom of the steps to my house before I add, "I'm seeing someone else."

"WHAT?"

That's exactly why I didn't go inside. I knew he was going to yell and I didn't want Stephanie to hear if she was awake. Don has a really deep, booming voice when he's calm, let alone when he's not.

"What the hell has gotten into you?" he barks. "Who is it? How long has this been going on? Avery, you barely ended things with Liz. Did this start before? Because if the media finds out, you'll lose deals. Look what happened to Tiger Woods."

I'm not even close to surprised that his first reaction is concern about how this will look. He honestly probably wouldn't care if I had cheated on Lizzie; he just cares if people find out about it. "It started after Lizzie, I promise you. But it's serious."

He snorts. "If it started after Lizzie, it can't be serious. It hasn't been long enough to be serious, Avery. Jesus Christ, I don't understand you. I honestly don't."

I can't defend myself because that would mean admitting I felt something for Stephanie back in Seattle and admitting I let myself end up with Lizzie anyway. And that would make me an asshole, which I am and he probably thinks I am, but I don't need it confirmed out loud.

"It's an old friend, and it just evolved into something more," I explain as I climb the stairs to my porch and juggle my bag of bagels and the two lattes and the phone pinched to my ear.

"Who?" He says it with such bite and with such demand that it really pisses me off.

"Keep trolling your puck bunny gossip sites, Don. Maybe you'll find out," I say, and hang up on my father and manager and the navigator of my universe. Ugh. Talk about a quick way to blow a perfect morning to shit.

I shove my phone in my pocket and push the key into the lock. Stephanie is coming down the stairs, her brown hair mussed and her blue eyes sleepy. She's barefoot in nothing but an old Winterhawks T-shirt I gave her last night after sex. It barely covers the white lace boy shorts she calls underwear and I call boner bait. Her long, bare legs are tanned, and I debate having her as an appetizer before the bagels and coffee.

"Morning, scrumptious." I smile up at her, putting the bag of bagels and my latte on the hall table as I toe out of my shoes.

She scratches her bed head and giggles, her voice groggy. "Scrumptious?"

She stops on the last step and I hand her a latte and then wrap my arms around her. We're eye-to-eye now. I press my lips to the curve where her neck meets her jaw. "Because you're delicious."

I make a point to rub my unshaven jaw against her skin and she squirms. "I'm going to drop my coffee!"

"I'll buy you another," I promise, and do it again. She manages to wiggle out of my grip and gets around me, jumping off the last step and heading straight to the bag of bagels.

"Bagels? What kind?" Before I can respond, she glances inside and her bright eyes get brighter. "Everything? Oh, my God, get in my mouth now!"

"Don't tempt me," I murmur, and give her a predatory grin.

She laughs and her cheeks turn pink. She grabs the bag and skips toward the kitchen, flashing me glimpses of her lace-covered ass as she goes. I shift the growing hard-on in my pants and follow her.

She's already ripped the lid off the cream cheese container and is digging into it with a knife. I smile and sip my latte and sit down next to where she's standing at the kitchen table smearing cream cheese on a bagel. My phone starts to ring in my pocket. I stand up, yank it out and turn it off before dropping it with a thump on the table. As I sit back down, I look up and find her staring at me with wide, curious eyes. She hands me the bagel covered in cream cheese.

"Thanks." She smiles, but her eyes are on my phone. "My manager is on my case."

"About managerial things or parental things?"

I bite off a big piece of bagel and chew. "He doesn't like the girls' stuff for the clothing line. I need to review it."

"Is that all?"

I kind of shrug.

She finishes chewing a bite of bagel and then adds in a softer voice but just as calm, "Does he still want you to get back together with Liz?"

I take a long, slow sip of my latte. That's all the answer she needs. Her face falls. I take her hand. "It doesn't matter what he wants."

She nods, but I can tell she doesn't believe me. I don't blame her. She's known me for years, and she's watched me make all my decisions based on exactly what he wants. I put the latte on the table and stand up, leaning toward her with my hands on the table between us for balance. "He influences my professional decisions, not my personal ones."

She still doesn't look convinced. "Trey was a personal decision."

Wow. Okay. I should have known Stephanie would call me on the one thing that proves what I just said isn't the total truth. That's what attracts me to her. She has no tolerance for bullshit or half-truths.

"This time is different." I reach out with one hand and slide it into her messy hair before cupping the back of her head and bringing her lips to mine. The kiss is long and slow, and I can't help but feel I'm more into it than she is. And I hate that.

When we break apart, she gives me a weak smile and then reaches for her latte and changes the subject. "Can I see the women's clothing?"

I nod, even though I still want to talk to her about this and find a way to make her believe me when I say Don's preference for me dating Lizzie makes no difference. Instead I walk over to my laptop on the built-in cabinet I use as a desk in the corner of the kitchen. I flip it open and a few seconds later the design sketches for the women's clothing line are on display. She's leaning over my shoulder, staring at the screen, her blue eyes narrowed critically as she takes in the tights, tops, jackets and hoodies.

"Thoughts?" I prompt. When she bites her lip, I add, "Be blunt."

"You're catering to the puck bunny crowd," she announces, and gives me a sympathetic smile. "Those are the girls who want in your pants, not the ones who want to buy your pants."

She's looking at me with a serious but kind expression. As I pull my eyes from her and back to the screen, I see what she's talking about. All the designs are tight with far too much sparkly fabric and too many plunging necklines.

"I'm betting they'll hire some big-titted model with collagen lips and no athletic ability in the ad campaign," Stephanie explains, and turns to walk back over to her bagel and coffee on the table. I grab her wrist and spin her back to face me, pulling her right up against me.

I let my lips graze hers softly. She looks…closed off. Not distant, but definitely not like she's looking into the eyes of a man she just let be inside her for half the night. She's putting up walls. She's pushing me back into the friend zone. Or at least it feels that way.

"I'm not into big tits and collagen," I tell her quietly, but with truth anchoring my words and giving them weight. I let my lips wander to her cheek and her jaw. "I'm into athletic builds and proportional breasts."

My lips tickle her neck and she wiggles. It makes me smile. I lift my head and kiss her. It's hard and dominant because I'm fucking needy and worried that she's not going to let this happen. Let us happen. My tongue touches hers and I feel her melt and submit to her feelings. She's not just letting me kiss her now; she's kissing back. When I finally pull my lips from hers, I finish my sentence. "And I sure as hell don't like collagen lips. I like soft, natural ones that have a beautiful pink color to them after I kiss them."

She smiles despite herself. "Well, you might get outvoted."

"I won't. It's my decision. I'll send them my changes based on your feedback tonight." She nods, but again it's not filled with any kind of confidence. I hate that so much. "Steph. Hey."

She looks up at me, and the lack of certainty in her eyes is painful. "I know what I want and it's not a slutty clothing line."

She smiles.

"It's also not Lizzie," I tell her, and hold her tighter around her trim waist. "It's you."

Her arms are around my shoulders and her fingers snake their way into my hair. "I want you too."

"Good." Her admission is better than an overtime goal during play-offs. I lean in to kiss her again, but she pulls back.

"But let's just...keep this to ourselves for now."

What? I loosen my grip on her waist. She scrapes her fingernails against my scalp and pulls me in for a hug. "I just...it's so new and you know as soon as we make it public it becomes this...thing that's bigger than us. The media will ask questions; your dad will have opinions. Seb will try to check you through the boards."

She smiles at that last comment, but she's probably not totally kidding. Still, I'm more than willing to risk a few hard hits by her overprotective brother. Besides, I hate hiding things. I've done it before. Every one-night stand has been in secret while other players flaunt them. I don't want to do that with Steph, which is why I was honest with my father.

The look on my face must show my dislike for what she's suggesting, because she suddenly seems desperate. "I just want to enjoy this. Quietly. For a little bit." She kisses my neck and then my cheek. Her hands start slipping down my spine, to my lower back and then to my ass. As she grips my ass, the front of my pants gets tight and any thoughts, other than ones about getting her naked, fall right out of my head.

Chapter 23

Stephanie

It's raining when I step out onto Avery's porch. Maddie is standing there holding two umbrellas. She hands me one while I hand her one of the lattes in my hand. Avery went for a run this morning in this drizzle and he brought back three lattes, knowing that Maddie would be driving me to work because of the rain.

She takes a long sip of her latte as I open the umbrella. She's smiling at me, brighter than the nonexistent sun, while we scurry down the steps to her car, which is parked out front at the curb. Once we're tucked away inside and fastening our seat belts, she turns to me with a wide grin.

"How are you? I haven't seen you in, like, a week," she says as she starts the car.

"You see me every day at work," I remind her, even though I know exactly what she's talking about.

I haven't slept at home all week. The Saints are on an extended home game run, which means Avery's been here for five days straight and I've been in his bed for five nights straight. That ends after tonight, unfortunately. They're off to San Francisco tomorrow morning.

"Okay, coworker Maddie has seen you a ton, but roommate Maddie barely remembers what you look like." She pauses before putting the car in drive and gives me a dramatic once-over with her big blue eyes. I squirm under her scrutiny. "And you know what? You're lucky I even recognize you. You look different. You look…happy and glowing in…in love!"

"Oh, my God, stop!" I wave my hand in her general direction. "You're being silly."

"So you don't love him?" Maddie asks, and cocks a manicured eyebrow.

"We've only been dating for like a week," I mutter, and point at the clock on her dash. "Drive or we'll be late."

"It's raining in SoCal; everyone is going to be late. They treat water from the sky like it's an apocalypse," Maddie quips, but she's not kidding. It doesn't rain here often. In fact, it's probably only rained three times in the last six months. But when it does rain here, everyone forgets how to drive and the freeways become a bumper car ride from an amusement park. They say it's because the oil from cars is baked into the pavement and the water brings it to the surface and makes the roads slippery. I say it's because people are idiots.

Maddie pulls away from the curb, but she's not letting the conversation about me and Avery go. "I know you guys are trying to keep it low key, but everyone at the game tonight is going to know what's going on just by looking at you."

"That's not true."

She laughs. "Totally true. He looks at you like you're edible, and he never looks at anything like that, not even the Stanley Cup. You know how the media likes to linger after games, even after they've gotten their interviews. They're totes going to know you two are in love."

"Stop saying that!"

She stops laughing and her smile gets sober. "So are you going to tell me what scares you more? Admitting to yourself that you're in love with Avery Westwood or admitting to the rest of the world you're dating him? 'Cause I can't tell which it is, and that's just plain weird."

I swallow too big a gulp of my piping hot latte and burn the roof of my mouth. I curse and then sigh and glance at Maddie who, thankfully, is focused on the road and not the look of terror on my face.

The truth is, I am kind of completely terrified by both prospects. Avery and I have been in a very nice bubble all week. He goes to practice and games; I go to work, come home and do my schoolwork, and then I cross the porch to his place and we take off all our clothes and have sex until the sun comes up. It's a simple, highly pleasurable little bubble. But tonight, it will most likely burst. I'm going to the game with Maddie and they're playing the Winterhawks again.

The good thing about Sebastian playing for a West Coast team means I still see him a lot. That had been a pro when I first decided to take the job transfer, but now it feels like a bit of a con. I still wanted to see Seb, but I don't want him to see me—with Avery. He'll be worried and probably mad at me for starting things with Avery without telling him about my past. And he has every right to judge me for that. Even I know it isn't a smart move.

I know I'll have to tell Avery soon, but I'm going to delay it as long as possible. I feel like the more time together living in the present without the past, the better this will turn out. Avery will see who I am now—really see—and know without a doubt I am not that broken girl who messed up her life over pills. The worst thing in the world to see is the doubt on someone's face when you tell them, "I'm clean now." My mother still looks at me with that doubt, which is why I don't see her much.

I have yet to fully convince myself Avery won't feel the same way now about my issues that he felt about his friend Trey's issues. Well, except they weren't issues anymore. I haven't touched a prescription drug—or any drug, not even Advil—for more than five years. Maybe that will be enough for Avery. After all, he is more than willing to be friends with clean and sober Trey, so he might be more than willing to fall in…to be in a relationship with someone who is too. I think he really likes me, and I really like him.

"Hello! Earth to lovebird! Answer my question already!"

I sip my latte again, more cautiously this time, as she eases toward downtown San Diego, braking every couple of seconds due to the congestion caused by the rain. I take a couple deep, cleansing breaths I learned from my brother's girlfriend, Shayne, who is a yoga instructor and now learning transcendental meditation and keeps sending me how-to YouTube videos.

"I'm worried about people finding out about us," I admit. "I'm worried about the viciousness of puck bunnies and the intrusiveness of the media, and I'm worried I'll screw up Avery's image and the brand his father has worked so hard to build."

Maddie makes a noise that's kind of like a snort. "Please. I mean, yeah, the media will be excited he's with someone, because even they know his monklike reputation, but you're going to be like the Princess Diana of hockey WAGs. Everyone will love you."

"Look at you with the lingo."

"I also know there are puck bunny websites, like this one called the Warren where they rate the players' abilities off the ice. Ty has twelve listed encounters and an average rating of eight point five out of ten." Maddie wrinkles her freckled nose with distaste.

"Oh, my God, you've been on there?" I'm shocked and even a little concerned. I know most wives and girlfriends avoid that stuff like the plague. First of all, not all of it is true, and second, these girls are sometimes vulgar and downright mean.

"I got curious one night." Maddie shrugs. "It's fine. I know he was…liberal with his sex life before he met me. But I also know that he isn't now. And that he must care about me a lot because he performs way better than an eight with me."

She grins and it's making me grin. "He loves you, Maddie."

"Yeah. I think he does. And the feeling is mutual." She pauses, braking abruptly as the guy in front of us swerves. "Like you and Avery."

"Shut it," I murmur, but I'm smiling.

We finally make it to work only half an hour later than normal. Maddie is right; everyone else is having commute issues because of the weather, and the place is a bit of a ghost town. My phone rings just as I'm slipping into my desk chair. It's the ringtone I have set just for Seb—a One Direction song that he has on his iPod but would never admit to. It makes me laugh every time it goes off.

"*Petit frère.*" He hates it when I call him *little brother*.

"*Soeur geante.*"

I burst out laughing, because he hasn't called me that since we were really young. He thought it was the same as big sister, but really it means *giant sister* and I always thought it was ridiculous, which is why he kept doing it well into our teens.

"It's good to hear you laugh."

"I laugh all the time, Seb."

"Maybe, but every time I call you lately you seem uptight and rushed," he explains.

I feel guilt bubble up in my gut. He's right. I've been answering because he called me out when I tried avoiding him, but I've been short and distant because I don't want him to find out about Avery just yet. Someday...maybe soon...ish. But not now. I know exactly what Sebastian is going to say, and I don't want to hear it.

"Sorry. But it's a good thing," I assure him, and then lie about the details, which I hate. I promised myself when Seb helped me get out of the life I was drowning in and start a new one that I would never lie to him. "I've been busy with interior design classes and having a good time exploring San Diego with Maddie."

"And work is going well?" he wants to know. "You're not overwhelmed or too stressed out? I know you said there'd be more work with your lawyer making partner."

"It's honestly not that bad." And that isn't a lie. I work well with my lawyer and the additional work is manageable. Seb's worried because he knows I don't do well when I'm stressed or feeling inadequate. This position is kind of the opposite. I am overqualified so it doesn't challenge me and I get bored sometimes.

"Alex give you his pass for the game? You're all set for tonight?"

"Yeah, I have a pass. Avery's."

There's an expected silence. It makes me want to smile and panic at the same time. I enjoy throwing curveballs at Seb for two reasons: because it's fun to throw him off and because I actually learn from how well he handles everything. Avery giving me his pass is a curveball for sure.

"That girlfriend of his isn't going to the game? Laurie or something?"

"Lizzie, and no, they broke up a few months ago."

"Not according to his Instagram," Seb replies. "Oh, by the way, I want to go out after the game. With you. Nothing crazy, like not a late night or anything, but maybe we grab takeout and head to your place. I'd love to see it. Last time I was there you barely had furniture."

"What do you mean, not according to his Instagram?" I say, because that's the last thing I heard. The rest was just *blah, blah, blah.* "Avery has an Instagram?"

Sebastian laughs the deep, rumbling laugh he's had since puberty. "I know. I was as shocked as you. He started it this summer, I guess because everyone was on him to engage with fans and, you know, be human."

I try to swallow, but my throat is dry, so I grab the water bottle I always keep on my desk, push back my chair and start to make my way over to the watercooler in the small kitchen across the floor. "What's his username?"

"AWestwoodOfficial," Sebastian tells me. "I gotta go, Steph. See you tonight."

"Yeah. Have a good game. See you after," I mutter, and end the call. In the kitchen I fill my bottle and then lean against the sink and pull up Instagram on my phone. I'm not a huge fan of social media, but I have Facebook and Instagram. I mostly post pictures of nature and the ocean on Instagram and use it to keep track of my friends' posts and lives. Seb's not on there, but his girlfriend, Shayne, is and so are Jessie Garrison and a few other friends from Seattle. I search the username Seb gave me and find the account.

Avery clearly doesn't use it a lot if he's had it since last summer.

There are fewer than twenty pictures. All of them have Avery in them and none look like media shots. They're all personal. There's him at a picnic table with the ocean behind him in Dieppe holding up a lobster roll with the caption "Cheat day." Then there's a short video of him practicing, just messing around with the puck, bouncing it on his stick like a million times before slapping it from midair into the net.

A few shots of him here in San Diego. One is a selfie of him sitting on his front porch steps smiling but looking away, like he's unaware of the camera. Another was posted three days ago. It's Avery at the beach, wind blowing his hair all over the place, with Liz tucked under his arm smiling brighter than the sun. My stomach is suddenly in my high heels, or possibly under them. I reach for my water bottle and take a sip, closing my eyes and trying to make sense of this. He wasn't with Liz three days ago. I know that for a fact, so why do I still feel betrayed?

Daniel walks into the kitchen and stops at the sight of me. I straighten up and shove my phone in the pocket of my pants. He gives me a small, superior grin. "Catch you on your phone on company time? Tsk, tsk."

I ignore his comment. "I'm about to make the coffee."

"But you got distracted by your hockey boyfriend?"

"No. I…" I shake my head and slip past him to the coffeemaker on the counter. It's not technically my job to make the coffee for the floor. In fact, my boss and I don't ever drink it. But it's an unspoken rule that the first legal assistant in gets it started. Besides, it'll distract me from my thoughts of Avery two-timing me.

"I'm just kidding around," Dan says as he steps closer—too close—to me. "I'm not looking for coffee anyway. I need some water."

I grab the tin of gourmet coffee and open it as I watch him move to the watercooler and stick his coffee cup under the spout. "I've got an old college basketball injury and it's acting up again. It's my lower back and it's a total bitch."

I nod and scoop the coffee into the filter. I see him pull a small pill bottle from the inside pocket in his suit jacket. He rattles it and smiles. "These little babies make it possible for me to sit at my desk all day without moaning in pain. I doubt a moaning lawyer who can't stand straight would go over well."

He laughs at his own joke and pops two of the oval pills into his mouth, chasing them with water. I instantly identify them as tramadol. One of the odd "perks" of being a recovering pill popper is I can identify pills by just their shape and color most of the time.

When I'm done, I flip the on switch and turn back to face him, and once again he's standing way too close for comfort. He's smiling, but for some reason it doesn't feel friendly. It feels lecherous and it makes me want to shiver. I fight the urge and subtly slip away from him.

"Are you really with that hockey guy? Avery Westwood?" Dan questions. He sounds incredulous, which is super insulting. "Like, *dating* him?"

I turn to face him, hands on my hips and shoulders back. "Yes. I am. And it's none of your business."

"Hey! Whoa!" Dan puts up his hands and looks at me like I just boiled his pet rabbit or something. "No need to get snippy. I wasn't in shock because I don't think you'd attract someone like that. You're a pretty girl, Steph. Definitely hot enough."

"You do realize this is inappropriate workplace conversation, right?" I can't help but snap back.

"It's a compliment. I think you're smart," he blathers on, taking another step closer to me, and once again invading my personal space. "Smart enough to know that professional athletes are dogs. You deserve better than a dog, Steph."

"Avery is not," I reply, but it's not as convincing as it would have been twenty minutes ago, before I saw his Instagram account. Still, I cross my arms and take a step back so now I'm mostly in the office and not the kitchen. Out of the corner of my eye I see another legal assistant, Joyce, standing next to her desk. She glances up. Good. I'm not alone with this pig. "And for the record, my brother is a professional hockey player, so you may want to rethink your stereotypes. Thanks."

I turn and storm back to my desk, trying not to get too worked up. Daniel is a douche. I've known that almost since day one. But he shouldn't be talking to me like that at work—or at all. I'm about to text Maddie and ask her if she thinks I should go to HR when my boss walks in. His smile falters when he sees the look on my face. "Are you okay?"

"Yes. I'm…" I take a deep breath. "I'll be fine. Latte?"

He pauses, like he doesn't believe me, but then decides not to pursue it. He smiles. "Yes please, Steph. How about caramel today?"

"Oh, getting adventurous." I smile and he chuckles.

I grab the company card out of my desk and gladly head downstairs to the Coffee Bean. Hopefully, Douchey Dan will have gone back to his office by the time I get back.

Ten minutes later I'm balancing a hazelnut latte for me and a caramel for my boss as I march back into the office. I notice Dan's bottle of pills on my desk and freeze. There's a Post-it stuck to them.

You left this in the kitchen. Joyce.

FUCK. I look up. Joyce isn't at her desk, so I can't tell her the error she just made. I grab the bottle. I want to leave it on Joyce's desk with a note telling her they're Dan's so she has to return them, because I want nothing to do with that jerk, but Conrad calls from his office. "Steph! Can you get my Outlook calendar working? It's all messed up again."

I shove the pills in the pocket of my suit jacket and grab his latte and head into his office. I get so busy after that I honestly forget the pills are in my pocket until I get home that night. I had taken off the jacket earlier in the day and just grabbed it off the back of my chair and carried it with me. It wasn't until I dropped it on my bed and the pill bottle rolled out that I remembered. I stare at the bottle as it rolls out onto my bed and curse in French under my breath.

Fucking hell. I stand there in nothing but my bra and underwear, holding the jeans I'm about to change into, and stare at it. That little bottle is as scary to me as a loaded Glock and just as dangerous. I should give it to Maddie and ask her to take them back to Douchey Dan or at least hold on to them over the weekend, but I don't want to make her deal with him. Also, then I would have to explain why I don't want the pills in my possession. Honestly, it's not that I'm tempted. I'm not...yet. But there is always that possibility. I have never tested myself. I even opted for the ring contraceptive over the pill because even the motion of taking a pill regularly scares me. It just has bad associations for me.

One day I might need antibiotics, which aren't a narcotic so I should be fine, but I hope I never have to find out. When I was living in Seattle, Sebastian even went cold turkey on medication. I used to housesit for him when he was on road trips and there wasn't even a bottle of aspirin there. He refused painkillers from the team doctor, which is a big deal because my brother gets hit and punched a lot. He's a bit of a goon on the ice.

I take a deep, cleansing breath and toss the bottle in my purse. That way it'll be easy to return to Dan on Monday and I won't forget it. Then I continue getting ready and force myself to shove any thoughts of the pills out of my mind. Instead I concentrate on what, if anything, I'm going to say to Avery about that Instagram account.

Forty minutes later, Maddie and I are outside the arena at the will call window and I'm opening the envelope with Avery's family pass inside. I loop the lanyard around my neck and walk with Maddie to the VIP entrance. She's already got Ty's pass around her neck.

"Where to first?" Maddie questions as we pass through security. "The lounge? The visitors' room to see your brother? Or should we sneak in a pregame good luck kiss with the home team?"

"You want to kiss the whole team?" I kid, and give her a wink. "Make sure you use Listerine after Larue. God knows where he's been."

She laughs and gives me a playful shove. I know she wants to go see Ty, but I suddenly feel like avoiding Avery. He's got a whole bunch of pregame rituals and superstitions, and I don't want to throw those off. Plus, I'll probably blurt out something about the Instagram and I'm one hundred percent certain that a confrontation with your girlfriend about your ex is bad luck before a game.

"You go see Ty and I'll go find Seb," I suggest. She hesitates. "You know how Avery is about his pregame rituals. I don't want to throw him off."

She finally shrugs and turns left down the tunnel toward the Saints' facilities while I turn right toward the visitors' facilities. It doesn't take much to find Sebastian. He's standing in the hall in workout shorts and a blue Winterhawks T-shirt chugging a Gatorade. The green one, which is his favorite. I smile automatically at the sight of him and a flood of warm, happy feelings fills me up. I love my brother and I didn't realize how much I missed him until I saw him standing there.

He hears the click of my high-heeled boots on the concrete and looks up. As the Gatorade bottle leaves his lips, it's replaced with a wide, happy grin. *"Bonjour, soeur geante. Mon dieu, tu es tellement beau ce soir!"* He opens his arms and pulls me into a bear hug. "It's not cool to wear yoga pants and sweatshirts to games in California?"

Right. I never dressed up when I went to games in Seattle. In fact, one time I honestly considered wearing my pajama pants but thought that might be pushing it. I'm not exactly in a prom dress or anything tonight, but I'm wearing a pair of nice jeans and a sexy shirt and my hair is styled and I've got on more makeup than I wore to work today.

"Yeah. It's a scene here, like everything. I have to keep up," I snark, and tickle his side briefly. He squirms away. I've been doing it since he was six. It's ridiculous because now he's this big, tough hockey goon who is reduced to a giggle fit if you run your fingers over his ribs.

"Seriously, Steph, you look great," Seb tells me. He tries to ruffle my hair, but I duck. "California must agree with you."

"I think it does." This thing with Avery is icing on the cake, but even before him I was enjoying my life. A lot. "How's Seattle?"

"Good." He smiles. "I mean the team is weird without Avery. But Dix is a good captain. And we're smoking Avery in the standings, so that's fun."

I roll my eyes but grin. "You're such a competitive jerk. As always."

"Hey! Stephanie!" I see Jordan Garrison standing in the doorway to the locker room. He's in workout shorts, too, but he's shirtless. His blue eyes sweep over me, totally checking me out, but it's innocent. He's smiling at me with his usual friendly lopsided grin that causes a dimple in his cheek. "You're looking good, Steph!"

"Hey! You're married," Sebastian barks at his teammate and friend.

Jordan shrugs, still smiling as he jokes. "Weddings don't make you blind, Seb. You'll figure that out soon enough. I'm not hitting on her, just noting a fact."

"No noting anything about my sister. Siblings are not notable!" he replies sharply. I want to think he's kidding because he's kind of smiling, but it doesn't reach his eyes, which makes me think there's a pinch of truth in there.

"If that were true, then Dev and I wouldn't be married to sisters like a bunch of hillbillies," Jordan retorts, and both Seb and I can't help but grin at that. Jordan's older brother Devin married Jessie's younger sister, Callie. "Anyway, nice seeing you, Steph. Jessie told me to give you a hug if I saw you, but I'll skip it now, thanks to the threats. Seb, we gotta get dressed."

Seb nods at Jordan and then turns and reaches out for another hug. I squeeze him extra hard. "What was that Jordy said about you finding out about marriage soon enough?"

"I made the mistake of mentioning to him that I know I'm going to marry Shay," he explains simply, like he's telling me something as mundane as his weekend plans or favorite movie or something.

I pull back from the hug and stare at him, my hands gripping his shoulders. "Are you kidding me? You're going to ask her to marry you? And you told Jordan but not me?"

He looks confused by my complete and utter shock. He laughs and unhinges my hands from his body. "Steph, to be fair, I would have told you, but you either avoid my calls or cut them short lately," he explains with a judgmental gleam to his blue eyes. "And it's not like I have anything decided. I just started looking at rings and I'm thinking I'll ask her to move in with me first."

I'm hit with another wave of love for him. He's not just a great brother; he's a great man. He hasn't made the giant, irredeemable mistakes I have, so he deserves to be happy. I feel my eyes flood with tears so abruptly I can't fight them. Sebastian looks suddenly terrified. He grabs my hand.

"Hey! *Pourquoi tu pleures*?!" he asks, his deep voice sinking lower with concern.

I shake my head and squeeze his hand before letting go and stepping back. "Don't worry. They're happy tears. I love Shayne. She's perfect for you, and I'm happy. For you. I am. It's so great! Now go. Get ready. I'll see you after the game."

I turn and stride down the hall as fast as I can. When I round the curve in the hall, I slip into the women's bathroom to grab a paper towel and dab at my eyes, trying to save my makeup. I take some deep breaths, and for the first time in a long time, I realize I need to go to a Narcotics Anonymous meeting. Those weren't tears of joy for my brother. Of course I was genuinely happy for Seb, but the tears sprung at the thought that he was worthy of love and I wasn't.

I decide I'll go to a meeting tomorrow night. It's not because I feel like I want to use again; it's because I realize that I'm starting to feel like that damaged, unworthy teenager again. The one who tried to numb her feelings of inadequacy with pills. The one who feels like she'll never be loved. The one who isn't good enough to be the girlfriend of the star of the National Hockey League.

Chapter 24

Avery

We're losing. I am really getting fucking sick of losing, especially against my former team. Again. I know I'm scowling as I skate to the bench. I know the fucking television cameras will pick it up and the fucking commentators will talk about it and then the fucking reporters will ask me fucking stupid questions like, "You seemed very tense out there. Was it because the team is still struggling to score?" And I'll have to give some carefully crafted, passive answer when all I want to do is yell, "YES! I hate being on a team that perpetually sucks!"

"Easy, boss. It's only two goals. We can make that up," Ty says as I drop down beside him. Clearly my expression is as pissy as I think it is. "Fuck, you and I can make that up without these chuckleheads."

"So let's fucking do that," I growl, and he nods and butts the side of his helmet against mine.

We have twelve minutes to make this happen. It's not impossible, but if the rest of the team could get their shit together and try even half as much as Ty, then we'd have better odds.

I've reviewed all my teammates' stats from previous years and other teams and they all have potential. They all earned their spot on this team, so why the fuck can't they get it together and make this team a contender? Ty stands and goes over the board with his line but not before giving me a reassuring nod.

Before his shift is over he's scored. "FUCK, YEAH!" I bellow, which turns the head of everyone on the bench, including the coach. Guys swear on the bench all the time, just not me.

The scowl on my face slips a little and I bounce, eager to get out there and add another one. It takes two shifts, but I score one, too, and we end the third tied, no thanks to fucking Echolls, who gives away the puck right in front of our goalie. On the quick pause, Coach writes up the shoot-out players. I know I'm on it. I always take the shoot-out. I have a seventy-six percent success rate.

"Larue, Echolls and Westwood, in that order," he commands, and my jaw drops. Echolls?

"No."

I don't realize I've spit the word out of my mouth until the whole bench turns and looks at me. The coach is glaring, as he should. "Got something to say, Seventy-Eight?"

He's calling me by my number. Never a good sign. "Sidebar?"

"No. You can say it in front of everyone."

I swallow. "Parsons played his ass off tonight and he has a fifty percent success rate in the shoot-out this season."

"Yeah. And…" I don't fill in the blank for him, so he fills it in. In front of everyone, including a furious Beau Echolls, because he knows what's coming. "And Echolls is only at forty percent."

I nod.

"Fuck you!" Echolls roars, skating across the ice and shoving Alex out of the way to get right in my face. "You're a fucking self-righteous bag of shit, you know that?"

"I'm the captain. I've studied everyone on this team, and I know you are underperforming. I also know we need to fucking win, so suck it up, princess." I put my hand on the front of his jersey and give him a shove. He shoves back.

Beau raises his fist. It almost feels like slow motion, but then everything speeds up as Alex grabs Echolls and yanks him backward, Ty gets in between us, and the coach bellows, "ENOUGH!"

He could bench me and give my shoot-out spot to someone else. He should. Never ever should a player question the coach's decision, especially not on ice, especially not in front of the player. And if I were any other player, I would be benched. But I'm not. Coach grimaces and growls his orders. "Larue, Parsons, Westwood. Echolls, you're fourth if we need a fourth."

Beau looks like he's about to turn into the Hulk. His face is red, his eyes are bulging out of their sockets and his lip is snarling like a rabid dog's. If he could froth at the mouth he would. He's not directing his anger at Coach; he's directing it right at me. And if looks could kill, I'd be in little pieces all over the blue line right now. But fuck him. I'm right. And I am so sick of fucking losing.

Ty doesn't score. But Alex does and I do and only Sebastian does for the Winterhawks, so we win. We actually fucking win. I realize it came at a huge cost, though. If our team morale was bad before, it's going to be worse now. But I needed to fucking win. I watch Echolls storm down the tunnel in front of me, hurling his stick into the wall with such force it snaps in half. He chucks his helmet across the room and storms into the medical room instead of the locker room. I actually appreciate that he's trying to avoid another confrontation.

Despite the win, the room is bleak. Everyone has their head down and no one is speaking. Larue isn't playing his usual crappy music on his iPod like he does after a win. I know I can't leave things like this. I know I have to be the bigger man. The leader. I also know that the mood is my fault.

I pull my sweaty jersey over my head and dump it in the laundry bin. As I sit to unlace my skates, I say, "I shouldn't have singled out Echolls."

Everyone looks up. Every single one of them. Some have stunned looks on their face. Some are scowling. Some, like Ty and Alex, look empathetic. All those expressions are justified. "I'll apologize to him when he calms down. But the thing is, guys, I'm not the robot everyone makes me out to be. I didn't get here by having no heart. I got here by having too much, just like the rest of you. And we desperately needed a fucking win."

Almost every head in the room nods at that. I pull off one skate and then the other and continue. "I'm well aware that Echolls and a few others aren't thrilled with my appearance on this team. And I am even more aware that I haven't shifted the team's trajectory all that much since I arrived. Not as much as people want. But I believe in all of you. Echolls included. So I apologize for ruining the win. I won't do it again."

There's a rumbling of responses. Everything from nods, grunts, to "no worries" and "okay" and, thankfully, a few "it's all good, Captain" and "apology accepted." Out of the corner of my eye I see the coach in the doorway; his expression is much less furious than it was on the ice.

He clears his throat. "We're not doing press tonight, boys."

He disappears, but what replaces him is a face with more fury than

Coach showed all night. The face of Don Westwood. What the fuck is my dad doing here? There's no saving this night now.

I stand up and walk over to him. Without a word I pass by him and continue down the hall. Beau is still in the medical room, the only other private space, so I walk into the training room. A few guys will come in to use the bikes to warm down in a couple minutes before their showers, but it's empty right now. And that's a good thing. The interruption will mean the conversation with Don will be cut short, and I already know that's a good thing.

When I stop, just inside the door, and turn to face him, he is so angry he essentially hisses and spits his words. "What the fuck was that down there? You're fighting with your own team now? What kind of leader does that?"

"I didn't start it," and just like that I feel like a whiny teenager again. For someone who has never acted much like an actual parent, he sure has a weird way of doing that to me. "And I fixed it."

"What caused it?" When I don't answer right away, he clarifies, even though I don't need it. "What made Echolls go after you? On national television. You know this is a nationally televised game, right, Avery?"

"Yeah. I know. And we won," I reply tersely, and then steady my voice to seem calm and rational. "I suggested Parsons be put in the shoot-out over Echolls."

Don blinks his hazel eyes. His jaw goes slack for a second, then tightens again. "Did the coach ask your opinion?"

"No."

"Holy fuck, Avery." Don swears a lot. I used to appreciate it because I wasn't allowed to and he'd always pick the right things to curse about. But not now. "You're pulling diva shit now?"

"I just wanted a fucking win. We haven't beaten the Winterhawks all damn season," I retort, and his eyes dart around the room to make sure it's still empty.

"You don't get to talk like that. And you don't get to be a fucking diva. Nobody buys products from a diva."

Here we go with the endorsements again. "Okay. I get it. I fixed it. I need you to let this go. What the hell are you doing here anyway? I didn't have your visit on my agenda."

"Stop with your mouth," he snaps, referring to the *hell, fuck* and *damn* I've dropped. "You are clearly going down some kind of path that isn't the planned route, so I came here to get you back on track."

"What the..." I pause, run a hand through my sweaty hair and re-phrase before I drop another f-bomb. "What are you talking about?"

"Living in that condemned cottage, dumping your girlfriend, re-designing your clothing line, starting brawls with your own team and"—he pauses to lower his voice—"messing around with some player's sister."

"How do you know?" I demand, awe overtaking the anger in my tone.

"You said she's an old friend," Don explains with a huff. "Your only old friends in San Diego are Larue and your neighbor, Deveau's sister. I made an educated guess."

Oh, my God, he seriously flew across the country for this? Actually, to a different country? I inhale and hold it for a long minute, gathering my thoughts. "Her name is Stephanie and, yeah, she was a *very* good friend before things developed. I hear that's a good way to start a solid relationship."

"Lizzie was a good way to start a solid relationship."

That's a weird statement. I guess the way I met Lizzie, at a family friend's barbeque, was good. And then I kept running into her at places like the farmer's market or the gym. But I just never felt I knew Lizzie the way I know Steph. "I don't have a connection with Lizzie the way I have with Steph."

Don makes a face at that. "Is the connection in your pants or in your head?"

"I'm going to pretend you didn't just say that, Don," I reply in a deathly serious tone. He backs off right away, which is a good thing for him.

A couple of the guys come in and hop on the bikes. Good. I am so done with this conversation. Don sighs and scratches his nearly bald head. "I suppose you have plans with this girl after the game?"

"I do."

"I'm staying at the Palomar," he says. It doesn't surprise me. Even in Seattle where I had a four-bedroom house, Don didn't stay with me. He likes his space and I've learned to like mine. "I'm here for at least two days. I'll call you tomorrow to arrange a meeting. We have more to discuss."

"Yeah. Sure." I just don't feel like arguing anymore. He wants to talk, we'll talk, but just like my decision to play in San Diego over L.A. or New York, he won't be changing my mind—about the revamped clothing line, where I live and especially not about Stephanie.

We shake hands, like a manager and an athlete would do, and I head back into the locker room to shower. I notice the medical room door is open and Beau isn't inside. I should track him down, but I just want to shower and change so I can find Stephanie.

Chapter 25

Stephanie

My legs are aching and my feet hurt, but I keep jogging because the pain is helping me forget all the stuff in my head that's making me hurt in a different way. After the game last night, I waited in the family lounge for Avery, but my brother showed up first. When Avery showed up, we all went out for a late bite to eat.

I didn't get alone time with Avery until we got home. And after two hours of sitting next to each other and acting platonic, he was apparently more than ready to drop the charade. He spent the drive home, after Sebastian hopped in a cab back to his team's hotel, with one hand on the wheel and the other sliding higher and higher on my thigh. He was kissing me before we got up the front porch and we never even made it to the bedroom. We had sex until we passed out on his living room couch.

When I woke up at six, I decided to go for a run and clear my head and figure out exactly what I was going to ask him about that damn social media account. Besides, I knew if I was still in bed when Avery woke up, he'd be inside me again before I got a word out. Because he would want it and I would too.

Sex with Avery is more addictive than any narcotic, and I've tried more narcotics than I want to admit. It's slightly terrifying. I promised myself I would never be addicted to anything ever again, but I never realized I could be addicted to the feel of someone between my legs.

I crave Avery.

I'm passing the Coronado Hotel, trying to focus on the burn in my legs and the sound of the waves crashing beside me when I feel hands touch my hips from behind. I spin, arm raised, hand in a fist, and am greeted by familiar, but shocked, caramel eyes. I drop my arm.

"Crap, Avery, I thought you were a rapist or something," I confess, and struggle to catch my breath. Apparently being terrified while exercising winds the hell out of a person.

He steps forward and wraps an arm around my shoulders, pulling me into him. My cheek rests on his sweatshirt near his collarbone, and I breathe in the fresh-laundered scent of the fabric mixed with the lingering smell of that woodsy, dark cologne he wears. It starts to calm me, so I take a deeper sniff.

"Sorry!" He squeezes me tighter. "When I woke up and found you gone, I figured this is what you were doing, so I thought I would join you. Like old times."

I laugh at that. "You mean in Seattle, when I would somehow always run into you when I was sweaty and gross."

I pull away from him and turn back to my route. I start to jog, but much more slowly than before. I'm not running from my fears anymore. They're running beside me now. He gives me a sheepish sideways glance as we continue down the path. "I'll let you in on a secret. It was no accident. I knew your workout schedule and showed up where you'd be."

My step falters, and I slow down even more. "What?"

He speeds up and turns around so he's running backward, facing me. This gorgeous boy is telling me he went out of his way to run into me? Really? Is he joking? He doesn't look like he's joking.

"You what?"

"Seb mentioned that you like to go running after work in the park by your house," he admits, and his grin gets bigger. "Come on, I have hockey practice just about every day and games and a personal trainer and state-of-the-art facilities to train in. You really think I needed to jog in that park in the soggy Seattle evening rain?"

I laugh. He's right. It rained a lot of the nights I ran, because it's Seattle and that's what it does. But Avery was still out there a lot. Almost every night he didn't have a game. I did think it was odd at the time, but I believed his explanation about it being a way to clear his head more than a way to stay in shape. "You wanted to run with me."

"I wanted to spend time with you. I had a major crush." He winks at me, and then spins around to face forward and drop back next to me.

"Avery... really? While we were in Seattle?" I'm honestly blown away.

"You're gorgeous and you had no problem challenging me and calling me out on my shit," he explains. "And it was hot. And I needed it. I needed you. I just wasn't ready to admit it to you or myself."

I don't know what to say to that. I'm so blown away, there are no words, so we jog in silence a little farther, until we turn off the beachfront path and head down the street where our houses are located.

I slow to a walk. "So you go home for the summer and start dating Liz?"

His smile drops, and his gaze slips to his sneakers as we walk. He shoves his hands in the kangaroo pouch on the front of his sweatshirt. "That wasn't planned. When I got home from Seattle for the summer I told my…Don that I was done with his mandatory no-girlfriend rule. I told him I wanted a relationship. I was going to ask you out at Jordan and Jessie's wedding, but you shut me down suddenly."

"The cold lake water shut you down," I counter softly, and he grins insightfully.

"You tipped that canoe on purpose," he replies, and doesn't wait for me to confirm, his eyes shifting to his feet. "So I gave up, went home and tried to move on. Then Seb said you were moving here."

Avery finally looks up from his feet. "And then I called my agent and had him ask the Saints if they wanted to make an offer."

"So you knew I was here when you signed with them?" I swallow hard. "But you were in love with Liz."

"I was never in love with Liz," he replies swiftly, but without contempt. He's not being mean, just stating something he believes to be fact. "But I didn't think I had a shot with you, and Lizzie was…what I was supposed to want."

"What does that mean?"

"You've said it yourself, more than once," Avery explains, running a hand over his unshaven face before pushing it back into his hair. "Lizzie was a perfect match. She volunteered, she taught kindergarten, she was from my hometown, she didn't go bar-hopping, she wasn't interested in the media, she didn't even have a social media account…"

His sentence trails, whipping away with the wind, and he pulls a hand out of his hoodie pocket and casually takes my hand in his. The pictures from his Instagram fill my brain again, but before I can say anything he starts talking again. "But something didn't feel right. That's what was crazy. She just didn't fit. But I still felt like you might."

He stops walking, turns to face me on the sidewalk and tugs on my hand, turning me toward him. He looks so earnest and so vulnerable. It's breathtaking on a man who is nothing but stoic confidence to the rest of the world. "I took the contract with the Saints because you were here. That's how much I was hoping for this."

"But I don't volunteer. I'm always tense and quiet with strangers. I would be horrible at those events the WAGs put on for the fans. I'm not well spoken or well educated. I've got a paralegal diploma from an online college. I don't have Lizzie's perfect past. She's a good fit for your life. I'm not, technically," I say, and my throat starts to feel tight.

I try to pull my hand away from him, but he won't let go. In fact, he steps closer, tucking his free hand under my ponytail, behind my sweaty neck, and tugging my lips to his. The kiss is brief but scorching, and he only pulls back far enough so that I can see the look of certainty on his face.

"Fuck good. This is a *perfect* fit," he replies, and oh, how I want to bask in that. Drown my fears and uneasiness in his words, but I can't.

"So why are you still posting photos with her on your Instagram?"

I have a bird's-eye view of his face as it morphs from certainty to confusion so quickly it looks like it hurts. "What are you talking about?"

His hand behind my neck slips away and I take a step back. He digs in the pocket of his track pants and pulls out his phone, not waiting for my explanation. A second later he's swearing. Loudly. "Mother. Fucker. Are you fucking kidding me?"

"Avery…shush," I advise quietly as a mother with a stroller glances up, horrified, from the sidewalk across the street. He glances up, the amber in his eyes darkening as he holds up his phone toward me, gripping it in his fist so his knuckles are white.

"I don't run my social media," he explains to me. "I don't even know the password, so I promise you I didn't post any photos of her and me. Ever."

"Who runs it?"

"My sister." He turns the phone around in his hand, fingers moving briskly across the screen as he closes Instagram and starts to dial a number. "My father insisted I get on social media, so I hired her to run the account. She's supposed to post generic but personal shots of me."

He starts marching down the street, phone pressed to his ear. "That beach photo isn't recent. It's from this summer in Dieppe."

He's furious, but I'm relieved. His sister must answer the phone because suddenly he barks. "Kate? What the fuck are you posting on my Instagram?"

I slow my pace, so I'm behind him a little, giving him some privacy to yell at his sister. I can hear most of the conversation, though. He's really angry, and whatever she says just seems to be getting him angrier. "I gave you direction when I gave you control of the account. You were supposed to follow what I said, not what he says!"

He stops in front of our places but doesn't move to climb the stairs to his house or mine. He just stands rooted on the sidewalk, rigid like an angry tree. "Give me the password. I'll post some stuff on my own. If you post one more picture of Lizzie, I will fire your ass."

He listens to her for a second, and then seems to hang up on her without a good-bye. He turns back to me, but his eyes are on the phone, and his fingers tap away on the screen. He mutters, half distracted, "Come here."

I step closer and suddenly he wraps his arm around my shoulder and nuzzles my neck. "Smile, beautiful."

With his arm out in front of us he snaps a picture. "What are you doing? You can't post that!"

He looks shocked. "Why not?"

"You know I haven't told Seb," I remind him. "I thought we were keeping this to ourselves for a while."

He smiles softly and turns me to face him, his arm slipping to my waist and holding me flush against him. He's all hard muscle wrapped in soft, warm cotton. I push his hood down as my hands slide around his neck. "About that. We should tell him."

"I know. It's just…" I pause and let my fingers play with the ends of his dark hair and the base of his neck. "When the world knows, it'll start to get complicated."

"It will, but it'll be worth it," he whispers, and his hand slips from my lower back to my ass, sliding over the smooth spandex and grabbing on as his lips cover mine.

I kiss him back with more passion than I think I ever have before, because it will be my last kiss before I tell him about my past and in some deep, dark place in my heart I'm worried it'll be our last kiss, ever. I open my mouth and slip my tongue past his lips. He meets mine and his hand on my ass squeezes and pulls me roughly against him.

It's a Saturday morning and the neighborhood is just waking up. Anyone could bear witness to this passionate display of PDA, but I don't care. I want to savor this moment, his lips, the feel of his tongue, the heat of his body. I take my time, absorbing every sensation, and as soon as the kiss breaks, leaving me breathless and wanting, I regret every second of it. Because my brother is standing on my porch staring at us.

Avery doesn't see him, but as my whole body tightens instantly, he follows my gaze. His hand flies off my ass and he steps away so suddenly I almost tip over. I hadn't realized I was using him for support. Sebastian isn't moving, isn't speaking, and I can't for the life of me figure out what has got his light blue eyes blazing. Anger? Shock? Both?

I run up the steps and throw myself at him. "Hey! I didn't know you were going to stop by!"

I'm not so much hugging him as trying to anchor him to the porch, in case his plan is to fly off it and attack Avery like an overprotective goon. Avery is either brave or stupid because we walks up the path to the stairs, bringing himself precariously close to the wild animal that is my brother. "Hey, Deveau. What's in the bag?"

I look down and notice for the first time that Seb's holding a paper bag with grease stains on it. "The severed head of the last guy I caught kissing my sister."

"Sebastian!" I flush so quickly I almost feel light-headed.

Avery doesn't even twitch. "I had no idea that severed heads smelled like bacon."

Sebastian doesn't even crack the slightest hint of a smile. "Breakfast burritos for my sister and me. Sorry, none for you."

Avery remains unfazed as he climbs the steps to his own porch. I grab my brother's hand by the wrist. I couldn't hold him back if I wanted to, but I'm hoping the gentle squeeze of my hand will be enough to make him realize I don't want him to jump the railing and murder my boyfriend.

"That's okay. I have to meet my dad for a breakfast meeting anyway." He turns his beautiful face to me. "I'll call you later."

I nod because I seem to be unable to make words come out. Avery disappears into his house and I quickly unlock the door to mine. Sebastian follows me inside and shuts the door a little too forcefully. It rattles the pictures on the wall next to it. I frown as I call out Maddie's name and toe off my running shoes. There's no response. I turn to Sebastian.

"She must have stayed at Ty's."

Sebastian strides down the hall and into the kitchen. With each wordless step my anxiety grows. He's never silent. Sebastian is a talker. He has all the best smartass lines on the ice and all the most thoughtful insights for friends and family. So silence is scary. I follow him and watch as he opens the bag and hands me a breakfast burrito wrapped in foil. "They're from the gourmet shop by my hotel. Organic everything, and they still taste great."

I nod and start to unwrap it, my mouth watering with the smell of cheese and bacon. He aggressively bites of a giant chunk of his and chews harshly, like a lion devouring his kill. I take a much daintier bite. He's right—it's delicious.

"Stephanie." He swallows and levels me with his eyes, which are almost identical to mine. "When the fuck did you start sleeping with Westwood?"

I almost choke on the chunk of burrito I'm swallowing and head to the fridge to grab a bottle of water. I knew a question was coming. I just didn't expect it to be so blunt. "I'm not sleeping with him," I argue back and then pause. "Well, I am sleeping with him, but not *just* sleeping with him."

Seb looks stunned. "Who else are you sleeping with? I'm not judging, Lord knows I got around before Shay and I don't regret it, but, *mon Dieu*, Steph, this seems out of character. In Seattle you were the queen of celibacy."

I realize he took my statement completely the wrong way, and I actually laugh. It's nervous and sounds garbled because I still seem to have bacon wedged in my windpipe. Ugh. I cough and take another swig of water. "I meant Avery and I are doing more than sleeping together. We're dating."

"Avery doesn't date," Sebastian states firmly. "Well, other than that blond chick you said he broke up with who's hanging off him on his Instagram."

"Yeah, his sister runs his social media. I think she didn't get the memo Liz and Avery were dunzo," I explain, and toss him his own bottle of water from the fridge before heading back to the counter to grab my burrito and attempt to eat it like a normal person.

He watches me, silently chewing on his own breakfast. He swallows another chunk—he's already halfway through his in two bites—and twists open his water bottle, which looks minuscule in his big mitts.

Sebastian is a hulk of a guy. He knows it and he knows how to use it. I've watched him mess up tons of opponents on the ice, and I don't want him doing it to Avery, which is why I'm trying to explain the depth of our relationship to him so he doesn't think I'm being used.

"I really like him. And he really likes me." I jump up so I'm sitting on the counter. "We didn't rush into this. It wasn't a whim. We've talked it out and we both know it's not some random hookup. Did you know he used to accidentally on purpose run into me while I jogged in Seattle?"

"No. I didn't." My brother doesn't look nearly as impressed by that fact as I am. He finishes his burrito and tosses the tin foil into the garbage next to my sink. Then his head snaps up and our eyes lock. "He knew you had moved here when he picked San Diego."

I stop chewing and nod. "He did."

Sebastian stares at me incredulously and whispers, "Holy shit he *followed* you here?"

"He says he did without really totally saying it anyway."

"The Saints suck. It's a virtually impossible team to turn around. Los Angeles and New York would have been easy teams to get to the finals, and San Diego probably won't even make the play-offs." Sebastian runs a hand through his brown hair and whispers, "He must love you."

"I…I mean…" I drop the rest of the burrito on the counter as emotions fill up any empty space in my gut. "Do you think so?"

"Do you love him?" Sebastian asks instead of answering my awed question.

"I've never felt this way about someone," is all I can figure out to say. "It's terrifying."

Sebastian smiles at that, but it's fleeting. "So…he knows…everything?"

I know he doesn't want to ask. I can tell by the stunted way the question makes its way out of his mouth. But he has to ask because he knows Avery. He knows that his whole life is calculated, well thought out and planned. The fact that I don't say anything is answer enough. Sebastian groans.

"It's the past," I remind him. "And I was actually about to tell him when you showed up."

He cocks an eyebrow to make sure he gets his sarcastic point across as he replies, "Yes, because all serious conversations start with his hand on your ass and your tongue down his throat."

"I really was about to tell him," I repeat firmly, ignoring his little snarky, albeit accurate, comment. "And last time I checked, you and Shayne weren't big on the communicating in the beginning either. You didn't even know her dad was a hockey player until after you'd seen her naked. More than once."

He smiles at that, like he's reminiscing in his head about his girl-friend's nakedness.

"Hello! Stop walking down naked memory lane and focus. I will tell Avery about my not-so-stellar past. I promise. It's just not easy to talk about. It's not like, 'Hey, I used to own a cat.' It's, 'Hey, I used to be a runaway with a drug problem.'"

"When did this start?" he wants to know as he takes another sip of water.

"A couple of weeks ago, officially," I explain, and hastily add, "Well, after he ended things with Liz, or 'the blonde,' as you call her."

"But you've been hanging out with him a lot, right? Like in Seattle and when he moved here. He couldn't live any closer if he tried." Se-bastian motions toward the wall behind him that is the shared wall with Avery's unit. "And you never, not once, told him about things?"

"You know I don't talk about it," I reply, and hand him the rest of my burrito because I'm not going to finish it. He takes a bite so big there's hardly anything left. "I haven't told Maddie yet either."

His rugged face starts to soften and he tilts his head. "Hey. You know you have nothing to be ashamed of, right? I know you know this."

"I'm not ashamed. I'm proud I got through it," I tell him—what I've always said. What I've always believed. But somehow...the words don't hold the weight they used to. "But that doesn't mean I have to emotionally vomit everything at everyone all the time. Hey! Look at me! I'm a survivor. I was in the bell jar and found my way out."

Sebastian tosses the last bite of burrito in the garbage and startles me by grabbing me and pulling me into a hug. "You're worrying me, Stephanie. This thing with Avery is worrisome."

"I'm fine. I'll be fine."

"He's not an easy person. He's constantly under pressure, and I've watched him make some harsh decisions because of his public image. It's like he spends his life in between a rock and a hard place, you know?" Sebastian explains, and when he lets me go I nod. "The thing he hates more than anything is being blindsided—on the ice and off—so don't blindside him. Your past shouldn't matter to him. But…if it does, wouldn't you rather know that now, before it gets too serious?"

"You think he might break up with me because of it?" My voice it high and weak, cracking on the last few words. My brother is voicing my biggest fear. The one I've had all along. The reason I didn't want to get involved with Avery and the reason I didn't tell him the minute we got involved.

"I know him well enough to know he doesn't make the same mistake twice," he replies. I know he's referring to the fact that Avery once abandoned Shayne's brother when he was going through rehab. Sebastian hugs me again. "I like to believe he's honestly a good guy. But I also know trust isn't something he gives lightly. He trusts you, and by not telling him everything you're kind of lying to him. If he hears it from someone else first, he'll feel betrayed."

"No one knows."

"Shay knows and Trey and Jordan and Jessie and—"

"I'll tell him," I promise, and Sebastian glances at the clock on the stove.

"I've got to get back to the hotel. We're leaving in an hour. Busing it to Los Angeles." He kisses my forehead and then musses my hair, causing half of it to fall out of the ponytail.

I yank out the elastic and follow him to the door. "Give my love to the Seattle gang. Especially my future sister-in-law."

His whole face lights up at that comment, which warms my heart. He steps out onto the porch and glances at Avery's door. "Let me know if you need me to introduce his face to the ice. I bet it would be kind of fun."

"Sebastian!"

He just shrugs innocently and gives me a wink before adding, "I love you. If you need me, just call."

"*Je t'aime aussi, petit frère.*"

Chapter 26

Avery

I glance at the phone in my lap one more time. Still no message from Stephanie. I texted Jordan on my way to the hotel to meet my dad to find out when their bus to L.A. left, and he said eleven. It's almost one now, so whatever confrontation or conversation Steph had with Seb is well over. I thought she'd get in touch with me by now.

"Avery!" Don snaps in my face. I hate when he does that. It's been his go-to move since I was a kid and I used to zone out while he taught me about set plays and shooting trajectories. When I was a hormonal, bitchy teenager I used to have to clench my fists to keep from slapping him out of my face. Today I just sigh.

"Sorry, Don, I'm expecting a text." I reluctantly shove my phone in my pocket and force myself to focus on the sketches on the laptop screen in front of me. They're of the newly redesigned clothing line.

"As I was saying, I think they got it right this time. The clothes are functional but fun," Don explains, and points out one top in particular. "Look at the colors and pattern on this. It's flirty and fun but also something you could actually do CrossFit or something in."

I look up at him and bite back a smile. "Did you just say flirty and fun?"

His perpetually solemn face breaks into an uncharacteristic smile. "Your sister's words when she saw the designs. But I thought they were fitting."

I smile. "Yeah. They are. I'll approve this."

The designers implemented every single ounce of the feedback I gave them, most of which were Steph's ideas. I can't wait to tell her. Don shuts the laptop and sits back in his seat, picking up his drink, which I think is some kind of kale smoothie. We're sitting on the patio at the restaurant in his hotel. We've been going over business for almost two hours. Since we're playing again tonight, I really need to get home and start my pregame rituals, which include taking a nap, then heating up some chicken parmesan that I have delivered weekly from an Italian place nearby, followed by a blue Gatorade on the way to the game.

"So that's it for now? Because I have to get back."

Don looks perplexed. "To follow your ritual or find that girl who isn't texting you?"

"Stephanie," I say. "Her name is Stephanie. If you're coming to the game tonight, you'll probably meet her, so I suggest you write that down somewhere."

Don frowns. "Don't get flip."

I stand up. "So I'll see you tonight?"

"I talked to Lizzie this morning." He says it so casually, like he's muttering a grocery list, that it adds to the anger the statement brews in me. He raises his hands before I have a chance to voice my rage. "Calm down. If you're not going to care about her feelings, I have to."

"I do care about her feelings, but it's not like I was going to marry her or anything," I reply. It's an effort to keep my voice low and even. "It was six weeks. We were only together six weeks and she's acting like I broke up a ten-year marriage. So are you, for that matter."

"Well, I was hoping for more than ten years when I set it up."

His words don't register fully at first. Not the full meaning. Then it's like a grenade that's had its pin pulled. It lands smack-dab in the middle of my brain and there's nothing…and then *BOOM!*

"When you set it up? Set up what? Lizzie and me?" I question, glaring at my father/manager/matchmaker, apparently. "How?"

He has the nerve to roll his eyes like I'm the one being dramatic. "You came home from Seattle last summer like a moody teenage girl who didn't get asked to prom, and you wouldn't stop bitching about wanting a real relationship."

Is he for real right now? Is he actually belittling me after I followed all his damn rules my entire career and busted my ass, sacrificing most pieces of a normal life in order to become the best of the best and create the life he's living right now, at this fancy hotel with his twenty-dollar fucking smoothie I'm sure he's expensing to me? Is he really fucking doing that?

"Look, I get it, you need to get laid, and you want it steady, like other guys get." He leans back even farther in his chair, either completely oblivious or completely unruffled by the fury building inside me. "But you aren't other guys. Everything you do, everyone you do, can affect your bottom line. I knew what type of girl would work with your image—local hometown girl, sweet, does charity work, no crazy half-naked party pictures on social media—so I started doing a little looking and found Lizzie. I told her about you and invited her to that barbeque. The rest was supposed to be happily-ever-after history."

"How the fuck did you find her? Did you take out a fucking ad and interview women like it was a job? And, no, I won't stop fucking swearing," I finish before he can berate me.

He stands up now so we're almost face-to-face, but my dad is barely five-nine, so I have a couple of inches on him, not to mention pounds. Thankfully, the restaurant is almost empty so no one is paying attention to the father and son who are about to kill each other.

"She's the daughter of a guy I went to college with," Don replies. "Now calm down."

"Don't tell me what to do," I reply sharply. "You don't get to do that anymore. You can advise me on business matters, but that's it. You're nothing but a business manager, do you understand?"

His scowl softens around the edges with something I can't comprehend, because it looks like remorse or hurt or something equally as uncharacteristic to this man. "Avery, I only had your best interests in mind. I was trying to help."

"You want to help, do your job and only your job. Or I *will* fire you." I don't wait to see what new expression that comment gets. I just leave.

We have never had a fight like that. Never. And we've had some doozies. I can't fucking believe Lizzie was a setup. Of course now that I know, it all makes sense. He probably advised her on me the way he advises me on business. He probably told her what to say, how to act, what food I liked, what music. That time she made me chicken parm before a game was probably because my father told her to do it and not the amazing coincidence I thought it was.

Jesus. What the hell kind of lie was I living? No wonder I felt like something was missing with her. Our relationship was never real or authentic, so of course it didn't feel right. And Lizzie never told me either. That part bothers me the most.

210   Victoria Denault

When I get home, I head up Steph's staircase and knock. Maddie answers the door and looks surprised to see me. "Hey!" She smiles brightly. "Stephanie's not home. She went for a ride up the coast, I think. You know how she loves to ride near the beach on a sunny day."

"Oh." I can't hide my disappointment. "I was hoping to talk to her before my nap. See how things went with Seb."

Maddie leans on the door. "She told Sebastian about you two?"

I nod. "I think she kind of had to since he caught us making out."

"Ha! That's awesome." Maddie laughs and I give her a pained look. "Okay, well, there were subtler ways to tell him, but I think Steph needed that kind of kick in the pants. She was really nervous about being public with you for some reason. Now that Sebastian knows, there's no reason to keep it secret."

I think about that and realize how right Maddie is. Stephanie was the one who wanted things on the down-low, which is strange because it's usually me asking for secrecy. Was she really that worried about her brother's reaction? Because he didn't freak out, at least not in front of me. He didn't try to kill me or even maim me.

"Yeah. We can be public now." I smile at Maddie, but it's still uneasy.

Something isn't sitting right. Why didn't she call me after Seb left? She once told me that long rides down the Pacific Coast Highway clear her head. Why does she need her head cleared?

"Cool!" Maddie is more enthusiastic than I am. "So we need to plan a double date. I love double dates. Maybe we do a weekend at Catalina Island? That'd be fun, just the four of us."

I just nod and hop over the railing dividing our porches. "Sure. Let's figure it out later. Right now I need my pregame nap."

"Yeah, Ty's snoozing in my room." Maddie's blue eyes drift up toward the ceiling for a minute. "I'll tell Steph you stopped by. See you tonight after the game."

"Later."

I wave and unlock my front door and slip inside. I drop my keys on the hall table and walk into the living room. I always take my pregame naps on the couch, with the same knitted blue-and-gold throw blanket that used to be on our couch at home. I snagged it when I turned pro and moved it to Seattle with me. I pull it out from where I keep it in the bench by the window and pull the curtains closed before dropping onto the couch and getting comfortable.

I stare at my phone screen. Not a word from Stephanie. That makes my gut roll uncomfortably, but I'm not sure why. I decide not to bother her because she's on her scooter and I don't want her to be distracted by a phone buzzing in her pocket. So I pull up Seb's contact instead. The Winterhawks should be settled in L.A. now, and since they don't play until tomorrow night I know I'm not interrupting a pregame nap when I dial his number.

He picks up on the second ring with a gruff, cool, "Yeah?"

"Hey. It's Avery."

"I know," he replies, still gruff and cool.

"Everything okay? With you and Steph?"

"Yes."

I pause. He is not going to make this easy. I don't fully get it because Kate, my sister, and I don't have this kind of sibling bond. I don't know if that makes me an asshole or not, but it is what it is. As kids, we were never in the same place all that often. I was always off playing hockey and went to a boarding school, so we spent maybe eight weeks a year in each other's presence. I sigh and ask the only question left to ask. "Are *we* okay?"

Now it's his turn to pause. I wait patiently for his response. When he gives it, his voice is a little less chilly. "For now. Because from what she's told me, you really like her."

"I do. We're really hitting it off," I confess. "I'm sorry you found out so…abruptly."

"Hitting it off? Abruptly? Avery Westwood, always the king of politically correct answers," Seb chides, and I can't tell if he's mocking me or kidding around, so I decide to go a different route.

"Stephanie is an amazing human being and she makes me crazy in all the right ways," I blurt. "I've never fallen in love before, but I'm pretty sure that's what's happening here."

There's another pause and then I hear him whisper a French swear word. Then he heaves a heavy breath that creates a static sound on the line. "She's traveled a long, hard road to become the amazing person she is. And to be honest, I don't know if you can handle her—the real her—and that scares the shit out of me."

"What do you mean 'the real her'?" I question because I'm completely baffled by that statement. "We spent a lot of time together, even before we got involved, and I know her well. I intend to get to know her really well. I'm not going anywhere."

"I hope not, because she likes you. A lot. And that's a big risk for her," Sebastian replies. "You always seem to think you're the one risking something by letting someone into your life because you have to protect your image and brand and crap. But have you ever stopped to think of what Stephanie will be exposing herself to by dating you?"

"What?"

"You've never deemed a girl worthy enough to publicly acknowledge, so the media will be all over this. All over her. They'll want to know everything about her," Sebastian explains. "And the puck bunnies will rip her to pieces on the Internet because someone got into Avery Westwood's jock and it wasn't them. She's been a very private person for a reason, and because she likes you that's going to be blown to shreds, and I don't think she's really considered that."

"Did you tell her this?" I can't help but ask. I feel a tingle of anger prick at the back of my neck and shimmy down my spine as I sit straighter on the couch. "Are you trying to convince her to end this or keep it secret? Because I'm done with all that bullshit. I want a normal relationship with a normal girl—your sister."

Sebastian sighs again. "I would never try to get her to break up with you if that's what you're asking. But I'm not sure I trust you not to hurt her, and that's the problem."

"I won't hurt her." I don't even think about the words before they come out of my mouth. They don't need thought; they're coming from my heart. I would never hurt Stephanie.

"Even if it means hurting yourself?" Seb counters back. "Even if it means hurting your precious image?"

"Why would it mean that?"

"If you hurt her, Westwood, I will fuck you up. I know you know that."

"Yeah. I do, but thanks for making it official," I mutter.

"I gotta go," Sebastian tells me. "If we keep talking about this, I'm going to picture your hand on her ass again, and then I'm going to have to break it with my stick the next time we play each other."

I smirk at that. "Fine. But I'm serious. I'm not going to hurt her. No matter what."

"I want to believe you," Sebastian replies, and then there's a click as he ends the call.

I drop the phone onto the coffee table, switching off the ringer and setting the alarm before dropping back on the couch and lying down. I don't even know what half that conversation was about. Sebastian was acting like he knows something I don't. Something big. What the hell is going on?

I close my eyes, but my brain won't shut off, and it's starting to frustrate me because my pregame nap is a must. Everyone makes fun of me, calling me superstitious, but it's not really that. It's order. I play better when I follow a routine. Everything is simple, planned, with no unexpected interruptions and I can focus on what's ahead: the game, winning.

But thanks to all this weirdness with my dad, Lizzie, Stephanie and Sebastian I'm not sleeping. I pick up my phone again and open Instagram for the second time today, which is two times more than I've opened it since I downloaded it this summer. Then I log into the account using the password Kate gave me over the phone earlier.

Sebastian doubts my commitment to Stephanie? He's worried that I'll be concerned about my image. I'm done with having an image. I want to just be me, and if people don't like it, fuck them. I scroll through the pictures Kate has posted and I delete the most recent one of Lizzie and me because it's false advertising. It makes us look like we were together just last week. Once it's gone I load the picture of me and Stephanie from this morning and caption it *Morning run with this beauty*. Then I hit publish and immediately turn off my phone completely. I don't want my father or Kate or anyone bothering me. I have to get this pregame nap in.

Chapter 27

Stephanie

When I got home from my ride along the coast, I was ready to head straight over to Avery's and tell him about everything. I have nothing to be ashamed of. My past is far from perfect and I have made a lot of mistakes, but I bounced back and I am who I am today because of, not in spite of, what I went through. If Avery is the person I think he is, the person I'm falling in love with, then this won't be a big deal.

As soon as I walked in the door, Maddie ran at me squealing and holding her phone in my face. She couldn't seem to get a word out other than a high-pitched "Oh my God!" and "You're official!"

I didn't understand so I grabbed her phone. She had Avery's Instagram account open; the picture he took of us this morning was up on the screen. I grabbed the phone from her and read the caption ten times before it sank in what he'd done.

Emotions started to whirl—shock, fear, and even a little happiness formed a tornado inside me. And then I did the stupidest thing ever. I started to read the comments.

A lot of them were just emoticons—everything from smiley faces to shocked faces to crying faces from women who obviously had a crush on him. But some of them were words and they weren't that nice. Someone called me cute, but someone else wrote "You can do better." Ouch. And then there were a couple comments asking what had happened to the blond girl and someone even called him a player.

I scrolled through the rest of his photos and realized Avery had deleted the one of Liz that Kate had put up recently. Ugh. Doesn't he know you can't delete anything on social media without looking guilty of something? This is not good.

I handed Maddie back her phone and turned to the door to head to Avery's. "He went out for pregame food with Ty," Maddie explained. "And believe me, you don't want to see him right now. He's in a mood."

"Why?"

"I guess the restaurant where he gets his pregame meal delivered the wrong thing." Maddie rolled her big blue eyes and scrunched her nose. "It was just chicken piccata instead of chicken parm, but you'd think it was laced with arsenic the way he was freaking out."

I smiled despite myself because it reminded me of the chili night he insisted on doing back in Seattle because they'd done it before their successful Cup run years earlier. He was obsessed with wanting every single thing to be the same. "I guess I'll see him at the game, then."

Now we're sitting in the Saints arena watching the jubilant crowd start to filter out. San Diego won, which is great because they need it. It's also great because Avery scored and played well, which he always says he doesn't if his pregame rituals get screwed up. So maybe now he will calm down on the superstitious stuff.

I watch Maddie bounce up excitedly. "Let's go down to the lounge so we can see the boys and check on Alex."

Alex was slammed into the boards near the end of the second period and didn't play the third. I stand with her, but with much less bounce. I have to have a talk with Avery about everything, and I still don't know how I am going to start that. I feel like I have a lot riding on this, like my heart, for one thing.

We start to inch out of our aisle and head to the ice level instead of up to the plaza. After flashing our badges at the guard, we make our way down the concrete hall toward the lounge.

Avery's standing at the end of the hall, still in his skates and helmet. He's talking to a trainer or doctor or someone, and I wonder if it's about Alex. Our eyes connect, and he motions me over. We're not supposed to be in that area right after a game—it's players and media only—but I tell Maddie I'll meet her in the lounge and I make my way over.

Avery, his gloved hand on my lower back, guides me past the locker room and the rush of reporters pushing their way in. He turns me down a hall with a bunch of closed doors and stops. Moving his gloved hands to my shoulders, he turns me and presses my back to the wall.

"How'd things go with Seb?" he blurts, letting go of my shoulders.

"Good. I don't think he's going to try decapitating you next time you play him," I joke, and Avery smiles. "But I need to talk to you. Can we go somewhere, just the two of us, after you're changed and everything?"

"I can't, Steph," he says quietly. "We're heading straight to the airport tonight for the East Coast road trip."

"Oh. Right. You mentioned that, didn't you?"

"I did. Last week." He nods, but his thick, dark eyebrows pull together under his visor. "Is everything okay?"

"Yeah."

He leans in and if it wasn't for his helmet, I get the feeling he would kiss me. His hand is around my lower back again, pulling me closer. I can smell how hard he was working on the ice but I don't even care. And that's the problem. My attraction to him overshadows everything, even common sense.

I put my hands on the front of his jersey and take a step back. "I have a GED."

"What?" He blinks.

"I dropped out of high school and I got a GED instead."

Avery's dark brow pinches and his mouth goes slack, his panty-wetting smile gone. "But you went to Catholic school. I saw the uniform."

The smile is back, but I'm too sick with worry to return it. I twist my fingers nervously. "Until I was sixteen and then I dropped out. It was a horrible place, and I was in a horrible place."

The smile falters again. "Okay. Why are you telling me this right now?"

"Because it's something you should know," I reply, and pause as someone in a suit marches by, giving us side-eye. "I told you I wasn't Liz."

"Okay, well, I'm surprised because you never said anything." Avery shrugs. "But I know now."

"There's more," I say, and swallow hard.

"Avery!"

The stern voice is like a bucket of cold water, and we jump apart. A woman in a tailored suit is standing there looking annoyed. "You need to do interviews."

"Right. Sorry, Marsha. I'll do the interviews ASAP." Avery gives me a quick kiss. "I'll call you tomorrow after we're settled at the hotel in Toronto, okay?"

I nod because I can't find my voice, and it wouldn't matter if I could. I know he doesn't have a choice.

Now he looks worried again. "Steph, just tell me what's wrong, because clearly something is wrong."

"Avery...," Marsha says tersely.

"We can talk when you land in Toronto," I say firmly, and then reach up and tug off his helmet. To prove my point I rock up on my toes and kiss him lightly. Well, it's supposed to be light, but he puts a gloved hand to my back again and holds me to him as he opens his mouth and deepens the kiss. Like every time I feel the forceful press of his lips and the dominant touch of his tongue, I melt. I forget where we are and what I'm thinking and just lose myself in him.

Marsha clears her throat like a trucker with a phlegm ball, and we grudgingly pull apart. He gives one quick, chaste kiss before clomping down the hall in his skates after the annoyed PR lady. I watch him walk away and then turn and make my way down the hall back toward the lounge. The last thing I want to do is drop all this on him over the phone, but if that's the way it has to be, then that's the way it'll be.

Chapter 28

Avery

I never sleep on the overnight flights, even though every seat on our private plane reclines into beds, like first class on most jumbo jets nowadays. This flight, while everyone else slept, I grew increasingly uneasy and I couldn't figure out why. The Saints aren't exactly a top-ten team, but we won last night and Beau hasn't gotten in my face about anything since that last incident. I still owe him an apology, but since he has actually been leaving me alone and not causing shit, I don't want to poke the bear. Instead, I have just kept my distance.

By the time we get to the hotel, I'm bleary-eyed and exhausted. I text Stephanie and tell her I miss her and I had a crappy flight and I'm going to take a nap. I wait a couple of minutes for her to respond while I open my suitcase and change out of my travel clothes, but when she doesn't respond right away I just turn off my phone and crawl under the crisp sheets. I'm out as soon as my eyes close.

I wake four hours later to Ty knocking on my door and calling my name. We're not playing until tomorrow night and there's no practice until tomorrow morning, so I don't know why he's bothering me at first. But by the time I stumble over to the door and open it, rubbing my sleepy eyes as I take in his appearance, I realize we have press. Sometimes on a nongame away day the PR people set up press time in a hotel conference room so local media and some of the larger networks, like ESPN and NBC and TSN, can get a chance at in-depth interviews.

"Ah, crap. Am I late?" I scratch my bed head.

"No, but you will be if you don't get ready now," Ty says, and pushes into my room. I yawn and try to focus. "You've got twenty minutes to shower and turn yourself into the clean-shaven, bright-eyed angelic Avery the media adores."

"I'm hardly an angel," I mutter as Ty drops into the chair in front of the window.

I head into the bathroom, pushing the door mostly closed. I turn on the shower and dig around my travel kit for my shower supplies.

"Name one law you've broken," Ty calls out.

I shove my underwear off and frown at my reflection in the mirror. "I don't break laws."

I can hear him chuckle. "See? Angelic Avery. You've never even had a parking ticket."

I'd argue that, but he's right. I haven't. So I choose not to answer and get into the shower instead. Roughly ten minutes later I walk back out into the hotel room with a towel around my waist. I feel five hundred percent better than I did when I went to sleep. I grab some clean clothes out of my suitcase on the rack at the end of the bed and glance up at him. "Have you talked to Maddie?"

"Yeah. I had Skype sex with her before my nap when we got here," he says absently as he scrolls through something on his phone.

"TMI, dude," I mutter, and pull on my underwear and pants. We don't have to wear suits for this so I'm opting for some jeans and a black Saints T-shirt with our motto on the front—*Strength, Passion, Persistence—Saints.* Ty is wearing one of our branded black golf shirts.

"You haven't talked to Stephanie?" he asks as I make my way back into the steamy bathroom to put some product in my hair.

"I texted her, but she didn't respond before I turned my phone off to sleep," I explain, wiping the steamed mirror with my palm before I grab my hair stuff and twist it open. I style my hair into a more casual tousled thing that I usually only do on weekends and then I glance at my five o'clock shadow but ignore it as I walk back out into the room. I grab my phone off the night table and a protein bar I always travel with from the front pocket of my suitcase and wave at Ty. "Come on, let's go."

He glances up and blinks. "But you haven't shaved."

"Oh, no. What will the world think?" I fake a gasp and he flips me his middle finger, but he gets up and follows me out of the room.

"I think the only time you've done an interview without your face looking like a baby's ass is during play-offs when beards are required," Ty laments as we walk down the empty hall to the elevator.

"Yeah, well, things change," I say with a shrug.

"I like this new, less uptight you," Ty replies, and runs a hand over his own face with its two-day-old scruffy beard. Ty is never clean-shaven. His face goes from barely there scruff to full-on caveman depending on his mood. "Maybe this rougher Westwood image will land you an Axe Body Spray commercial."

"Fuck off," I bark, but I'm laughing, until a hotel room door opens just in front of us and I swallow it down and snap my lips closed before I can say anything else. It's the reaction that's been drilled into me from years and years of being in the public eye. Be quiet, polite and indifferent.

Luckily, the person who comes out of the room is Beau Echolls and not a random guest who might be offended by my potty mouth. Beau glances at us and actually smiles. "Hey."

That throws me off. I don't think I've ever seen him smile in my general direction, let alone *at* me. Ty nods at him and grunts. I decide now's the time to make up for that on-ice bullshit I caused. "Hey, Beau."

He falls in step beside us. I clear my throat as we reach the elevator bank and Ty hits the button. "Listen, Beau, I've been meaning to tell you I'm sorry about interfering with Coach's decision on the ice during the shoot-out."

Beau looks over at me, his expression like stone. "You did what you thought was right."

The elevator dings and the doors slide open. Luckily, it's empty so we can continue this conversation. I let them both step in before getting in myself. Beau hits the button for the conference room floor. "But it wasn't right. I was wrong. I'm sorry."

Both Ty and Beau are staring at me, not even trying to cover their surprise. It's like my apologizing is a sign of the apocalypse. That's embarrassing. I shrug under the weight of their stares. "Seriously. I apologize."

"Okay," is all Beau responds.

I'm okay with that. The silence in the elevator is weird—not awkward but just weird, so Ty starts yammering on about the game tomorrow night and how the Toronto Titans are doing worse than us so we should win it. I dig my phone out of my pocket and turn it back on. The message and voice mail alerts go nuts. Now they're both staring at me again.

"Sorry," I mutter, and open up my messaging. There are four from

Don; all of them say the same thing. We need to talk; I need to call him. They get more and more urgent with each one, which is made obvious by the fact that the last one is in all caps with five exclamation marks. I ignore those. I'll call him after the interviews. He'll understand me putting media first, since he's the one that taught me to do that.

There's one from Stephanie, which she sent about half an hour after the one I sent her. She says, *I know you're napping. Hope you're dreaming of me the way I dream of you. Skype me when you get a chance. We need to talk and I want to see you when we do it. xo Steph.*

"Skype. Nice! Someone's getting virtual sex!" Ty says, because the nosy asshole read the message with me. He claps my shoulder, but I shove him.

Beau watches us. "That Sebastian Deveau's sister?"

I nod and wait, my shoulders tense because I don't know what to expect from small talk with Beau. We've never done it before. He starts to smile, but it's weird and somehow not at all friendly. I wonder if I'm reading too much into it because of our past, or maybe this is what he looks like when he smiles. I've never seen him do it before so I wouldn't know.

"Guess she's *addicted* to ya," Beau mutters, and his smile deepens but doesn't gain any warmth. The elevator doors open and he's the first to step off, walking briskly into the conference room.

"What the fuck was that?" Ty says under his breath, his face reflecting my feelings of confusion exactly. "That kid is fucking weird."

"Yeah. I guess." I shrug and push Beau from my head as we enter the conference room. It's big and dimly lit except for the spotlights and camera lights shining in specific areas where chairs are set up facing each other for the reporters and the players. Beau is already situated in a chair across from his brother Chance, who works for NBC Sports.

Nikolai is being interviewed in the corner by a guy from TSN and as soon as we enter I'm waved over to talk to the girl from ESPN. I walk over, shake her hand and settle into the seat across from her. As she fusses with her mic and a guy comes over to attach mine, I send Stephanie a quick text telling her I'll call her as soon as I'm done with interviews and then turn my phone off and shove it in my back pocket.

The questions start off simple. What do I expect from this road trip? How do I feel the rest of the season will go? And then they turn to the personal questions. How am I liking San Diego? How is it different from playing for Seattle? I give her my standard upbeat answers where I say how much potential the team has and how great the weather is in San Diego and blah, blah, blah. Honestly, I could do this in my sleep. But then she throws in something I've never had to deal with before. A girlfriend question.

"So I saw your Instagram account..." She lets the sentence trail, like she expects me to pick it up. I'm that type of interviewee. I play ball. I give them what they want.

"And you want to know who the girl is in the photo?" I finish for her.

"We know who it is," she replies, smiling brightly. "It's Stephanie Deveau. The sister of Winterhawks defenseman Sebastian Deveau."

"Yes, that's her." I nod and start to rub my palms on the front of my jeans but stop myself. It's a nervous habit I haven't done in interviews since Juniors. Why the hell is that popping up again?

"It's just very rare that you post photos with anyone, and then two pictures with two different girls in a week." There's an incredulous lilt to the reporter's voice, and I try not to frown as she mentions two photos. I guess deleting something online is really as useless as people say.

I shrug and give her a friendly smile, because the last thing I'm going to do is start trying to explain the whole Liz thing. "I do have a life outside of the rink. And friends."

"So those girls are your friends?"

"No. I mean, yeah. Well, Stephanie is my girlfriend." Wow, that was as graceful as a drunk kangaroo. But at least I got it out.

Her eyes flare and I chalk it up to the fact that I haven't publicly admitted to ever having a girlfriend. Out of the corner of my eye I can't help but notice Beau is no longer being interviewed by his brother. He's standing beside him and both are looking over at me. I have no idea why. They have no reason to care about my personal life.

"Wow. That's a first for you. I mean…that you talked about. There were rumors this summer…" Again she lets the sentence trail off.

"I have had girlfriends. Contrary to popular opinion, I'm not a monk." I give her a big, friendly grin. "Although obviously hockey is my first priority."

"So I know you give a lot of your time and money to children's charities," the reporter starts, and it feels like a jarring left turn. I have no idea why she's switched topics so suddenly. "Mostly you donate to pediatric cancer foundations. Will you be donating to youth drug treatment centers now?"

"I…umm…I'm always open to worthy causes," I stutter like an idiot. How did we get onto my charity work? I watch Ty stand up from where he's being interviewed. It's abrupt, and he's got a scowl on his face as he unclips his mic and shoves it at the reporter from TSN.

The door to the room, way at the other end, opens and the manager of the Saints is standing there. He's in a dark suit wearing a darker look on his face. He's with Coach Meisner, who looks like he just swallowed a bag of glass. They whisper to each other, hands motioning tersely. My reporter is still talking and I realize with horror I've tuned her out, so I ask her to repeat herself. "I'm sorry, could you repeat that?"

"I was saying what about runaway advocates like the Canadian nonprofit Roadways, which provides housing, medical help and education for teen runaways?" she repeats, staring at me with curious, innocent eyes. "I know they're closing some locations due to lack of funding. That must be very close to you heart now, considering your girlfriend's past."

"I'm sorry, what?" I've never said that once in an interview, let alone twice.

Suddenly there's a huge crash. Everything stops as every head in the room spins to see the source. Ty is standing near where NBC is set up wearing a sheepish look as he stands next to a toppled light and stand. He raises his shoulders. "Oops. My bad. Sorry, Echolls."

Chance Echolls glares at him. "You didn't see a giant light on a six-foot pole? Really, Parsons?"

Ty ignores him and descends on me along with the coach and Peter Doughty, the team's manager. He gives me a weird look, but it's the reporter he talks to, asking for a moment of her time. Coach grabs my arm. "Go up to your room, Westwood. We'll meet you there."

"Okay," I reply, because I am completely lost. I feel like I'm standing in invisible quicksand and with every moment I stay in this media room it inches higher and higher around me, threatening to suffocate me.

Ty nudges me. "Let's go. Now."

I don't speak again until we're at the elevator bank. I realize I still feel like I'm in quicksand. "My reporter was asking some weird questions," I say, my voice sounding tinny and pitchy, even to me. "What the hell is going on?"

The elevator opens and Ty yanks me inside, repeatedly jamming the close door button so no one else slips in with us. When the doors are closed and we're alone, he pulls his phone out of his pocket and replies. "I don't know. My reporter asked me if I thought that you had a drug problem, which I laughed at, and then he said something about how players on your junior team did and so did your girlfriend."

"What?"

"He referenced—" Ty's voice cuts off and then he hisses out a swear and turns his phone screen toward me. "He said there was a story online. Here."

I look at the Google page on Ty's screen. He punched in my name and Stephanie's and the page filled with articles from twenty different websites. Each headline is slightly different but every single one has three things in common: *Westwood, girlfriend, drug addict.* I grab his phone roughly and punch the link for the first article, which is a credible sports news site. I read it at lightning speed and then take a deep breath and read it again, just to be sure.

"Did you know Steph had a problem?" Ty questions quietly.

"No. She doesn't," I argue back in a monotone. "She would have told me. This is some kind of lie someone is spreading."

"Is it?" Ty sounds as convinced by my theory as I am saying it, which is not at all. But…how can this be? Stephanie is Sebastian's sister. He never mentioned anything like this the whole time I've known him and neither has she. I don't understand.

"Do you want me to call Maddie?" Ty asks. "I mean Maddie would know, right?"

"I don't know," I mutter as the elevator opens on our room floor. "I need to talk to her."

As we make our way down the hall toward our rooms, I pull my own phone out of my pocket and turn it back on. It screams with alerts. Three text messages from my dad along with two voice mails from him, two from my agent and fourteen others from numbers I don't recognize, which are probably reporters. There's none from Stephanie. Why the fuck isn't she contacting me about this? And what the fuck is going on?

Chapter 29

Stephanie

Hey, Stephanie," Dan says quietly as he passes by my desk.

I fight the urge to shudder. The sound of his voice, as always, has the same gross and creepy effect as having a spider crawl across your shower floor, while you're naked and defenseless.

"Hi, Dan," I mutter back, and watch as he heads across the open floor to his own office. He reaches behind him and rubs his lower back through his suit jacket, and that's when I remember his pills. I quickly unlock the desk drawer where I keep my purse and dig around inside it until I find the bottle; then I march across the office, tracing his steps.

I knock lightly on his open door. He looks surprised to see me. "Does Conrad need me for something?"

I shake my head and take a tentative step inside as I hold out the bottle toward him. "You left these in the kitchen."

He looks at the little white bottle in my hand and his eyes grow wide. "My pain medication? I've been looking everywhere for that! I had to get a new script."

"Well, here you go," I say as he stands and comes around his desk to take them from me. His brown eyes narrow. "You've had these since Friday morning? And you didn't get them to me sooner?"

"I got called into that deposition with Mr. Archer on Friday. It took all afternoon and it was off-site," I explain, suddenly feeling defensive because he's looking at me like I'm some kind of criminal. "Sorry. Anyway, I'm glad you could get it refilled, and now you have extra."

He takes the bottle from me and mutters a very ungrateful "Thanks."

I beeline it out of his office only to find Maddie standing at my desk looking more unraveled than I feel. Her big brown eyes are pained and her full, usually upturned mouth is set in a tight line. I feel my heart skitter with fear inside my chest. My steps slow as I approach her. "What's wrong?"

Her eyes dart left and right and she crosses in front of my desk so she's right next to me, her voice barely a whisper. "I think you need to go home. Use a sick day."

"Why? What's wrong?" I repeat, my voice jumping up and down in octaves with every word.

"I'll walk you out, and I'll tell Mr. Archer you're sick and had to leave. Grab your bag," she orders calmly, but I feel like there's something heavy sitting on my shoulders, like a baby grand piano or an elephant, and I can't seem to move. She takes my arm and tries to tug me, her eyes wide and pleading now, almost panicked. "Please, Steph. You want to go home. I promise."

"Is it Seb?" I ask, and I suddenly hate myself for not memorizing this year's Winterhawks schedule. I used to know every day he was on the ice. But today is a Monday. Why would he have a day game on a

Monday? They don't play day games in the middle of the week. Did something happen to him off the ice? Is it Avery? Is it…

"Steph." She says my name sharply, but not angrily. "Everyone is fine, but you need to go home."

"Stephanie, I need you to…" Mr. Archer is in his door, which I swear was closed a minute ago. "Is everything all right?"

"She isn't feeling well, Mr. Archer," Maddie lies, and this time when she gently tugs my arm it unroots me from my spot and I step toward my desk. Maddie opens my drawer and takes out my purse. "I was going to drive her home because, you know, the scooter probably isn't a good idea when she's feeling ill."

"Oh. Okay," Mr. Archer says. He looks sympathetic as he gives me a small smile. "Feel better, Steph. Send me a quick text if you won't be able to make it in tomorrow."

I nod wordlessly and follow Maddie to the elevator. We get in with a few other people and ride in silence to the parking garage. Once there, Maddie turns to me. "The media is saying stuff about you. It's not nice."

"What?" I shake my head. "What are you talking about? Why would the media be talking about me? What media?"

"It started on sports sites and then grew and now a whole bunch of places are reporting about it." Maddie bites her lip and takes my hand in hers again. "Steph, do you…did you have some issues when you were younger?"

That elephant is suddenly back on my shoulders with a grand piano and a compact car. My whole body feels like it's being crushed into the ground. And my heart has somehow slipped from my chest to the bottom of my shoes and it's being ground into oblivion under the pressure.

"I…" I swallow, but my mouth is dry and it's painful. "I'm fine now. I've been fine for a long time."

"I know." Maddie's face twists in sympathy. "I live with you. I know. I just…you never mentioned you used to…have issues."

"It was a long time ago," I reply hoarsely, and stare at the cracked pavement between us before looking up at her again. "The media says I'm not recovered?"

"No. I mean not anything I've read, but I guess…" She pauses and pulls me into a hug. "They're still making it look bad. Like you're a criminal or something, and I guess they asked Avery about it at a press thing today. Ty said he was blindsided."

Her comforting gesture just feels like more suffocating weight, so I gently squirm free. "Oh, my God, they did WHAT?"

"You didn't tell him about this?" Maddie asks; there's judgment in her words. It's soft and ever so slight, but it's there.

"I was going to, but I didn't…" I struggle to take a deep breath. "I was going to tonight. I just…I don't tell people. It's my past. I'm not that girl anymore."

"Okay. Okay." Maddie tries to hug me again, but I dodge it and start toward the exit. She scurries after me, our heels echoing in the cavernous concrete structure. "Let me take you home. It's okay. Everything will be okay."

"It won't." I shake my head and feel heat climb my neck and face and create hot tears that I wipe before they can fall. "I was going to tell him but I didn't, and now it's going to wreck everything."

"No. It won't," Maddie insists. "Let's get you home. You can call him there."

On the drive home I turn on my phone, which I had turned off like I try to do every day. It lights up with a voice mail notification. I quickly listen to it. It's Sebastian.

His message is in French. He says he loves me. It's going to be fine. He will make sure it's fine and he loves me and wants me to call him immediately. I check my text messages. Nothing from Avery. That makes me feel nauseated.

I call him first, before calling Sebastian, but it goes straight to voice mail without ringing, so I assume he's on the other line. I don't want to talk to Sebastian. I don't know why, but I don't. I just want to talk to Avery. I need to talk to Avery. So I hang up every time his voice mail kicks in, count to twenty, and hit redial, but it goes to voice mail four more times. Then Maddie is parking in our garage.

I get out of the car and walk numbly into the house. Maddie follows, looking helpless and lost. When her eyes land on me, it's with sympathy but also with confusion. I should have told her. Then maybe she wouldn't be looking at me like I'm suddenly a stranger.

I drop my purse on the kitchen counter and walk over to the fridge. I want to reach for a beer. Hell, I want to reach for twelve, but numbing myself in a time of pain is what got me a past I'm not proud of to begin with, so instead I grab a pressed juice and twist off the lid. I take a small sip and realize I'm not thirsty, so I put it down on the counter.

"I'm sorry." My voice is a broken whisper and a hot tear escapes before I can stop it. I brush it away with my fingertips.

"You have nothing to be sorry for," Maddie says firmly. My God, I wish I could believe her. "You do not owe me an explanation or an apology. So you had a rocky childhood. You don't owe anyone an apology for that. You're here, you're a great human being, an amazing roommate and the best girlfriend Avery Westwood could hope for. The end."

I burst into tears. She makes a shocked sound, like a squeak of fear and a gasp of horror mixed into one, and rushes to me, but I turn away and a wave her off with a flailing hand. "It's fine. I just…" I fight for control and gain it, tenuously. "I just I hope he feels the same way."

"I'm sure he does," Maddie says, but then she adds, "Or he will."

I wipe at my damp cheeks as my phone shrills. It's Sebastian's number on the screen, not Avery's, and my heart cracks a little like the vicious little lines a pebble makes in a windshield if it hits it hard enough. I shove my phone at Maddie. "Can you tell him I'm fine, but I need a minute to myself? Please."

She nods reluctantly, but I hear her answer the phone as I walk out of the kitchen and head upstairs to my room. There, I peel off my business clothes and pull on a pair of running shorts and a tank top and curl up on top of my bed. I stare across the room at my laptop on top of my desk. I know the last thing that I should do is read the stories. The words people will be saying about me—in the stories and the comments—will likely take those hairline fractures veining out across my heart and turn them into fissures the size of the Grand Canyon. I need to keep it together. At least until I talk to Avery.

Maddie is in my open doorway a couple minutes later. She walks in and holds the phone out to me. "It's Avery. He called while I was on the other line with Seb."

I bolt up from my fetal position like I've been Tasered. With a trembling hand, I take the phone from her and swallow hard. Maddie leaves my room, pulling the door closed behind her.

"Avery?"

"Steph." It's him. But it doesn't really sound like him. His voice is tight and thick with tension. "Are you okay?"

I exhale. He's asking about me? "I'm okay. Are you okay? I'm so sorry."

He doesn't respond to that right away. It takes half a second and then he says, his voice sounding a little bit less tense, but now masked with confusion, "Is it true? What everyone is saying?"

"I don't know what they're saying, exactly. I refuse to look," I explain, my voice trembling. "But if it's about the fact that I ran away from home at sixteen and that I was addicted to prescription drugs, then yes. It's true."

"Holy shit." He whispers it; it almost sounds like a sigh but I catch the words. Those hairline fissures in my heart start to grow.

"Yeah."

Everything is quiet. I don't even think he's breathing. I don't know what to do or what to say. I start to feel panicked. I bite my lip to keep myself from trying to explain or apologize for my past because I know that will just make me feel worse. And although I owe him an apology for not telling him sooner, because of this very thing that happened, I don't owe him an apology for my past. He wasn't there when I was living it. I didn't hurt him. I hurt Sebastian and my mom and my dad, and I've apologized to them.

"I just wish you'd told me," he finally says.

"I was going to. It's why I asked you to Skype me tonight," I say, and sigh. "I wanted to explain everything."

Avery is quiet again, and an ache starts to develop in my chest; the longer the silence goes on, the harder it is for me to keep myself from asking the question that needs to be asked. The one I don't want the answer to. I slip lower on my bed, my head pushed back in my pillows and, because the silence is deafening, I ask it. "Does it matter?"

He erupts. "Of course it matters! They asked me about it on camera and I looked like a goddamn idiot. I just sat there with my mouth hanging open, and when I did speak it was a clear evasion tactic. I gave non-answers because I was blindsided. That matters. And Don is losing his mind. I guess he saw the articles before I went into the interview and was trying to reach me. He knew before I did. Do you know how much I hate that?"

I make a sound. I don't mean to, but it bubbles up from my chest anyway. A sob. Only because I'm trying to force it back down as it claws its way up my vocal cords, it comes out more like a weird hiccup. But at least the sound stops Avery's rant.

"Jesus, Steph, why couldn't you have just told me? Even in Seattle! I mean we've known each other forever and Seb never mentioned it. I've known him longer. You would think—"

"That he would blurt out painful, private family business to you?" I cut him off, my voice much more venomous than I expected. I just hate his reaction. "Because you're so easy to talk to?"

"Wha…what?"

"Avery, you're a machine. You eat, you sleep, you hockey, that's it," I blurt, wiping my wet cheeks on the back of the arm of my sweatshirt. "You say it's just for the cameras, but you don't give your so-called friends much more. Why would they open up to you about their secrets when you don't share yours?"

He's more than frustrated now—he's angry. I am, too, which is actually a bit of a relief compared to the guilt and shame that filled my heart moments ago.

"He should have told me because it could have become a controversy back in Seattle, for him and the team. Even before it became my personal controversy," he snaps. He may be right, but he's still an asshole for saying it.

"That's the difference between Sebastian and you," I reply harshly. "Seb is in it for the love of the game and nothing else. He doesn't give a fuck about his image or his brand and he definitely wouldn't put it before his sister's needs. I didn't want people to know, so he didn't tell anyone."

"Well, now people know, and I look like a fucking idiot."

I hear a click in the line and he lets out a string of expletives that sound like one giant swear word. "Don has called three times during this conversation. I have to deal with him. I'll call you back."

"Sure. Whatever."

"Whatever?"

"What do you want me to say, Avery?"

"I'll call you later," he barks, and the line goes dead.

Chapter 30

Avery

Maddie sounds truly remorseful as she tells me that she can't pass her phone to Stephanie because Stephanie didn't come in to work today. She called in sick. I want to put my fist through something so badly. Maybe if I trash a hotel people will stop asking me about my girlfriend's past.

"Can you please call her and ask her to call me?" I request in a voice that relays every ounce of my desperation, and I don't even care.

"I did that last night when you called my phone because hers was turned off," Maddie explains, and sighs. "But I'll do it again when I see her tonight. I'll even call you and shove the phone in her face if I have to."

"Thanks."

"Avery, she's not avoiding you," Maddie promises, but even she doesn't sound like she believes it. "I mean, not just you. Reporters got her number somehow and she's avoiding them. And the HR department at work came by looking for her too. This is a nightmare for her."

"I know," I reply swiftly, and then it dawns on me. "You don't think I know that?"

"It kind of feels like you're mostly concerned with how it's affecting you," Maddie says quietly. "And if I get that vibe, maybe Stephanie does too."

"Well, if she would talk to me, I could try to fix that," I counter, even though I have no idea how to fucking fix this. Still I find myself defending my actions. "It is affecting me—every waking moment since the story broke—and it's hell. But at the same time, I know, obviously, that it's more hell for Steph. This is her story. Her life and something she overcame just to have it shoved back in her face again, like the person she is now suddenly doesn't matter anymore."

"Exactly!" Maddie almost squeals; it's jarring to have her go from somber to elated so quickly in the conversation. I jerk back a little where I'm sitting in a chair in the corner of the hotel lobby. "Have you said this to her?"

"I didn't," I admit, and I feel Maddie's disdain through the phone. "I only talked to her once and she's been ignoring my calls. That first call I was…shocked and I didn't have time to react fully. Or properly. She needs to talk to me, Maddie."

Ty walks over, adjusting his tie and looking over his shoulder as the last of our team makes a trail from the elevators to the bus parked out in front of the hotel. It's time to head to the game. I still want to punch something, which is the worst way to go into a game. Fuck.

"I promise I will make her call you," Maddie says firmly.

I stand up as Ty motions at me. "Thanks. Ty says he'll call you later."

"Tell him if he gets a goal tonight he gets a blow job tomorrow night."

"I am not telling him that," I reply hotly, and hang up as she laughs.

"What did she say?" Ty asks as I hand him back his phone.

"I would rather die than repeat it," I tell him with a frown. "But you need to score tonight."

"Okay." Ty shrugs. "Any word on Steph?"

"Maddie says the reporters somehow got her number and are calling, which is why she turned off her phone."

We make our way out the front doors and onto the waiting bus. I listen to the players' idle chatter as the bus makes its way to the arena. No one speaks to me and I'm glad. It's been like that since the news broke. My teammates are giving me a wide berth, probably because for the first time in my professional career my face isn't devoid of emotions. I look as furious as I am, all the time, and I don't care.

Somehow Coach and the general manager sweet-talked the reporter into editing out all the Stephanie questions and my ridiculous bumbling responses for the final aired broadcast. I couldn't believe that the reporter had allowed it, but she did, and so she was now officially my favorite. I was going to go out of my way to make it up to her. This was a juicy story—as my father made clear every time we talked. The mighty Avery Westwood has fallen off his high horse. And this reporter had the first scoop on it, the first person to ask me about it, and she willingly vetoed the footage.

The game is painful. I can't concentrate, and I'm not playing well at all. Everyone else on the Saints seems to be following my lead. By the beginning of the third we're down 4 to 1 and by the final buzzer we've lost, 5 to 2. I did nothing to help us or prevent the massacre. I didn't score; I didn't get an assist—hell, I didn't even get a penalty. I was a ghost out there, and I loathe myself for it.

The coach storms into the locker room before the media, as we sit silently tugging off gloves and helmets. He glares at each of us. "We were one win out of a play-off spot until tonight. Now we're two wins away. We're sliding the wrong way. We need to turn it around. Practice tomorrow ten a.m."

No one dares to groan or murmur their discontent, even though we won't be landing at home until some ungodly hour of the morning, and the first day back from an East Coast road trip is usually practice-free. The media strolls in a few seconds after he's left. As expected, because it's what happened after the game in Toronto, they crowd around me.

I shove a Saints hat over my damp, sweaty hair, take a deep breath and wait for the first question. "Avery, you seemed to struggle a little bit out there," someone comments.

I barely look up to see who it is, keeping my focus on the wall of microphones in front of my face. "Yeah, I didn't have my best night, that's for sure," I reply. "I need to do better if I expect the team to do better, and I do. We've all got to dig deeper next time."

It's a canned response. Nothing new or enlightening, just the same old sound bites. Someone else asks me about a specific play in the second where I overshot the puck and it bounced off Ty's stick and almost into our own net. I give a typical answer—I made a mistake and there's no excuse. It's my standard answer and one I believe. I never forgive myself for being anything less than perfect at this job. And then Chance Echolls asks a question.

"So do you think the disruption to your game is being caused by the reports your girlfriend has drug problems?"

A hush blankets the room, filling the air with tension. I look up and find his blue eyes and wolfish face staring down at me. "I don't know what you're talking about."

"Stephanie Deveau spent eight months in a rehab facility outside of Seattle less than five years ago," Chance informs me, and everyone, because not one reporter has turned their cameras and mics off. I know because I've finally looked up. Sure, some of them are wearing sympathetic expressions or even horrified ones, but no one is turning away. Assholes.

I sit up straighter on the bench, rolling my shoulders back and tilting my jaw up. Marsha takes a step into the scrum like she's about use all her PR powers and halt the questioning. I raise my hand lightly, stopping her in her tracks. I take a second to make sure I'm going to present this as calmly and in as detached a manner as possible, and then I tell him. "Five years is a long time. People change a lot in five years. Look at you, Mr. Echolls. Five years ago you thought you were going to be an NHL player, but here you are asking NHL players questions about their personal lives instead."

Someone snorts and there's a chuckle from the back of the pack somewhere. I keep my face calm and simply enjoy the shades of red taking over Chance's face. He's like a really angry mood ring or something. Then I turn my eyes down, focusing on the mics again, and add, "It wasn't our best game, except for Furlov. Tonight would have been a lot worse if he hadn't stopped twenty-nine shots. You guys should go give him some love."

They take the cue, all of them except Echolls, who is still standing in front of me, his face crimson, even though his cameraman has scurried off with the pack. If he could blow steam out of his ears, he would. That makes me crack my first smile since this thing happened.

I stand up. He's got about an inch on me, but I eclipse him in width. I slowly adjust my hat, tugging on the brim. He opens his mouth, but he closes it without a word and stomps off.

Marsha walks over. "That was…well, it wasn't as big of a disaster as it could have been."

I nod. "With the way things have been going, I'll take that as a win."

Marsha gives me a small smile. "You know this thing will blow over."

I nod and she nods back before she marches over to where all the reporters are standing in front of Nikolai. I look down at Ty. "That was fucking intense. You're a badass with the dig about him not playing. But isn't your dad going to flip? It wasn't exactly Saint Avery material."

I shrug. "Fuck Saint Avery and fuck Don Westwood." I pull my Under Armour off and turn to make sure the reporters are out before dropping my pants. "I fired him."

"You what?"

"Don's not my manager anymore," I repeat.

Ty stands up so quickly he almost knocks me over. "When? Why?"

"Because I'm sure he's the one who told the press about Stephanie's past," I tell him, and head to the showers.

He watches me go in shock. I'm sure I'll end up explaining it to him later. It isn't hard to put the pieces together. I did it instantly. My dad knew about Steph and me. He was ticked off that I announced our involvement without consulting him. He must have done a background check on Steph. After all, he did one on Lizzie. He admitted that. And he probably leaked Steph's past to the press because he knew just telling me wouldn't get me to change my feelings.

Then he suggested the only way to fix the situation was to break up with Steph. That was his big solution? He made it seem like it was the only solution—he was so convincing with his laundry lists of reasons. The two that hurt the most were: "You have to distance yourself from this, at least until people forget about it. Two of your endorsements have already called asking about it." And "Avery, if she lied to you about this, what else is she lying to you about?" The first because I'd been trained to care what companies thought about me since I was ten and the second because…what if he was right? What if the girl I thought I knew so well I didn't really know at all?

After my shower I walk back into the locker room and change into my suit. Ty doesn't bring it up again until we're on the bus. "Did he admit he did it?"

"No, and I didn't expect he would. But if he can basically hire Lizzie to date me, he can throw a story to the media," I reply. "He's overstepped his bounds as a business manager way too much. This was a long time coming."

"Dude." Ty shakes his head, scrubbing a hand over his face. "He's your dad."

"He hasn't been my dad in a long time." It's pathetic, but it's the truth.

The bus is going straight to the airport, so the trip is long. As we chug along the freeway, I check my phone. There's a message and, thankfully, it's from Stephanie. I listen to it twice I'm so happy to hear her voice.

"Hey. Maddie told me I should call you. I'm sorry. I'm not trying to avoid you. I'm just avoiding the press. My phone is ringing nonstop. Maddie says you guys are coming back tonight. You can use your key to come and wake me up. I know I said it's for emergencies, but this kind of feels like one, so…if you want to, I want you to. I don't care what time it is."

As soon as we get off the bus and I can get a little privacy, I call her back. I don't expect her to answer, and she doesn't, but I want to hear her voice anyway. I decide not to leave her a message. I'll just take her up on her invitation and crawl into bed with her. And then this will all be all right.

Chapter 31

Stephanie

I am so drunk it's not even funny. Drunk and filled with a giddy hope. Maddie and I, arms locked together, are wandering down the sidewalk toward our place. Alex is slightly behind me, whistling as he walks with us, his left arm in a sling. He showed up at our place just before six as Maddie was getting home from work and insisted he take us out for dinner. I tried to refuse, but he said he didn't want to sit around and watch his team play without him. Honestly, I didn't want to sit around and think about my problems anymore, so I went.

He never said a word about this whole thing, but I know he knows. How can he not? Still, I appreciated his silence on the matter because I was so over talking about it. And I was even more over thinking about it, which is why I agreed to dinner—and drinks. Lots of drinks.

We pass the street that borders the ocean where both Ty and Alex's condos are located and we pause. I think it's to say good-bye to Alex, but then Maddie turns to me. "I always meet Ty at his house after a road trip," she slurs. At least I think she's slurring. Maybe it's the alcohol my brain is swimming in that makes it sound funny. "But I can text him and tell him to come by our place instead."

"Why? Just go. It's okay. I know my way home." I give her a little hug that for some reason makes me almost tip over. I've honestly never been drunk. My youth was spent getting buzzed on weed and pills. I'd maybe have a beer or a cooler with the pills, but it only ever took one or two to make the pills stronger. Tonight, I am definitely drunk.

"You're kind of drunk, so I should go back with you...," Maddie argues.

"Maddie, I don't need a babysitter," I blurt, and my voice sounds weird. Higher than normal. "And if I do, Avery can babysit me."

"Stephanie..."

"Do not 'Stephanie' me," I tell her, and grin. "I'm fine. I'll be even better tomorrow."

"You'll be incredibly hungover tomorrow, that's what you'll be," Alex chirps from beside me. I look over and he's grinning. He doesn't seem drunk, at least not as drunk as Maddie and me.

"I can handle a hangover. I can handle lots of things," I reply, and smile. "I don't have a choice. I have to handle things. Lots of things."

His mischievous grin grows deeper, causing a dimple I didn't know he had in his scruffy left cheek. "I'd be very interested in finding out exactly what you can handle, little one."

God. Always the sleazy flirt. I roll my eyes, which makes me a little dizzy somehow. "You couldn't handle knowing what I can handle," I reply, and wink.

He blinks, stunned for a second. "You head on up to Parson's place," Larue tells Maddie, and wraps an arm around my shoulder. "I'll make sure she gets home."

Maddie bites her lip. I don't want her to feel like she has to take care of me. I don't want anyone to take care of me. So I nod. "Go. Seriously. I'll be fine."

Maddie turns her brown eyes to Larue and narrows them, crossing her arms over her ample chest like she's trying to look intimidating. "Avery is coming over later. You know that, right?"

"Yeah." Alex shrugs. "I'll get her home safe and sound, for Avery. That's it."

"You two are acting like I'm a drunk high school virgin," I announce, and shrug out from under Alex's arm. "I'm fine. I can get home by myself. And then Avery will be there and everything will be fine. Maddie, stay. Alex, go home."

I turn and keep walking down the street toward our place without looking back. But it's not a graceful or speedy retreat because the ground seems completely uneven. When did that happen? I pause a second to steady myself on the side of a parked car by the curb and then continue down the sidewalk. I make it about twenty feet when Alex's hand hits my shoulder like a fifty-pound weight, and I almost tip into his wide, strong chest.

"Easy there, kid," Alex tells me, and without even looking up—way up—at his face I know he's smirking. *"T'es maladroite, belle."*

"I'm not," I argue, even though he's right. I *am* clumsy right now. "The air is sobering me up."

It is sort of true. There is a strong ocean breeze, and it is cool and salty. It feels good on my skin and burns off a little of the alcohol haze. Alex keeps his big hand on my shoulder anyway. "So Avery's dealing with this well?"

"I think so. I'll feel better about it…and us…when I see him later," I explain. Hopefully by the end of the night, Avery and I will be solid again. That's what I want more than anything.

I need to make coffee when I get home, to get rid of this buzz. I want to be clearheaded and alert when he gets to my place, even though it'll probably be four or five in the morning. I need to be awake—to see him and talk to him—because it is the only way I will believe that this hasn't ruined everything between us. Avery's past, unlike mine, has always been out in the open; I know he abandoned his friend Trey when people found out he was an addict. He doesn't seem to be abandoning me, but I won't feel secure until I see him and talk to him in person.

I trip over my own feet and Alex reaches out and catches me effortlessly with his one good arm. It's starting to make me feel like I'm a toddler learning to walk and he's my dad. He pulls me into his side and holds me to him. He's a wall of muscle and strength. It feels good. Not Avery good, but good. I let him guide me down the street because it's easier than trying to keep myself upright.

"I hope you plan on going straight to bed, young lady," he advises me. "You are in no condition to be somebody's naked mambo partner tonight."

"I'm fine."

He doesn't say anything for a minute, and when I look up at him he's grinning mischievously the way that makes you realize why girls find him adorable. "Well, for Westie, maybe. I mean if he's all about the boring, slow missionary thing, the fact that you're beyond drunk probably won't matter. I mean you could even pass out and he might not even notice."

I glare at him…at least I think I'm glaring. "For your information,

Avery is not Mr. Boring Missionary. He's not the monk you guys think he is. He's definitely more experienced than me."

"Avery is experienced?" Larue snorts as my house comes into view. "Did he pay you to say that? How much? Is that what he does with his millions?"

I put one hand on his chest and one on his side and push away from him. I stumble but, luckily, don't fall over. Alex smirks at me. We reach my porch steps. "Go home, Alex."

He glances up at my house and Avery's and back down at me. "Team's plane won't land for another couple of hours. Let me come in and make sure you're settled, okay?"

My skeptical face must not be muted by alcohol because Alex smiles—innocently this time—and says, "Whoa. As friends. I promise. I'm not suggesting it because I'm looking to get in your pants. I'm suggesting it because I'm your brother's friend and he asked me to keep an eye on you."

"Sebastian asked you to check on me?" I ask, cocking my head to the side like a puppy that doesn't quite understand the command. "But I'm not shutting him out. I talk to him every day since this whole thing happened."

"Yeah, but he just didn't want you to be alone. And I don't want you to be either," Alex says quietly.

"I don't need…" I pause. My stomach flips. Uh-oh. I swallow it down. "I don't need company. I'm just going to sit here and wait. Avery will be here soon. I told him he could just use his key and come…"

I climb the porch stairs, turn and drop into the rocking chair near the door. A chair that moves was probably a bad decision. The motion feels quick and jarring and my stomach lurches. I jump back up and run to the side of the porch and barf into the bushes. When my body finally stops rioting, I hear Alex's deep belly laugh. And then I'm totally embarrassed. I wipe my mouth on my sleeve and can't look at him as I try to bustle by him, pulling my keys from my pocket.

"Thanks for walking me home. Sorry about that," I mumble, and promptly drop my keys. Alex scoops them up before I can bend down, which is a good thing because bending might mean puking again.

"Don't get all shy on me, drunkie," Alex says. "You think I've never handled a drunk girl before?"

He puts the key in the lock and opens my front door, then puts his hands on both my shoulders and steadily guides me inside.

"When I was a junior player, I used to be the guy who would hold the drunk girl's hair while she puked," he explains to me. "I was a shitty hockey player back then, barely held my place on the team. I didn't have the panty-remover known as a future first round NHL draft pick. I also wasn't the smartest and not nearly the best looking. I earned my girls by being the funny one who made sure they didn't get taken advantage of or choke on their own vomit."

This revelation makes me almost as dizzy as the alcohol. I look up at Alex in the dim light filtering in from the living room. He gives me an honest, soft smile for a second before it turns snarky and cocky. "Luckily, now I don't have to be the sweet guy. I've got an NHL paycheck to get me tail without any nice guy bullshit."

He gently uses his hands to shift me and heads down the hall toward my kitchen. "I'm getting you some water. Lots of water."

"I might puke it up," I say, and walk in anything but a straight line over to the couch, which is calling my name. I crawl slowly into a lying position on the couch. I close my eyes and the room spins, so I groan and sit up.

"I didn't know you were such a lightweight. You only had a few drinks." Alex's voice is getting closer, but I don't see him. He must have gone through the dining room instead of the hall because suddenly he's behind me and his head is tilted down, hovering above me. He hands me a full glass of water. "Drink."

"Ugh," I protest, but sip more than half the glass down anyway. "I've never been drunk. My buzz of choice was narcotics, or haven't you read the Internet lately?"

He disappears again, and when he comes back he's got the bucket we use to mop the kitchen floor. He places it next to the couch and drops down beside me. I turn away. I can't even look at the bucket without wanting to barf. He rubs my back softly. "Yeah, I've read the Internet. But I didn't have to. I knew in Seattle."

That statement sobers me up. "You knew? Sebastian told you?"

He shakes his head; his eyes crinkle a little in the corners as he smiles. "I'm a smart guy. I figured it out pretty soon after you moved to Seattle and I got drunk and crashed at Seb's and there wasn't so much as an Advil in his house to fight my hangover with. And then he started refusing painkillers when he got injured. And he was way overprotective of you. Like absurdly so. Do you know he said he would gut me like a sewer pig if I touched you?"

All I can do is blink at that statement. Alex's face is incredulous. "Sewer pig. His words. All because I hit on you. Which reminds me, is he going to be gutting Avery? Because I want advance notice so I can videotape it."

I try to picture a pig in a sewer, but mostly my mind just starts picturing a sewer…and sewage—like poop and…"Bucket."

After puking one more time, I tell Alex I am going upstairs to change. And after stumbling upstairs, changing my clothes, and tripping into the bathroom to pee and brush my teeth I open the bathroom door to find Alex stretched out on my bed. That's not where I left him. I left him downstairs on the couch. His eyes are closed and his hands are behind his head. He's got all my pillows stuffed up behind him, and I have a lot of pillows.

Without opening his eyes, he says. "Your phone made a silly noise."

I walk toward the night table where I dropped it before I got changed. It's still there, facedown the way I dumped it. I feel a flutter of hope that it's Avery. That he's landed and he's coming to see me. He never did actually confirm he'd come over. I invited him but he never responded. In his defense I told him I wouldn't be answering my phone so there's no reason to call me back, but I really wish he had. Halfway through our liquid supper I turned my phone back on hoping he had called and never turned it off, hoping he still would. I flip it over and see a text alert, but it's from Maddie. She's just making sure I got home okay. Despite the fact that it feels like my heart has turned to cement, heavy and cold in my chest, I text her back that I'm just fine, safe and sound at home.

I drop the phone back on the nightstand and stare down at Alex.

"Did you hit on me before or after you figured out I was a recovering addict?" I ask, my words kind of stepping on each other. I'm also getting really sleepy, which is annoying because I don't want to sleep. I want to wait up for Avery.

"After," Alex says, opening his eyes to level me with a curious stare. "Why?"

I can't help it. I start to cry.

Alex sits up instantly and reaches for me. His hands grab my arms at the elbows and he gently pulls me to the bed. I end up sitting on his lap. I don't even care how inappropriate this is. I just care about the fact that he's hugging me and I so need a fucking hug right now. God, alcohol sucks. It makes me feel everything. I hate feeling everything.

"Hey. Hey. What's this all about?" he says tenderly.

"I don't think he would have," I blubber. The tears are coming like a waterfall—fast and unstoppable. "I don't think Avery would have gotten involved with me if he knew about things beforehand."

"You don't know that, Steph," Alex replies, patting my back gently. "Westwood is a goddamn idiot, but I don't think he's that big of an idiot."

"It's why I didn't tell him. I knew he would run and I didn't want him to. I like him. I really like him, so I let it happen." I sniff and feel so pathetic and useless. "I wanted him to feel how right this was before I told him so that it wouldn't matter. But then I didn't get to tell him and now it's ruined."

Alex squeezes me hard and I curl my head into his neck. "It's not ruined. Avery knows you're right for him. The kid isn't as stupid as he looks. It'll be fine, Steph. You just need to sleep this off. He'll be here in the morning and you'll see."

Despite his kind, supportive words, I keep crying and he keeps holding me.

Chapter 32

Avery

I get out of the car and walk around the house instead of walking in my back door. It's late. Really stupid late. Almost five in the morning. I should have been home an hour ago, but the flight left half an hour late and then there was traffic—yeah, fucking traffic. Only in California would the freeway be backed up at four-thirty in the morning. I'm exhausted and all I want to do is sleep—with Stephanie. And I mean sleep. But with her in my arms. With things settled.

I look up at our attached houses. Both are dark. She must have given up and gone to sleep. I was hoping she would wait up, but I don't blame her for falling asleep. In fact, I realize because I never called her back she's probably not even sure I'm coming over. The thought makes me feel sick. I don't want her to think that I would blow her off.

I climb the stairs to my door, but once on the porch I jump the low railing and fiddle with my keys until I find the spare one to her house that she gave me when I moved in. I unlock the door and I let myself in.

The downstairs is quiet and dark. As I make my way up the stairs, I cringe at every creak. I'm trying to be quiet, but the old wood and my two-hundred-pound frame make it impossible. At the top of the stairs, to the right, her bedroom door is open just a crack. I head straight for it. The only light is the moon filtering in from the window behind her bed. She's neglected to close the curtains.

My eyes, having already adjusted to the dim light, roam to her bed as I take a step into the room. I see her tiny frame is twisted away from the door, her quilt pulled up over her. At first all I see is her hair fanned out on the pillow and then I realize...her body is curled into someone else's body. I step closer.

Alex.

She's got her head on my teammate's chest and her right leg is draped over his thighs; I can tell by the position of the bumps and lumps under the quilt. It's how she likes to sleep on me. His thick arm is curled around her shoulders holding her in place and his fat head is tipped down like he fell asleep with his lips buried in her hair. Just the way I do.

Everything inside my body turns cold—my blood, my limbs, my heart. It's like I've been injected with liquid nitrogen. She's sleeping with Larue. She *slept* with Larue.

I turn and walk out of the room, down the stairs and out the front door. By the time my feet hit the porch I'm shaking with rage and I'm flushed with humiliation. I was falling in love with her. She was...she was supposed to be the one. I blindly threw my hard-earned reputation on the line for her because I felt things for her I never thought I would feel. And...she just fucked my buddy?

How could she do that? Why would Alex? I mean, sure, he chirps about it, but I didn't think even he would break the code. I honestly thought he was not just a teammate but also a friend. And she…she would do this?

My father's cautious words, the ones that seemed to sting more than the others, float back into my head. *"How well do you really know her, Avery, if you didn't know this? I mean, what else isn't she telling you? If she lied about this, then what else is she lying about?"*

Is Don right? Is she really not who I thought she was? What the fuck is wrong with me that I didn't know this? Why would I ever let myself have feelings like this for someone who would…Christ.

I take a deep breath and storm off the porch and back to my car. I'm done with her. I'm done with these stupid feelings. I'm sticking with what I know. What I'm good with. What doesn't hurt. Hockey. Being alone. Maintaining my fucking image.

I storm around the house again and jump back into my car. I don't know where I'm going, but I know I'm not sticking around here.

Chapter 33

Stephanie

The first thing I notice as I wake up, even before the hangover drum session taking place in my skull, is the heavy, comforting warmth of the male limbs I'm tangled up in. Instead of opening my eyes, I pinch them shut tighter because I know the pounding will only get worse with light, and I don't want to leave the comfort of the bed or of the body holding me close.

I stretch a little, and his arms circle my waist a little tighter, his palms flat against my stomach. My shirt is lifted and his skin on mine is rough and delightful. I take a heavy, deep breath and feel his face curl into my neck and his breath tickle my ear right before his lips graze that spot behind my lobe.

"Avery…"

His fingers spread, tickling my abdomen. "Try again, princess," he whispers softly.

I freeze for a second and then my body goes into flight mode. I grab his wrists and yank his hands away from me and kick at the covers, crawling toward the edge of the bed and jumping out at lightning speed. I stumble as my feet hit the floor and almost topple over. My eyes dart down with my hands that are moving to cover what I think is my naked body, but, luckily, I am fully clothed. Thank God.

"Relax, Steph. It's okay."

"It's not okay! What are you doing in my bed?!"

"Absolutely nothing, and that's the first time in my life I've said that in a woman's bed," he snarks, and then turns serious for a second. "But last night I was just cuddling a very sad, very beautiful girl while she slept a fitful sleep."

"Cuddling?" I echo, and rub my temples where the hangover drums are beating.

"Yes, honey. Cuddling. That's all. I swear on my Stanley Cup ring."

I stare at him, unblinking, unmoving. He stares back, relaxed, smirking. My head pounds even harder.

"Oh, God, I regret this so much," I mutter, and yank the blankets off him. "Get up. Go home. Before someone sees you."

"You regret what? Letting a friend comfort you in your drunken time of need?" He rolls his eyes as he slowly pulls his hulking frame to a sitting position and swings his feet around to the floor. "If it makes you feel better, I didn't intend to spend the night. I was just going to stay until Avery showed up and he could take care of you. But I'm on pain meds for the shoulder and we were drinking, and when you passed out, I passed out."

"Oh, my God, Alex...Avery." I moan.

"He didn't show. I'm sorry, Steph." He says it quietly and with so much sympathy it actually hurts. I can't deny Avery rejected me when I see it on someone else's face. So I grab his hands, tugging him to his feet with all the strength I can muster. "Go home."

"They have practice in an hour and a half," he replies, glancing at my alarm clock. "I'm supposed to join and test out my shoulder. I'll just wander next door and hitch a ride."

"And tell Avery what? I was in the neighborhood spooning Steph and need a lift to practice?" I retort.

He smiles down at me and lets out a short, healthy laugh. "Okay I'll wander over to Parsons's instead."

"Good call." I march out of my room, down the hall and to the front door with Alex lumbering along behind me. As we reach the front hall, I grab the door handle and Alex grabs my shoulders, turning me around to face him. He's not wearing his usual jovial, slightly smartass expression.

"You okay?"

"Yes. I mean I'm incredibly hungover, but I'll be fine."

"I'm not talking about that," he says pointedly.

I move my eyes away from his. "I'll let you know after I talk to Avery," I say, and he hugs me.

"Okay, well, if you need to talk, I'm actually good for that, too, not just for drunk cuddling," he says with a friendly smile, which looks weird on his face because I'm so used to seeing it with a more lecherous smile.

"Thanks," I reply, and can't help but add, "You're a lot less of a slimeball than you let on."

"If you tell anyone, I'll deny it," Alex quips with a wink.

I open the front door, and he walks out onto my porch and down the steps to the empty street. I watch him stroll west until he's almost out of sight and then close the door. I'm about to head back up the stairs when something in the living room catches my eye. It's Maddie. She's holding a cup of coffee and curled up in the corner of the couch like a cat. A very disapproving, judgmental cat.

I blush under her blue eyes and that makes the disapproval turn to disappointment.

"Why would you sleep with Alex?"

"I didn't!" I walk into the living room and plop down beside her. My stomach, which is completely empty after the puke-fest last night, rumbles. I run my hands through my bed head. "I was so drunk."

"I know."

"I threw up."

"I thought you might."

"Alex took care of me while I waited for Avery."

"Of course he did." Her voice holds a sarcastic note.

"I'm an emotional drunk and I just started to bawl and Alex comforted me and I guess I passed out and he fell asleep." I ignore her tone and keep confessing. "I swear, Maddie, it was platonic."

"I don't think Avery knows that."

"Avery doesn't know anything," I reply, and sigh.

She shakes her head, her eyes clouded with concern. "He saw you. Last night. He showed up at Ty's at like seven this morning and he was completely screwed up. Kind of like a quiet rage thing. Ty took him out to breakfast to talk."

Oh, my God, Avery came over last night? He saw Alex in my bed? With me? No. It can't be. No. No. No. I grab my tangled hair in my hands, pressing my palms against my temples, trying to quell the pounding and the horrible thoughts running through my head.

"I don't know what's going on," I murmur, confused and still dealing with the throbbing in my head. "How does this keep going from bad to worse?"

"You should call him," Maddie suggests.

I stand up and start walking toward the front hall and stairs.

Upstairs I grab my phone and turn it on. It takes a second to boot up and then a bunch of alerts start to beep and buzz. I'm instantly overwhelmed, so I ignore them all and dial his number. It goes straight to voice mail.

"Avery. Call me. I did NOT sleep with Alex. I know what it seems like, but just ask him."

I hang up and feel a little spark of anger start to catch inside me. Does he really think I would sleep with his teammate? Honestly? Shouldn't he know I wouldn't? If he thinks I would cheat on him, we have much bigger problems than my past.

Chapter 34

Avery

About three-quarters of the way through the practice, my curiosity starts to outweigh my rage. Now when I look at Larue I don't wonder about how good it would feel to put his face through the glass and instead wonder how the fuck he's just standing there looking innocent. He must know I know what they did. The fact that we drove right by him as he walked toward Ty's house this morning, ignoring him as he waved and yelled, probably tipped him off. But he's been acting like his normal self all practice. He's joking with Furry, yakking about baseball with Drew. He's even talking to Ty. The fucking asshole even had the nerve to talk to me. Said something like "Great shot, Westie!" when I scored in a drill. I promptly skated away and focused my rage on my next shot, which broke my stick.

Coach Meisner calls an end to practice and tells us to head home and rest up. Warns us no one is to have a late night. He wants us rested and focused for our game tomorrow night. I watch my teammates filter off the ice, but I don't join them. I start taking shots on net until Coach comes up and insists I head out.

"Your scoring touch isn't going anywhere. At least not on the ice. Relax. Go home and rest," Coach jokes, and chuckles to himself. Normally the humor would make me chuckle, too, but it makes me feel sick today.

Even after getting kicked off the ice, I don't head to the locker room. I go into the equipment room and fake some issue with my left skate to buy time. I don't want to see Larue when I finally go in there. Without the distractions of practice or the watchful eyes of the coaches I will, without a doubt, beat the living shit out of him. When I finally make it back to the locker room it's empty.

I strip and take a long shower. I have no one to go home and see, so I'm not in a rush. Eventually I'll have to talk to Stephanie. I just don't have the energy to do it now. I need to focus on hockey and only hockey. This game—winning—is all I can control in my life right now. It's all I've ever been able to control.

I take my time drying off and changing. When I wander outside to the parking lot, even the small gaggle of autograph seekers that usually gathers there is gone. I walk along the edge of the building scrolling through my emails on my phone. My father has sent me three, but I only open the one titled "Motion is pulling out." Motion is the name of the fitness company backing my clothing line. Don doesn't add anything; he just forwards the email from the company president. Apparently they've decided that we have creative differences on the direction of the line and they've decided it's not a good time to move forward with my line. They wish me well if I decide to pursue it elsewhere.

The whole thing is complete bullshit. Sure, I changed the women's line to be less…slutty from what they originally proposed, but they hadn't balked about that. Not until now…now that I'm making headlines for my love life.

I take a deep breath and let it out with a sigh. I'm more mad at myself than anyone else in this situation when I really think about it. I'm mad that I'd let my feelings cloud my judgment and influence my decisions. My life might have been lonely and isolated when I stuck to Don's rules—no parties, no public drunkenness, no girlfriends—but at least I felt like I was in control. This...this thing with Stephanie was completely out of control. Even before she slept with Alex.

I am mad at myself for wanting more than a soaring career. For wanting a relationship—and not with a safe, predictable bet like Lizzie. I wanted these things with Stephanie. I couldn't not want them with Stephanie. I complicated everything myself. I shove my phone back in my pocket and glance up. Ty is leaning against the back of his SUV.

"Hey. Sorry I took so long."

"It's fine," he says, and pushes himself off the SUV. As I get closer, I realize he's not moving from his position leaning against the trunk. So I stop a foot away from him.

"Are we going or...?"

"He didn't sleep with her," Ty says flatly. "Says she was drunk and throwing up so he was taking care of her. Then they fell asleep."

"That's bullshit."

"But isn't that kind of exactly what she said to you this morning?" Ty counters, lifting his baseball cap to scratch his head. "You think they'd both lie to you?"

"Yeah. Maybe," I reply quietly. "I saw them."

He folds his arms across his chest. "Did you see them doing it? Were they naked?"

"Parsons, if I'd walked in on it, he'd be dead," I blurt, then take a calming breath. "They were all curled up together. If he was just keeping an eye on her, why wasn't he asleep on the floor or the guest room or the…"

"Because she was crying, dude."

I hear him before I see him. He comes around the car a second later. He must have been sitting in Ty's passenger seat listening to everything. Ty takes a subtle step to his left, to block my direct path to Larue.

"You should have waited in the car, Larue," Ty turns and says. "Just hear him out, Avery."

Larue ignores him and keeps his focus on me. Tension rolls up my limbs and through my body. I'm taut and ready to fight.

"Avery, she was crying. Over you," Alex continues, and raises his hands like he's surrendering. "She was drunk and emotional, and she just burst into tears and didn't stop until she fell asleep. And she fell asleep on me. Not because she wanted to but because she was a drunk mess."

I don't say anything at first. I glance at Ty, who is staring back at me with no readable expression. He's clearly the ref here, not taking sides, just keeping an eye out for illegal hits or unsportsmanlike conduct.

"You've been crowing for weeks you want her," I spit out.

"Yeah. And I do," Alex replies easily and with confidence. His light eyes become softer, though, and the hard edge to his words fades. "But she wants you, buddy. Even though neither of you seems to know how to be in a relationship, she wants one with you. Not me. And last night she felt like she was rejected. And she was beyond drunk, so I was a friend to her—and to you. If I'd left her, she'd probably have choked on her own vomit."

"Gross," Ty groans.

I just stare at Larue wordlessly. The realization that I think he's telling the truth starts to create a swirling cauldron of regret in my stomach.

"But you're actually second-guessing this, aren't you? That's why you were so quick to believe she'd screw me behind your back. Because you're still thinking about your goddamn image, aren't you?" Larue questions. "You're looking for reasons to leave her."

I move my sunglasses from on top of my head to my face to hide my guilty eyes. Ty glances from Larue to me. I turn to Ty and mumble, "I need to get home."

I walk by Alex, and he reaches out and puts a hand on my shoulder, stopping me. "I'm not going to touch her," he promises quietly.

"Doesn't matter. I don't think we'll work it out," I mutter, and the realization is like touching a frozen metal pole with your tongue. It's a mistake and now I'm stuck and I can't fix this without more damage.

Alex nods and shrugs. "I'm still not going to touch her."

He reaches out and claps me on the back as he gives me a hug and I give him one back. I'm still not happy at what I saw last night in her bedroom, but once again the real person I'm angry with is myself.

Chapter 35

Stephanie

I keep my head down as I step off the elevator and into the lobby of my office. I spent the whole ride over here praying that none of them know. That somehow there isn't one hockey fan in the building, or that if there is, they only check scores and no one stumbles across one of the fifty articles about Avery Westwood and his ex-druggie girlfriend. But that hope is dashed as soon as I pass the receptionist, Letitia.

"Stephanie?" Letitia says quietly, and I pause and pull my eyes off the dark marble floor. She's wearing an expression of discomfort on her pretty features. "Mr. Archer needs you to go straight to the boardroom."

"He's here?" I check my watch. "But he usually only comes in at nine."

Holy crap, did I miss an early conference call with a client or something? Letitia's gaze drifts. She starts shuffling some papers in front of her and with every ruffle of paper another bird of doom seems to soar around my gut. "He's here. In the conference room. And he needs you to meet him."

She's clearly not going to tell me anything more, so I just thank her and make my way left to the conference room instead of right to my desk. Through the glass wall as I approach I see two other people in the room with Mr. Archer. A woman I don't recognize and Dan. I push open the door and step inside.

"Mr. Archer? You needed to see me?" I question, exuding confidence in my tone and smile. But on the inside I'm a quivering mess.

His eyes dart to Dan and then the lady sitting at the head of the table, and he doesn't do his usual "call me Conrad" line. Instead he nods sharply and clears his throat before motioning to a chair. "Yes, Ms. Deveau. Please have a seat."

I do what he says, even though I don't want to. Sitting makes me feel instantly weak and small, like a child in the principal's office. But I do it, so I don't seem contrary. I nervously smooth my skirt with my hands and perch on the chair.

"Stephanie…" He pauses. "I understand that you…may be having some personal problems?"

My eyes dart swiftly from Dan to Mr. Archer to the unnamed woman in the chair. When my eyes land on her, she seems to startle. "Oh. I'm sorry. I should have introduced myself. I'm Camille Leeds from Human Resources."

She extends her hand, leaning over the conference table toward me, and I take it. Her fingers are bony and cold. I glance up at Mr. Archer, who's still waiting for an answer. I swallow and struggle to craft one in my head. "No, sir. I'm fine. I won't let anything interfere with my job."

He looks at Daniel and then down at Camille, like he's silently asking for help. Dan is busy examining his fingernails, but Camille jumps in. She looks at her clipboard of papers in front of her. "Stephanie. The news reports about you have come to our attention."

"They're gossip pieces intended to create controversy about a hockey player," I can't help but correct her. "It's not real journalism."

"That's true," Mr. Archer says, and nods his salt-and-pepper head emphatically. He's on my side, I realize. He doesn't want me cornered in here just as much as I don't want to be.

"That's not the issue," Camille replies coolly. "The issue is that your history was not disclosed to the firm, and we are unclear as to whether it is in fact history."

"Excuse me?"

"Ms. Deveau…"

I stand up so abruptly the chair I was in rolls swiftly across the floor, bumping quietly against the wall. "The firm did a background check when I was hired and found nothing because there is nothing to find. I have never been arrested or charged with any kind of crime. I did not disclose my life as a teenager because, quite frankly, legally I am not required to do so."

Daniel looks up at me with a cold, hard stare. "You took my pills the other day."

So that's why he's here? That son of a bitch! I cross my arms so no one can see them shake. "Joyce found them in the kitchen and thought they were mine, so she put them on my desk. I forgot about them but returned them to you the first chance I got."

Camille's eyes move from me to Dan, and he lifts an eyebrow to signal his disbelief. Now I know what my brother feels like on the ice when someone cross-checks him. I want to climb across this table and put Dan through the goddamn wall. Instead I turn to my only friend, my boss. "Ask Joyce. Also, I have the Post-it she put on them at my desk somewhere."

"I believe you," Mr. Archer says, but from the expression on their faces Camille and Dan don't.

I look squarely at Camille. "Are you firing me?"

"No. No," she says swiftly, and almost looks shocked I would ask, but the fact is I don't even know if I want to work here anymore. I don't know if I can—not if everyone thinks I'm still an addict. She pulls a pamphlet from the paperwork on her clipboard and slides it across the table to me. "I'm required to give you this. In case you are still…if you need any kind of help, we have a program our insurance covers."

I look at the cover of the pamphlet. It's a rehab facility. I want to scream so loud I shatter the glass walls, but I simply shove the pamphlet in my purse and ask Mr. Archer if I can go to my desk now. He nods quickly.

As I reach the conference room door, I pause and glare back at them over my shoulder. "Camille, if you have any pamphlets on the fraternization policies here or the sexual harassment guidelines, I suggest you give them to Daniel. I'll be at my desk if you need me."

Only I don't go to my desk. I head straight to the women's bathroom, lock myself in a stall and spend the next ten minutes hyperventilating and crying.

How did this become my world? I might have been lonely before I let myself entertain the idea of Avery, but I was content. I was secure. I had left my past behind. Then I let the idea of him into my head…then I let him—the actual him—into my heart. And now my world is falling apart. I don't blame him. I blame me. I knew how this would end and I followed after it blindly anyway. Now every single thing in my life is unraveling and I don't know what to do to stop it.

After a few minutes I pull myself together, blow my nose, touch up my makeup and force myself to head back to my desk, intent on losing myself in the mountain of email that must have piled up in my inbox. As I start to glance over them, suddenly there's a coffee on my desk. I look up. Mr. Archer is standing next to it smiling softly at me. "I figured it was my turn to grab you a latte. Hope caramel is okay today."

"Yes." I smile gratefully. "Thank you, Mr. Archer."

"You're welcome, Stephanie."

I take a deep breath and am about to dive into my emails, when I realize he hasn't moved from the side of my desk. I look up and he gives me another tentative smile. "There's actually something I wanted to talk to you about. Before this all happened."

My heart sinks, and I honestly don't think I can take much more of this. He shakes his head. "This is nothing bad. It's actually something good. Could be something great."

I just stare up at him blankly and wait for him to continue. It's hard to believe that something great could be happening to me right now. "You know how Luxe Spas is planning on expanding into the East Coast. How they want to start by placing spas in several major hotels?"

"Yeah. We've been working on the first deal for over six months now." I nod and take a sip of my latte.

"Well, it's taking so long because we don't have someone on the ground over there," Mr. Archer says. "I've been heading to New York twice a month, but it's still not enough."

"You're moving to New York?" I squeak, because honestly the idea of losing my boss and having to start fresh with a new lawyer, one who would most likely believe all the stories that people would tell them about my past...ugh. I can't do it. I just can't.

"We don't really need a lawyer on that side, but we do need someone who can get the paperwork through and manage the acquisitions," he explains. "It would be for about three weeks, four tops. And of course the firm would put you up in an apartment, all expenses paid, and you can come right back to your position here when the contracts are completed."

"Me? You want me to go?" I put the latte down so firmly on the desk that some of it slops out of the drinking hole in the lid.

"I was going to mention it last week, but we got bogged down with the deposition and I wanted to clear it through the senior staff first," he explained. "They're on board. It makes sense. You're a paralegal, Steph. You've been working below your abilities as my legal secretary and we don't have a paralegal position open here, but this would give you experience to move up when a position opens."

I can't believe it. I never would have expected this opportunity—and I never in a million years have considered living in New York City. It seems magical and terrifying all at the same time. Mr. Archer is still looking at me expectantly, and I'm just staring back at him with my mouth hanging open.

"I know it's a lot to consider, and I don't need an answer right now. I'm hoping you can let me know by the end of the week," he tells me, and smiles. "Look, Daniel is an ass, we all know that. And no matter what people are saying, you're the best assistant I've ever had. That's why I'm offering this opportunity to you. It's just a few weeks, but it could mean a lot for your career. And maybe you're looking for some space from things here."

I nod and try to swallow, but my throat is dry and my pulse is racing. He pats my shoulder and walks past me, saying, "Just think about it."

I don't know how long I'm staring vacantly at my computer screen, but it's a long time, because when I lift my latte to my lips again it's cold. I decide to break the company rules and call Sebastian. I need to tell him about this offer. I need to talk it through with someone, and he's my best choice right now. I don't want to bother Maddie. She's too close to it. And I can't tell Avery because…I don't know what the hell I am to him or, quite frankly, what he is to me right now.

I dig my phone out of my purse and start to dial Seb's number when my office phone buzzes. It's reception. I hit speaker. "Mr. Archer's desk, Stephanie speaking."

"Stephanie, there's an Avery Westwood here to see you."

Oh, my God, he's at my work. I stand up and lean toward the phone. "I'll be right out."

I turn to my boss's office door and call over my shoulder. "I'm running a quick errand, Mr. Archer. I'll be back in fifteen."

"Okay," he calls back as I walk as quickly as I can without looking like an idiot toward the front of the building. I'm feeling panicky and emotional, and I don't like it. Still, I'm glad he showed up here unexpectedly, because I feel like it's a good sign. He wouldn't come all this way if he hated me, right? Oh, God, please let me be right.

I turn the corner in the hall and walk into the lobby. Avery is in jeans and a wrinkled T-shirt, his sunglasses still on, despite being inside. Letitia is typing at her computer behind the reception desk, but her eyes are glued to him. He's chosen to lean against the wall instead of sit in one of our white leather Barcelona chairs. I can't help but admire the lean, strong angles of his body and the golden glow the California sun has given his skin. His dark hair is perfectly mussed.

He turns his head and spots me standing there. Pushing himself off the wall, he takes a couple steps toward me.

"Hi. Sorry to show up like this."

"It's okay," I say quietly. I turn to Letitia, who is still staring. "I'm going to grab a coffee. I have my cell if anyone needs me."

She nods. Avery gives her a half smile and her face explodes in a smile. I'm almost one hundred percent certain she doesn't know he's a professional athlete. She just thinks he's hot. Because he is. He's hot, and funny, and sexy and…probably not mine for much longer.

We walk wordlessly to the elevator and step inside when it opens, standing on opposite sides like strangers. The doors swoosh closed and the car quietly slides downward. I wish he would take off his sunglasses. I want to see his eyes.

"I talked to Larue," he says quietly, but it fills the metal boxlike space.

"I didn't sleep with him," I say calmly.

"I know."

The doors open; he waits for me to exit and follows behind. I head through the small marble lobby and out the doors into the sunshine. Traffic is whipping by and feels louder than normal. He must agree, because he starts to walk around my building to the quieter side street. I follow. He's parked at the first meter on the street, next to a towering palm tree. He sits on the hood of his car, feet on the curb, and I stand across from him, my back against the palm.

"Why did you think he and I…you know?" I can't help but ask. "Did you see him leave or something?"

He shakes his head and then scratches the stubble on his jaw. "I took you up on your offer to come see you as soon as I got home. I used the spare key like you told me to. I saw you two together in bed."

"Oh," is all I can say. I shake my head. "I didn't know I was in bed with him. I was upset and drunk, and I think I passed out."

He nods. "I know. Should you be drinking like that? Until you pass out?"

"No, but should anybody?" I reply. "And it's only the first time in my life I've done it. I won't be doing it again."

"Do you need to…" He looks so uncomfortable right now and it's breaking my heart. "I don't know…talk to someone or something?"

"I've been clean for over five years, Avery. And it wasn't alcohol; it was pills. Don't be an asshole," I say quietly. And it's true. Last night was dumb and I know that. I have no urge to do it again. No matter what happens here with him.

He shoves his hands in his pockets and looks down at the grass. "I don't know how this works. I don't know what you can and can't do. I don't know what I should worry about."

"You should worry about whatever you worried about before you found out," I reply, trying not to sound harsh.

This is exactly what I never wanted—from Avery or any person I fell in love with. I didn't want them to look at me differently. "This can't change the way you think about me or feel about me."

We both stop talking and just stare at each other. I feel like I might cry again, only this time I'm not sure why…and I'm not sure I want to know why. I think my soul knows something inherently that my brain hasn't caught up to yet.

"But it does." His voice is deeper than normal. Thicker. Filled with something…something painful. "You lied to me about it."

Those words physically hurt. They're heavy and they press down painfully on my chest. "I never lied. I avoided mentioning it, but I never lied."

"We don't know each other as well as I thought we did," he finally says, crossing his arms over his chest.

What is he doing? Is he…breaking up with me?

"You know me. I know you. You and I were friends before anything got physical."

"Yeah, but even then I don't know if I really knew you." He shrugs a little, like he's giving up on something. And he is. On us. "I mean, let's be honest. We've both always been attracted to each other, so that probably made it different than if we were just friends."

"Did I always think you were good looking? Yes. But I'm not you, Avery. I don't put on fake smiles or hide my personality to create a fake image to get what I want," I say angrily. "I'm just me. The same person. All the time."

"By hiding your past you were showing me the real you? Really?" he challenges, his voice suddenly hard and uncaring. "I might have an image and hide stuff from the public, but I never hid anything from you."

"You're right. That's how I knew exactly how you'd react to this," I spit as the wind picks up and blows my hair across my face. I angrily push it back.

I went there. Brought up *his* past. The way he abandoned his friend who had an addiction to painkillers. If this conversation hadn't hit rock bottom before, I've just dug a deeper pit and flung us both inside it.

Avery stands up, off the hood of the car. "I was young and I was stupid. Cutting myself out of Trey's life was a stupid decision, and I've regretted it ever since. I told you that. But you think I'm that same person. You think I haven't changed at all?"

"Aren't you about to do it again?"

He freezes. His whole body just goes to stone, standing there on the curb looking down at me. I let go of the palm tree behind me I hadn't even realized I was gripping and take a step toward him. I don't know if this is good or bad. Is he shocked or even more horrified? It finally hits me. This is not going to work. Avery and me. It's just not going to happen. We've messed this up too badly.

"I still like you, Steph," he says softly. He reaches out like he's going to touch me, then shoves his hands back in his pockets. "I still want to like you, but I don't know what to do here. I don't know how to fix the fact that I don't know you like I thought I did."

"I can't change who I am or who I was. And you can't either. You need your image, and I don't fit it." I take a step back and bump into the palm tree, so I move to the left. I will without a doubt be crying within the next two minutes, so I need to get away from him.

"You fit fine when no one tried to make you fit," he says, pushing his sunglasses up so I can finally see his pretty eyes. They look so sweet, so hopeful, when he utters his next words. "Why don't we just date privately?"

"What?"

"You know, like in secret. No one needs to know except our friends."

"You want me to be your..." I pause to take a breath, but it hurts to breathe, so it's shallow and stilted. "Your dirty little secret?"

"Not like that. Steph, come on. You're the one who wanted to keep it private before, so why I can't I want it now?" he stutters. "It's just...I've got a lot going on right now. The team needs to make play-offs. I need to be focused on that. And I need to find a new company to back my clothing line because the one I had just pulled out. If we play it off like we're friends, the press won't make this into an unnecessary distraction. For either of us."

It has got to be the look on my face that makes his voice suddenly falter and stop.

"We're not friends. We're not anything, Avery. Bye," I choke out before turning and walking as fast as I can away from him. Once inside my building, I march right into the lobby restroom and burst into tears.

Chapter 36

Avery

The thing about hockey injuries is they're painful, but not relentlessly so. When you tear a muscle or break a bone, it hurts, obviously, but there's medication and surgery and rehab and a hundred ways you can ease that pain. And you know that, eventually, it'll be gone completely and you'll be right back where you were before.

The pain that losing Stephanie has caused is relentless. There's no medication, no surgery, no way to make it stop. It's this constant dull ache, and unlike with a sports injury, getting back to where I was before she ripped my heart out makes it worse. Because it's been four weeks and I'm back exactly where I was before she let me have her. I'm alone with nothing but a career and a brand to fill my time. The salacious articles have subsided. The personal questions in interviews have halted. Everything is back to "normal"—and that makes the ache in my chest worse.

I sit up, throw the covers back and walk across the bedroom to the bathroom. I pass my bag, which I packed at four in the morning when sleep wouldn't come. We're going to Seattle tonight to play the last game of the regular season. We have to win it to make the play-offs. It really all comes down to this. If you asked me how I'd feel in this situation a couple of months ago, I would have said there was nothing I wanted more than winning this game and getting the Saints into the play-offs for the first time.

But then Stephanie and I blew up, and I realized there is something I want more than winning a hockey game or turning this team around or more than my goddamn image. I want her.

The problem is I figured it out too late. When she walked away from me at her office that day, I felt numb. Nothing but numb. It took about twenty-four hours for that to wear off and that's when the incredible ache began.

It only got worse when, after a couple days, I finally grew some balls and went over to her house to see her. Maddie answered the door, her pretty face morphing into a scowl at the sight of me. "She doesn't want to see you."

"Come on, Maddie."

"She doesn't want to see you. She told me that. I'm telling you that," Maddie repeated, her voice flat and lifeless.

"I miss her."

"It's over," Maddie replied. "She told me that too."

"I don't like the way it ended," I argued. "I want to try and…I just need to see her."

I could see the war going on in Maddie's head from the flicker in her eyes. She wanted to let me in. She wanted to be loyal to Stephanie. She didn't know which urge to give in to. I leaned on the door frame and begged. "Please. Please just let me see her."

And just like that, Maddie's hand fell away from the door, letting it swing open. I stepped over the threshold and squeezed her shoulder in thanks. "She's upstairs," Maddie explained quietly. "Packing."

I stopped dead, my foot on the first step, my head flying back toward Maddie. "Packing?"

My heart is suddenly racing. I hear something at the top of the stairs and look up to see Stephanie standing there with a suitcase beside her. She looks down at me with shock.

"Where are you going?" I ask her. My voice sounds thick.

"Somewhere else," she responds, and starts down the stairs, awkwardly lugging the big bag behind her. I climb a few stairs, so we meet in the middle, and I take the luggage from her. She struggles to stop me, refusing to remove her hand from the handle, but as soon as I put mine over hers she yanks it away. The rejection stings.

I lift the bag and carry it down to the main floor easily, placing it on the floor near the door, but I position myself between her and the bag. Maddie is slowly creeping down the hall toward the kitchen. "I'll just head out the back door and meet you in the car."

Neither one of us acknowledges her. Stephanie doesn't look sad like she did the other day. Now she just looks angry and distant. So distant. She's looking at me like she did back in Seattle before everything happened, which feels like a million years ago. When she found out just how much of a bitch to my image I had become. It was that look that pulled my head out of my ass before, and it's got the same effect now. I realize that all I want more than anything is her back in my life.

"Are you going on vacation?"

She doesn't speak. She just shakes her head.

"I don't understand," I say.

"I'm being transferred for a while," she explains, and runs a hand through her hair, absently pushing it back over her shoulder. She looks tired but still so fucking beautiful. "For work."

"You're moving?" My voice rises with every word. "Where are you moving?"

"It's not permanent," she replies, and tries to slip past me to get her bag. I don't let her. She glares at me. "I need to go. I have a flight."

"A flight?" I sound like a drunk parrot just repeating her words back to her. "It's far enough away for a plane? Where?"

"Avery, I don't want to tell you," she admits, and her pretty blue eyes start to water. "You need time and I need time."

"How much time?"

"I'll be gone a month or so."

"A MONTH?!"

Without even thinking, I grab her by the waist and pull her into me. Her body is warm but rigid. Before she can push me away, which I know is exactly what she's going to do, I kiss her. Kiss, actually, is an understatement. My lips are trying to speak the words my brain can't find: *Don't go, I'm sorry, I don't want this to be over.*

She decides to give in. Her hands fist in my shirt and when my tongue leaves her mouth, her tongue follows it, but only for a second. And then those fists in my shirt are pushing me back, and suddenly she's an arm's length away, her palm up in my face as a warning. "Don't. Just don't. That's not our problem—sex. And it's not our solution."

"Leaving's not a solution," I say, but I let her move past me and take her bag.

"It is for me," she replies, and opens the front door. "For now."

I follow her onto the porch, running a hand through my hair and clutching it so tightly, I'm surprised I don't yank it out. "Just tell me where."

She ignores me and continues down the porch steps to the curb where Maddie is standing behind her car with the trunk open. Together they put the suitcase in the trunk.

"Stephanie."

She gets in the car without another word, without another glance, and then she's just gone.

Now, four weeks later, I'm still "injured." That ache hasn't subsided, not for one fucking minute. I feel it even when I'm on the ice. Playing well doesn't help; playing shitty doesn't either—I've done both. Drinking too much doesn't help; being sober doesn't either. Working out more doesn't help; eating everything on the trainer's veto list doesn't help either. Nothing. Fucking. Helps.

I still have no idea where she's gone. No one would tell me, so I finally stopped pestering Maddie and Ty.

After the first ten days, I decided to focus more on why she left instead of where she's gone. She left because I was an asshole. She left because I did what I always do. I worried about my image over everything else. I asked her to lie about us because it would be easier than letting a bunch of people judge me on someone she used to be.

But, fuck, I never stopped to think in my self-absorbed panic that it meant I was treating her like she was a problem and like she was still that person with a problem. So I started trying to make amends; even though I knew I couldn't tell her how wrong I was, I could at least show the world how wrong I was.

I found a new company to do my clothing line with, and then I picked that charity the reporter mentioned, the Canadian one called Roadways that helps teen runaways, to give my profits from that clothing line to. I issued a press release and gave an interview to that same reporter, as a thank-you for not running that original footage.

We didn't mention Stephanie, but I did explain that I was a firm believer that a troubled youth didn't mean a troubled adulthood.

I shower, shave and get in my car, leaving early and stopping at a drive-through to grab a coffee on the way to the airport. My phone rings as I'm walking into the airport. Hope fills me like it does every time it rings, because I want it to be Stephanie. And like every other time, it's not. This time it's my father. I have sent his calls to voice mail for the last month. I fired him, but he is still working. Not so much as working but sending me detailed emails and leaving voice mails telling me what I need to do to keep all the projects he had been managing. There are a lot. I didn't realize how much my father actually did. Approving promotional shots, negotiating contracts and fielding new offers. My phone is constantly ringing and my inbox is overflowing.

I send him to voice mail again and ten seconds later my phone starts ringing. This time it's my sister, Kate. I pick it up even though I know that she's going to do nothing but bitch. "Hey."

"You can't keep punishing him for something he didn't do," she hollers so loudly I have to hold the phone away from my ear.

"Except that we don't know he didn't do it," I reply, calming her down because it's becoming habit. She calls to yell at me at least once a week.

"He said he didn't do it, so he didn't do it," Kate wails, then pauses and lowers her voice. "Avery, he's a lot of things—overbearing, distant, a jerk—but he's not a liar. He's always been honest. Brutally so. I know you know this."

I do know this. But if he didn't leak Stephanie's past to the media, then who did? It had to be him. "Do you need to talk to me about something else, Kate?"

"Yeah." She sighs. "When did you become such an asshole?"

"When my dad outed my girlfriend to the media," I reply as I push open the doors to the airport. "Anything else?"

"Avs, come on. Please," Kate begs, changing her tactic completely. "He's all we've got, and he's always been there for us."

She's talking about the fact that our mom died when I was four and Kate was two. Don Westwood might have been far from perfect, but he didn't give up on or ignore his two toddlers when his wife died. He was there for us; even if he was overbearing and treated me like more of a client than a son, he was still there.

For the first time since this thing with Stephanie blew up in my face, I start to feel bad about this fight with my dad. But if he really did this... Then again, if he didn't...

"Just answer one of his calls, okay?" Kate asks. "Just one. Come on."

"Fine. I'm getting on a plane, but I'll talk to him when we land in Seattle," I promise, and walk toward the security for the private plane area. "How's everything with you?"

"Fine," Kate says. "Except my brother is breaking my dad's heart."

"I have a broken heart."

She pauses at that admission. She's not used to me having feelings, let alone expressing them. "So maybe you should do something about that other than act like a selfish, ungrateful brat to Dad."

"Oh, my God, you're relentless." I roll my eyes. "I'm hanging up now."

"Safe travels."

I hang up and put my phone and belongings in the bin before passing through the metal detector. Once on the other side, I still have probably a good half hour before the rest of the team starts wandering in, so I make my way over to the waiting area and do what I always do when I have too much time on my hands. I scroll through the photos on my phone until I get to my favorite one.

It was taken before anything happened between us. When we were still flirty friends. She's sitting on her porch, the sun is setting behind her, making the sky pink and gold. She's holding her phone in her hand and laughing at me because I'd tripped over the railing trying to climb from my side to hers. She snapped a pic of me sprawled on the ground and was threatening to sell it to the tabloids. So I pulled out my phone and snapped one of her. I told her it was because she wasn't wearing any makeup and had six chins from this angle so I could use it for blackmail. But the truth was she looked beautiful in it. Cheeks flushed, lips parted, eyes sparkling, hair tousled.

I must stare at it for a long time, because suddenly someone gently kicks my foot. I look up and see Ty standing above me, coffee in his hand and headphones dangling around his neck. "What the hell are you staring at? You look downright morose, buddy."

"Morose? Look at you with the fancy words," I snark.

He laughs and drops down into the seat beside me. "My girlfriend is super smart. She's expanding my vocabulary," he says. "She's talking about going back to school to get her law degree."

"Good for Maddie." I smile. "What if she ends up at University of Wisconsin or something?"

"She won't," he says without the slightest worry in his voice. "We've talked about it. She's only applying to schools in Southern Cali. And she's going to move in with me next year."

"Holy shit. That's great, Ty. Happy for you." I smile at him and he grins back. I don't ask the questions that I'm thinking, like, *Will Steph keep the cottage or move somewhere else?*

He fiddles with the lid on his coffee. "Hey, so… Steph called Maddie."

I'm on edge instantly, because he told me weeks ago he can't talk about her with me, and now he's talking about her with me. I lean forward, my elbows on my knees, and turn to face him. His eyes are filled with compassion. "She's done her work thing, but she's taking some vacation time."

"Oh."

"Yeah."

"And you're not allowed to tell me where."

Ty shakes his head. "No. I could tell you, if they'd told me. But Maddie said she wouldn't tell me because I already told them I didn't like keeping things from you. So now we're both out of the loop."

I turn away from him and hold my head with my hands. "She's not coming back, is she? Ever."

"No, man, I think she is," Ty says quietly, and puts his hand on my shoulder. "I think she's really just taking some time. She didn't tell Maddie to look for a new roommate or anything. She's still paying her rent."

I nod stiffly. The "injury" just feels like it got a whole hell of a lot worse. How is that even possible? Fucking aching chest. Ty stands up. "I'm gonna take a piss before we board."

I just nod again and watch him go. I pull my phone out and pull up that picture of her again. I open Instagram and load the photo of Stephanie. I've left her voice mails and sent her texts since she left, but there's been no response, so I'm resorting to public declarations. I'm that desperate. I know this might create more hell than I'm currently in, but it also might be the only way to reach her. If there's even the slightest chance this makes her contact me, it'll be worth sparking the ashes of the media drama. Under the photo I write, *Missing this face more than ever.*

Alex walks over, always the last one to arrive. We've even had to hold planes for his lazy ass before. He smiles down at me. "Hey, Captain. Ready to go home and grab this play-off spot?"

"Yeah." I stand up and once at eye level I notice the giant hickey on his neck. "Dude. Really? Did you spend last night in a dark corner at a high school formal?"

He reaches up and touches his neck. "If you think that's bad, wait till you see the scratches on my back and bite mark on my shoulder. I'm still not sure if I fucked a woman or some kind of escaped zoo animal. Either way, best sex of my life."

He's grinning, and I try to give him a smile back, but it's hardly jovial. We walk toward the boarding door. "You could always move on and find someone to mark you up, you know?"

"Yeah. I know."

I do know. I just don't want to move on. Even if she does.

The flight is quick and painless. I listen to music and keep hitting refresh on my Instagram since we have Wi-Fi on the flight. By the time we land, the picture of Stephanie has more than two thousand likes. There's a bunch of comments too—about fifty—and I read every one. Only about four are super catty and mean. I delete all of them. It might not be social media etiquette, but fuck the haters.

The day goes by painfully slowly. I can't sleep during my pregame nap and the place I always ordered my pregame chicken parm from has gone out of business. I can't find another place that delivers at four in the afternoon, so both rituals are blown to shit. I'm feeling agitated and out of sorts as we walk through the bowels of the arena to the visitors' room.

Alex runs up beside me just as we enter the locker room. "I saw Sebastian. He's pissed."

"About what?"

"About you breaking his sister's heart," Alex replies, and when I glance over at him he's got the most serious expression on his face I have ever seen.

"So he should tell me where she is so I can fix it," I reply, walking into the room and over to my spot. I start yanking at my tie roughly.

"Stay away from him tonight. Seriously," Alex advises.

But of course I don't stay away from him, even though I can tell by the way Deveau glares at me from across the ice during warm-up that Alex really wasn't exaggerating. Sebastian's icy blue eyes are fiery, and his lip is curled as he glares at me. He wants to kill me. In a fucked-up way, that's a good thing. It means Stephanie isn't over me. It also means he knows that for a fact, which means he's talked to her, which means he knows where she is.

Deveau is a defenseman and I'm a forward—a center—so he's nowhere near me as we line up at center ice and the referee drops the puck. I win the face-off and get the puck cleanly back to Alex, who starts up the ice with it. I straighten, ready to follow, when all of a sudden I'm on my back staring up at the ass end of the Jumbotron above. White-hot pain on the left side of my jaw licks up the side of my face and down my neck. I don't hear anything for a second—it's complete silence, like I'm in a vacuum, while I fight to hold on to consciousness. And then I hear everything. Fans hollering, whistling squealing, players yelling.

I don't, however, realize he's on top of me until he leans forward and his face cuts off my blurry view of the Jumbotron and lights above. His skin is completely red, like he's been skating half the game already, but it's not from exertion; it's from rage. He leans over me, his gloves gone and his fists curled into the front of my jersey, and his voice rumbles out of him like thunder. "Come on, Westwood. Fight back."

He gives me a shake. I see a ref put his hand on Seb's shoulder, but he violently shakes it off. "Come on. Hit me. Fight back!"

"No."

"Fucking. Hit. Me."

"No."

The ref's hands are joined by the hands of the linesmen as they finally rip him off me and I struggle to sit up. Alex and Ty are in his face, being pushed back by the ref as they yell obscenities at Sebastian, who is being hauled off the ice. A Saints trainer appears next to me. "Take it easy. You may have a concussion."

I ignore him and get to my feet. I'm definitely wobbly, but I skate toward Sebastian. "Hey!"

He sees me and struggles to break free of the ref, but he can't. Another linesman and Ty start grabbing at my jersey to hold me back. Around me, there are several shoving matches happening because an ice-clearing brawl is always the next logical step when a player sucker punches the captain of the other team on puck drop.

"Hey!" I yell again, even though I can't get any closer to him due to my human restraints, and he's still being skated backward, away from me, against his will.

"Where is she?" I yell at him, knowing full well that every player on both teams can hear me, the coaches and probably even Chance Echolls, too, who's reporting from between the benches. Luckily, when this type of crap goes down, they cut his mic so it's not broadcasting our potty mouths to the nation.

"Fuck you!"

I break free of Ty and the linesman and move to skate toward him, but I'm dizzy. The trainer is suddenly in front of me again, holding me by both shoulders. "Avery, you gotta get off the ice," he explains.

"I'm fine," I lie.

"League protocol, buddy," he tells me, and I let him skate me toward the tunnel. "Quiet room time."

Right. When we suffer a hit to the head now, we have to spend time in the medical room while they check for concussion symptoms. I don't have a choice, and maybe if I take ten minutes I'll stop seeing three of everything. And sure enough, ten minutes later I'm feeling a lot better. I've got a bit of a headache and my jaw is going to turn black where Seb's fist connected with it, but my brain isn't foggy. Still, the trainer says, "Let's give it the rest of the period and reassess." I start to argue, but then he reminds me that it's better I sit twenty minutes than through the play-offs. I don't have a choice but to agree.

"What happened to Deveau?" I ask, because I didn't stick around to hear the penalty called.

"Game misconduct," the trainer says with a hard smile. "And that asshole will be getting a call from the league. No way he's not getting suspended."

The guy is probably right. You can't sucker punch anyone in this league, but you especially can't sucker punch me. I know how fucking egotistical that sounds, but it's true. As soon as he leaves me alone in the room again, I jump off the table I'm sitting on and head to the door. I glance into the hall. It's empty, so I leave and march down the familiar hallway to the home team side. I pass one guy—a janitor with a cart who must have been cleaning the VIP restrooms by the family lounge. He doesn't even look up as I slip into the Winter-hawks' locker room.

It's all too familiar and yet feels overwhelmingly foreign at the same time. Sebastian is sitting alone in nothing but some sweatpants, a towel around his neck, his head hanging down, eyes closed. I stand just inside the door, teetering on my skates, and clear my throat. He looks up, expressionless, but when he sees me, every feature of his face turns hard with rage. "Get the fuck out of here."

"I love her," I tell him calmly.

He stands up. "Yeah, well, you're doing it wrong, asshole."

"I know that," I admit, and fight not to take a step back as he moves menacingly toward me. "I fucked up. I was blindsided and panicked. She should have told me."

"Yeah, she should have," he agrees gruffly. "So you could have been a spineless asshole and disowned her before she fell in love with you."

I blink. "She's in love with me?"

"She was."

The word "was" stings worse than his punch.

"Where is she?"

"I'm going to punch you again. I don't care if it gets me kicked out of the fucking league," he warns, and takes another step toward me.

I open my arms. "Do it. At least one of us will feel better. And it won't hurt as much as I've already hurt myself, so go for it, bro."

Sebastian doesn't move. His hands are in fists, but he doesn't raise them from his sides. His eyes, so similar to his sister's, scan my face, like he's reading a book. And then he lets out a heavy breath, swears in French and sits back down on the bench in front of his stall.

"Why do you want to see her again?"

"So I can tell her what I've been trying to show her and everyone else," I explain, a desperate hitch in my voice. "That I know she's not that person. That I don't care that she was that person. That I love her."

"She is a good person and she's worked her ass off to beat her demons," Sebastian says in a gravelly voice directed at the floor. "And you asking her to hide the fact that she's with you made it seem like she had something to be ashamed of. She doesn't. You do."

"I know that," I confess, and rub a hand across my forehead. "I will spend the rest of my life making it up to her if someone would just fucking tell me where she is so I can do it."

"She's on vacation," he mumbles.

"Yeah. Ty said that, but Maddie won't tell him where," I reply, and lean against the wall. "You're going to get fucking suspended and miss the first couple of games of the play-offs, Seb."

"I know. And she's going to tear me a new asshole for doing that to you." He looks up and gives me a mirthless grin. "But it's worth it."

"Is she ever coming back to San Diego?" It feels like the scariest question I've ever asked because I don't want him to confirm my biggest fear.

He locks eyes with me, and after what feels like a millennium, he finally says, "She's probably quitting her job. But…she might end up back in San Diego anyway."

"Because of me?" I ask as hope seems to crest inside me like a wave engulfing my heart.

"No, you egotistical jackwad," he growls. "You're actually the reason she might not."

Oh.

He sighs again. "When Stephanie runs, she intends to stay gone from your life. Even if you want her back, you may not get her. She'll do everything in her power to keep you out once you're out of her life. She could have come to my mom and me at any point after she ran away and we would have helped her, but she didn't. We had to force ourselves back in her life when she hit rock bottom."

"I can't force anything if I can't find her," I remind him.

Sebastian stands up and glances at the clock. "The period is ending in two minutes. You have to get out of here."

"I know." I turn slowly, because I didn't get what I came for—her location—but I'm scared if I ask again he'll clock me again, so I don't.

"I'm going to get shitfaced after the game and then stay at Shay's," he announces, talking about his girlfriend, and I glance back at him, confused. Is he inviting me out for drinks or something? He scowls at me like he's in pain and adds, "I'd say my house will be empty, but that would be a lie."

She's here. Stephanie is in Seattle.

Chapter 37

Stephanie

I'm clutching the red throw pillow so tightly I'm certain the seams are coming apart. I'm not even breathing. I sucked in a breath about three minutes ago when my brother's fist connected with an unsuspecting Avery's jaw and I haven't let it out yet.

I pace my brother's large living room, back and forth, behind the couch for the entire first period. I wish I had gone to the game with Shayne and Jessie. At least then I'd have someone to calm me down. My brother begged me to, but I was worried I'd run into Avery. If I were there now, I would be able to know if he's okay. The fact that he isn't back on the ice is a sign he's not. I'm going to kill Sebastian! But at the beginning of the second period Avery is the first one onto the ice for the Saints.

He not only plays, but he also plays well. The Saints score three goals, two by Avery. But he's playing rougher than he usually does—more aggressively—and he takes two penalties, which is unheard of for him in one game. He also gets into a shoving match with

Chris Dixon, who I know he's good friends with. So clearly, the fight with my brother left him agitated.

At the end of it, they're tied two all, and after a round of overtime, it comes down to a shoot-out. For the Saints Ty scores, but Echolls doesn't and neither does Avery. For the Hawks Garrison scores, Asinov doesn't but Dixon does. Winterhawks win. Saints are not making play-offs this year.

Avery is the first person off the bench and down the tunnel. He moves so fast and with his head tipped down that the cameras can't catch him. But I don't need to see his face to know it's set in a scowl, and he's most likely irate. He left everything on the ice tonight and, for the first time in his career, he's not playing in the postseason. This is a big deal. This is soul crushing for him. He's going to be a fucking mess. Honestly, despite what happened between us, my heart breaks for him.

Is this my fault?

I hate myself for even contemplating that question. He made me break up with him. He is responsible for his own failure. And for *my* broken heart. Maybe karma has decided to take this moment to unleash all the hurt and pain I wished on him when we broke up. If so, it is kind of my fault. But if he hadn't decided his precious image was more important than the "unnecessary distraction" my past caused, there would be no reason for karma to kick his ass.

I sigh and head into the kitchen, busying myself with making a salad for dinner. My diet had been shit since the breakup and now that I'm trying to get through this instead of wallowing in the pain, I'm making a conscious effort to eat well.

An hour later, I'm on the couch trying to convince myself to change the channel, but I just can't. It's like a train wreck. I've watched the highlight show twice already. Of course my brother punching him ten seconds after puck drop is replayed ad nauseam. Everyone is sure it's going to be an automatic suspension; they're just guessing at how many games he'll have to sit. The general consensus seems to be three.

I fast forward through the fight on every replay, because it makes me sick, but I keep rewinding the postgame interviews. Well, Avery's interview anyway. Now for the third time his sweaty, angry, beautiful face fills the screen. He tries so hard to hide his rage, but it's a losing battle this time. The asinine, obvious questions from the reporters have his frustration and anger boiling over.

"Because he doesn't like me," Avery snips at some faceless reporter in the scrum when someone asked why Sebastian hit him. When asked why Seb doesn't like him, like an obstinate child, he simply snipes, "Because I did something he didn't like."

I roll my eyes at his response. I want to smack him and hug him at the same time. But I'll get to do neither because I'm not in his life anymore.

When his eyes shoot up to face the camera, they're the color of sandstone and as hard as it too. "He knows what it's about and I know what it's about. You don't need to know what it's about." He pauses and I can see him struggle to relax. He loses the battle. "Anyway it didn't affect my game. I left everything out there. And it clearly didn't stop the Winterhawks."

They've switched to the Winterhawks locker room interviews, and I'm about to rewind and watch Avery again to indulge my heart's masochistic tendencies when the doorbell rings. My heart skips and I immediately mute the television. I crane my neck, pushing my ear toward the front hall because I can't believe that just happened. It's after ten on Sunday night, Sebastian is out and I'm not expecting anyone.

It rings again.

I stand up and walk gingerly toward the front hall. The oak floorboards creak and I flinch—as if the serial killer on the other side can hear it and has started sharpening his machete.

"Stephanie. It's me."

I gasp. Because it can't be. But when I push onto my tiptoes and look through the small glass window in the top of my heavy wood door, there he is. Well there's his sweat-stained Saints baseball cap. He tips his head for a second and I glimpse those coffee-colored eyes and full mouth.

Holy fuck.

I take a deep breath trying to calm myself. There's nothing about this that's good, I remind my fluttering heart as I open the door. He's slouched over, but as soon as his eyes land on mine, he pulls himself up to almost his full height. I guess the pain of defeat makes it impossible to get the slump out of his broad shoulders entirely. I can't fault him that.

I fight to hold his gaze. It's hard because it's so angry—and desperate. I've never seen him look like this. Like an animal caught in a trap. And because I'm still so completely in love with him it hurts to look at him. He's not mine anymore.

"Can I come in?"

"What are you even doing here?" I ask without letting him inside. "You're supposed to be on your way back to California."

"I'm flying home commercial. Tomorrow," he replies, and takes a breath. "Can I come in?"

"Why?"

"Because."

"You say that a lot, huh?" I snap, and the anger darkens his already deep brown eyes.

"You watched the highlights," he confirms, his voice deep and somber.

He's wearing a pair of training pants and a Saints hoodie. It's pulled tight across his thick and wide chest. His hair is curling around that gross sweat-stained hat. The whole team probably didn't bother with suits after the game. They probably just boarded the bus and got the fuck out of there. And he came straight here. To me.

"You mean the lowlights?" I counter harshly. "Yes. And I watched that pathetic excuse for a fight too."

"He sucker punched me," Avery counters hotly. His jaw flexes. "Let me in, Stephanie."

It's not a question. He doesn't ask anyone for anything. He tells them. He's always got to be in charge. No one ever denies that. I tighten my grip on the door in my hand. The old bossy Avery is back. I didn't miss him. Much.

I move to shut the door in his face, but he steps right into it. His flat palm makes a loud smacking sound against the wood, and then he's pushing. Hard. I lose my grip on the door and it flings open. He steps over the threshold and right up into me.

Without an ounce of hesitation or decorum, he grabs my face roughly in his big hands and forces his mouth over mine. His hat falls off as I pound his shoulder with my small fist and wedge my other hand in between us and try to pry us apart. It's like a sparrow tangling with an eagle.

His tongue sweeps right into my mouth and I think briefly about biting down on it, but it feels so damn good. I grab the fabric of the hoodie that covers his chest and ball it up in my hand. He starts walking backward, pushing me back into the living room. The side of the archway clips my shoulder but he keeps pushing. When my legs hit the back of the sofa and I feel myself losing my balance, and my sanity. I shove him harder and this time he takes a step away.

"What the fuck is wrong with you?" I scream.

"I'm showing you I still care the only way left to show you," he says, his voice strained and loud. "I've tried calling, texting, I've done interviews, I've used social fucking media and so now I'm physically showing you."

I storm past him, back into the hall to the open door. He turns to keep his eyes on me but doesn't move to follow. He may be stunned and angry, but he's still not going anywhere. I reach out and wrap my hand around the door again. "I told you, I'm no one's dirty little secret. You don't get to come in here like a petulant child and just claim me like a consolidation ribbon after you fail at hockey."

His body is rigid. I've watched his shoulders get closer and closer to his earlobes the longer I rant. But I don't care. I'm not in his life to blow smoke up his ass like everyone else. I'm actually not in his life at all anymore. Even when I was in his life I didn't worry about pissing him off and losing him like everyone else. Maybe I should have.

"Because he doesn't like me," I mimic in what I know is a voice that makes him sound like the cartoon version of a sniveling child. "Because I did something he didn't like."

"He doesn't like me," he replies his jaw clenched. "I don't like me either since you left. Since I made you leave."

I try to take a breath, but it's ragged, like the air is catching on thorns in my throat. "You're just emotional over the end of your season."

"I did everything I could for this fucking team." His voice is low and deep and shaky with rage.

"Yeah. You did. So let it go," I reply tersely. I run a hand through my hair, which I had had up in a bun most of the day but was now around my face in messy blond waves. "They lost in spite of you, Avery. Not because of you."

He doesn't answer. He walks toward me, his shoulders slumped in defeat again. This time he stops a polite distance from me and keeps his hands to himself.

"I just can't handle the fucking pressure. I can't carry this team, and I can't keep giving perfect answers to the fucking press. I play for the Saints but I can't be one. I don't want to be one," he admits, and I know it's nothing he's ever said to anyone else and nothing that he ever will.

His dark eyes meet mine. They're so sad they make my heart ache. He bends down slowly to pick his hat up off the floor. As he stands, he chokes out, "I am so sorry."

As he steps for the door, I put a hand on his shoulder and flick my other wrist, causing the door to fly from my hand and slam shut. "You try to control everything and when you can't, when something knocks you on your ass unexpectedly, you give up or hide. Or expect me to hide. You're not a saint. You're a coward."

His chest tightens under my hand. "I was a coward. I've been one my whole life, hiding behind an image, but I've been trying to change. I fucked up, but I'm still trying. But I need you. I need you because you make me want to be better."

"You need me?" I repeat. God I want to believe it. I really do. I saw his interview about his clothing line. I saw the Instagram earlier today, but…I'm scared to trust him again. I know he can't do anything else to win me back. I walked out on us, and he didn't move on. He waited. He apologized—in words and actions. It hits me so hard I shudder—I either have to believe him or I have to let him go.

And the only thing that terrifies me more than forgiving him is not forgiving him. So I take a ragged breath and I whisper, "Prove it."

He drops his hat, reaches up and grabs my face again. This time, I don't fight him. His mouth lands on mine and I slip my tongue past his beautiful full lips. He holds my head with one hand, tangling his fingers in my hair and grabs my ass with the other. He squeezes so hard it'll leave a mark and then he bends his massive thighs, wraps his arms around my waist and lifts me up. His tongue never leaves my mouth. I've missed this—the way he dominates me. The way he manhandles me.

I wrap my legs around his waist. He carries me into the living room, right up to the couch and then he lays me on it. Hovering above me, he reaches over his head, pulls his hoodie off and drops it on the floor as he crawls on top of me. I spread my legs to make room for him. The minute he settles between them, he dips his hips and pushes into me. His hard-on grinds up my body, rubbing my slit through my clothes.

He pushes a hand into the couch beside my head, lifting his body up just enough to stare down at me as he snakes his hand between our bodies and grabs hold of the waist of my cranberry-colored sweats. In one strong movement, without me even lifting my ass, he yanks them all the way down to my knees. His eyes, narrowed in fury, hold mine as his hand moves to the white cotton of my boy shorts and shoves inside.

I'm soaking wet. He smiles and swipes his index and middle finger through my mess before pressing them into my pussy. My back arches in pleasure.

"Avery," I accidentally whisper his name.

"You still taste delicious?" he asks as I dig my nails into his scalp and he pulls his fingers out of me. I watch his long tongue slip from between his lips and lick my juices off the tips of his fingers. He smiles again. "God, I missed how you taste."

I pull myself to a half sitting position and tug his pants down over his muscular butt. Our faces are inches from each other. He roughly pushes me back down into the couch and shoves my shirt up to my neck. I'm not wearing a bra, which is good because he'd probably have just bit through it. He goes right for my nipple, swirls his tongue around it twice and then nips it hard. I gasp. As he moves to assault the other nipple, his hand moves into his underwear and he frees his hard, thick cock.

My body isn't used to his size and length anymore. But I want him so badly, I don't care. He pushes into me and I make a sound even I can't decipher and fight to keep my eyes open so I can watch his eyes roll back in his head and his cheeks flush. I bend my knees on either side of his hips and squeeze my pussy hard. I'm going to make him struggle more than any fucking hockey game. He whimpers. Literally fucking whimpers.

"Don't," he warns. "I won't hold on."

I squeeze down hard again as he swings hard into my hips, his balls slapping my ass. The vein in his neck throbs.

"Stephanie. Fuck. No," he demands. He drops his whole body on me. It's like being hit with a two-hundred-pound sand bag. The air whooshes out of my lungs. He curls his face into my neck, just below my ear. "Baby, please."

The emotion in his plea—the fact that he's begging at all—forces the air from my lungs again.

"I've missed this. I need you. Please."

I relax my core and gently wrap my arms around his back. Holding him to me, I kiss his shoulder and slowly rock my hips under him. He exhales loudly, a mix of pleasure and relief, and matches his thrusts to my rhythm. My eyes flutter closed and I concentrate on the perfect way he fills me up. He remembers exactly how to tilt his hips on his thrust, and I remember that if I just push my left hip up...

"Again. Harder," I demand.

He does it again. Harder. I can't catch my breath. My pussy quivers. He's on one elbow now and his eyes open. That dark chocolate color filled with anger and self-hate have melted into a caramel color filled with lust and love. That has to be love. Because I love him.

He looks down between us. "Let me make you come. Please. I want to make you..."

He pushes his cock deep and hard into me and grinds his pelvis into my clit. Keeping himself pressed right against me, he starts hammering me with short hard thrusts. The friction is too much and not enough. I arch my back and rub myself into his pubic bone. My fingers claw at his back as my orgasm ripples through me.

"Avery," his name slips from my lips in a ragged whisper. "Oh God, yes."

He pushes harder until my head bumps the arm of the couch above me. Then he pulls himself up and with one more thrust, he swears at the top of his lungs and explodes inside me. He seems to come forever, his body jerking and his hips twitching as his collapses on top of me.

Half an hour passes and we don't move. I keep my arms around his back but snake my fingers up and trace his hairline.

"For the first time in my entire life I lost. I really lost," he whispers finally.

"It's not the end of your hockey career. You'll win again," I advise him.

He lifts his head. His eyes are confused. His brow furrowed. "I wasn't talking about hockey. I'm talking about us."

I take a deep breath to make room for the swell of my heart roaring back to life in my chest.

"Concentrate on getting your team to win games next year," I tell him, and trace his lips with my finger. "Because that's the only thing you've lost."

I reach up and pull him in for another kiss.

Chapter 38

Avery

I wake to the sound of voices somewhere in the distance. My eyes open slowly, reluctantly. I was in such a good sleep. The best I'd had in four weeks, after we eventually made it up to the guest room. We still have a lot to talk about, but it was late and we were both drained emotionally and physically. So we both just fell into the king-sized bed and drifted off.

I look over at her now, on the pillow beside mine, curled up on her side, facing away from me. I roll from my back to my side, inching closer to her until my body is pressed against her gently and I can feel nothing but her warm, soft skin against mine. I reach over and lightly lift her hair, scooping it up and pushing it over her shoulder, so I can kiss her there.

I know last night was sex—great sex—but I don't know if it was breakup sex or makeup sex. Or if it was just angry, confused, undefined sex. Half of me—the lower half—is hoping we will do it again before we figure it out. But my brain tells me that wouldn't be the best idea, especially with those voices downstairs. Sebastian is home, and the last thing he would appreciate is listening to me pound his sister into the headboard.

She stirs beside me, eyes fluttering open. Her face is expressionless at first, while she pulls herself into consciousness. I graze her shoulder with my lips again. She blinks and then...she smiles. "Good morning."

"Good morning," I reply, and watch her shift so she's on her back, looking up at me with those incredible blue eyes. "Seb's home."

She pauses, listening. "Oh. Sounds like he brought Shayne."

"We should probably get up," I say, brushing the hair back from her forehead. "Go say hello and everything."

"As long as he doesn't talk with his fists again," she replies softly, and reaches up to run a hand over my jaw. I flinch when she gets to the tender part, which I'm sure is some shade of purple or blue by now. "He's a jerk."

"He was defending you," I reply. "Something I should have done. To the media."

She looks at me for a few seconds with serious eyes and then sighs. "You couldn't defend something I didn't tell you about."

"Yeah, I could have," I argue as she sits up, taking the sheets with her, leaving my torso exposed. I prop myself on my elbows and look up at her. "It didn't matter if it was true or not; you were the person I loved and I could have just said that. Instead I reverted into the shell of a person I'd been hiding behind for years. The person I hate."

She stares at me, her eyes wide and her teeth biting into her lower lip. I can't read her expression. It's not sad or mad, but it still makes me nervous. "What?" I prompt anxiously.

There's a knock at the door. "Stephanie? *Est tu là?*"

I know enough French to know he is asking if she is in there.

"Oui."

"Est-ce que tu peux venir en bas donc je ne drois pas lui frapper un autre fois?"

He says it too quickly for me to understand, but whatever he said makes Stephanie frown, her nose scrunching up and her eyes narrowing on the closed door. She looks at me. "He just said we need to come downstairs or he'll hit you again."

I roll my eyes.

"Be down in a sec," she calls back to her brother and adds, "And you'll be lucky if I don't hit you."

I smile at that, impulsively grab the back of her head and kiss her. It's my normal, savage, dominant takeover of her mouth. I can't help it. The slightest touch of this woman makes every single primal urge and instinct kick into overdrive. I climb up on my knees and cradle her head as I lean into her, my tongue pushing into her mouth as my body pushes her back onto the mattress. She lets the sheets drop and her hands slide into my hair roughly, tugging and scratching as they go, sending ripples of pleasure straight down my spine to my dick, which is rock-hard. She fucking makes me insane and insatiable.

Her bare legs part as her back hits the mattress and I settle in between them. "We really should go downstairs," she whispers breathlessly into the kiss before pulling her lips from mine. I start kissing her neck instead. "He'll hear us."

"I can be quiet," I promise, skimming the tip of my tongue along her collarbone.

"I can't," she replies. "Besides…we weren't careful last night."

I look up at her and kiss her lips softly. "I know."

"You didn't even ask if I was on birth control," she murmurs, her eyes darting away from mine.

"I assumed you were."

"You assumed?" she repeats, and looks stunned.

"Steph, I know you. You're smart and careful and you're not going to have sex with me without some kind of protection," I say, moving so I'm not on top of her anymore, because if she's serious about going downstairs I need to get rid of this hard-on, and that's not going to happen while it's hovering between her legs, inches from heaven.

"I could be trying to trap you," she says. She can't even get the words out without a smile, that's how ridiculous they are. "Isn't that what hockey players are always worried about? Isn't that what your dad thinks?"

I stand up and look around her room for my clothes, and then I remember the only thing I bothered to put back on before we came upstairs was my pants. "Yeah, well, you can't trap what's already been caught."

I spot my pants at the foot of the bed and reach over and grab them, picking up her T-shirt from last night and handing it to her. She sits up, beautifully, perfectly naked, but she's staring at me with her lip between her teeth again and that look I can't read on her face. "You're caught?"

"I'm yours," I tell her simply, and lean forward, putting my hands on the bed in front of her so we're face-to-face. "Whether you're mine or not, I'm still not sure. I don't know if last night was the big kiss-off or a reconciliation, but whatever the answer is, the fact is I'm yours. I'm not hiding it or talking myself out of it."

We stare at each other. The sun must break through the clouds because suddenly she's blanketed in a warm golden glow and I have to adjust the front of my pants. "Get dressed or I'm fucking you again and your brother will kill us both."

She pulls her shirt over her head and climbs off the bed, heading to her dresser and pulling on some underwear and a pair of shorts. As she moves to the door and opens it to step into the hall, I panic a little. I don't like that she hasn't said anything. She hasn't answered me—not that I asked a question, but I just professed my undying love to her and she has nothing to say. It's…Well, like everything about being in love with her—it throws me.

I grab her arm and turn her to face me. "Can you say something? Let me know where I stand before we go down there."

She smiles at me and reaches up and cups my face, the side that isn't sore from her brother's fist. "I told you last night. The only thing you've lost is a hockey game."

I hold her perfect face in my hands. "So we're back together?"

She takes my hand and tugs me downstairs. We reach Sebastian's front hall just as Shayne is pulling open the front door. Jordan and Jessie are standing there. Jessie sees us first and grins, her green eyes twinkling.

"Hey!" She walks in and meets us at the bottom of the stairs, hugging Stephanie and then me. She glances at my jaw. "Ouch. But something tells me you had someone to kiss it better."

"Stop hugging my shirtless enemies," Jordan tells his wife, and puts on his best fake annoyed face, which is actually pretty ridiculous and makes him look like he's constipated.

"Shut up, Jordan," I reply, and he laughs.

"Nice face." He motions at my bruised jaw, and every person in the room glances to Sebastian. He's leaning against the breakfast bar holding a cup of coffee. He takes a sip, looks up at all of us, face devoid of regret, and shrugs.

Stephanie lets go of my hand and walks over to Sebastian. "You're a jackass."

He lifts an eyebrow, the one with the slice through it from some previous on-ice brawl. "He breaks your heart. I break his face. Those are the rules."

"Yeah, well, you cost your team their best defenseman for the first round of the play-offs, I'm guessing," Shayne says to her boyfriend. "You couldn't wait to punch him off the ice?"

"I'll find out Monday. Have a call with Player Safety," he says, and for the first time his cocky attitude falters. He looks slightly remorseful, but I realize it's for the repercussions, not the act itself.

"You're getting two games," I announce, and every head in the room swings around to face me.

Jordan shakes his head in disbelief. "No way. It was unprovoked. The puck had barely hit the ice. Even though he's a first-time offender, it's gotta be more than that."

"I talked to them last night," I explain, crossing through the living room to hunt down my shirt. "I told them I said something to you that was derogatory and inflammatory, so that it wouldn't be considered unprovoked."

"You did what?" Stephanie stares at me with her eyes wide.

I find my shirt on the floor next to the couch and pull it over my head. "I called them."

"You can do that?" Shayne blinks and looks at Sebastian for confirmation. He looks as shocked as his sister.

"He can do it. I couldn't. Seb couldn't. No one else in the league could do it," Jordan says with a crooked grin. "He's Avery Westwood. This league is his bitch."

I laugh at that. "I've missed your interesting take on life, Jordy."

"You really did that?" Sebastian questions, his deep voice solemn.

I hold his gaze and nod. "While I was on my way over here."

Stephanie walks over to me and grabs my face in her hands and kisses me—hard. Someone starts clapping; my guess is it's Jessie. Someone groans, and by the baritone I guess it's Seb.

I wrap my arms around Steph's waist and kiss her back even harder than she's kissing me. When we finally break apart, she takes a ragged breath but turns to our audience with a smile. "My boyfriend's the best, isn't he?"

My hands are around her waist tighten, pulling her into my chest. "You won't regret this."

"I know," she whispers.

My phone buzzes from the front pocket of my hoodie and she jumps as it vibrates against her. I pull it out and see my dad's number on the call display. I never did call him like I promised Kate I would.

"I have to take this." I excuse myself, giving Steph a quick kiss on the cheek, and walk into the hall and out the front door. I stand on Sebastian's front porch and survey the incredible view he has. I miss Seattle in a weird way. It's rainy and cold compared to California but it's got a small town charm and everything is lush and green. I take a deep breath and answer the call. "Hey, Don."

"Avery?" It's a question, and I'm sure it's not because he doesn't recognize my voice; it's because he's just shocked I'm actually talking to him.

"Yeah. Hi." The slate tiles under my bare feet are cold and damp. I wiggle my toes a little and start to pace.

"Hi, son," he says, and it's odd. He hasn't called me that in…Jesus, I can't remember when.

"How are you?" I ask because I don't know what else to say.

"I'm not good," he replies bluntly. "I've lost my son over something I didn't do."

I don't know if it's because I've got her back or what, but I finally see things in a different light. And I'm finally, truly sick of fighting with him—or anyone, for that matter. "It doesn't matter anymore if you did or didn't do it. I handled the situation poorly and that's what almost ruined things between Stephanie and me."

"Almost?"

I stop pacing and stare out at the sound. "Yeah. She's willing to give me a second chance and I'm not going to screw it up. And if you do anything…"

"Avery, I'm not against you dating Stephanie. I never was," he replies, his voice taut with sincerity. Before I can balk at that, he continues. "Yeah, I wanted you with Liz, but I just wanted you to have a handle on what you were getting into, and you didn't and it blew up. I know I don't have the best way of showing it, but I was only looking out for you."

"Well, maybe sometimes I have to make mistakes," I reply, and sigh. "And that includes mistakes with my image."

"Maybe," he replies, and pauses. "But I think you'd make fewer mistakes if you had all the facts. You didn't about Stephanie and you don't about who leaked her past to the media."

I quietly debate cutting him off and hanging up, because I still don't see how it could be anyone other than him who did this. I know Sebastian wouldn't, and no one else knew. My father takes my silence as permission to continue. "Avery, I have a lot of contacts in the media and a few of them owed me favors since I've given them exclusives with you before. And they all said that the original information about Stephanie came from Chance Echolls."

I feel like I've been checked into the boards. I grab hold of the wall beside Seb's front door. "What? But he didn't break the story. If he was the one who found out first, why would he give the story away?"

"His excuse was that he was too close to the story with his brother on the team," Don explains. "But he was worried you'd figure out it was his brother who leaked the story."

I gave that shithead every opportunity to work with me.

"You boys treat the locker room like your own hen pen," Don retorts with a bit of a chuckle. "You must have mentioned something to Ty or Alex in front of him."

I did do that. A lot. And Beau was there every time. I just never thought he was listening. Or that he would be a big enough asshole to use personal information against me. Now I feel like an idiot. Of course he would. He hates me. He wants to make my life difficult.

"That piece of shit."

"Yeah," Don agrees. "I'm betting he got his reporter brother to do some digging into her past."

"If this is true…I won't share the ice with him again," I say hotly. "I want him off the team and I'll get him off the team. I'm done trying."

When Don doesn't say anything, I stop pacing again. "No opinion to share? No advice?"

"I'm not your manager anymore," he replies.

"You're rehired. Now spit it out."

"Your manager thinks if you get him kicked off the team and the media finds out, they'll paint you as a diva and a princess who threw a tantrum and cost a guy his career," Don says flatly, and then pauses, takes a breath and adds, "Your father thinks you've put up with enough from this asshole and with him gone you can focus on getting this team into the play-offs next season. And when you win them a Cup, no one will give a shit what happened to Beau Echolls."

"Thanks for the advice, Dad," I say quietly. "I think I'll take it."

I hang up and head back inside. Stephanie's face lights up when she sees me. "I've got to get to the airport. I have team business to handle back in San Diego," I explain, and take her hand. "Do you want to come back with me? I can get you a ticket."

"I'm going to stay here," she tells me, and my heart sinks. "I have stuff to do with Sebastian."

I nod because I don't want to get into this in front of everyone, but I'm suddenly nervous she may not come back to California if I leave her here. Seb said she might quit her job. I have a five-year contract with the Saints. I can't break it. I mean, I could, but it would be a costly legal battle and I'd be someone who gives up, breaks promises and abandons his team and responsibilities. And that's not just a slight to my image; it's not who I am.

"Relax, Westwood," Seb says with a wry smile, because clearly my expression is reflecting my thoughts. "I'm not keeping her."

"What time is your flight?" Jessie asks.

"In an hour and a half," I reply.

"Jordy and I can drive you," she offers, and I nod. She looks at Stephanie. "You can come along and make out with him in the backseat on the way there."

Jordan groans in protest and Steph laughs. "Let's go upstairs and get your shoes and socks."

She tugs me up the stairs and as soon as we're in the bedroom again she's got her lips on mine. I cradle the back of her head with my hand and deepen the kiss, using it to show her how desperately I need her. "You're coming back, right? To California?"

"Yes. I promise." She traces her fingertips along my hairline and down to the neck of my sweatshirt. "I'm starting a business with Seb.

A house-flipping business. He's going to invest the money and I'm going to oversee the renovations and design work."

"Really?"

She nods. "It's why I've been taking interior design courses. Seb became obsessed with renovating and real estate after he bought this place."

"But you'll be running it from California, right?" I need her to promise me. I can do long distance if I have to, but I really don't want to. I want her with me, in my heart and in my bed every night.

"We're trying to buy a place in San Diego to flip right now," she explains, and grins deviously. "Our place."

"What?"

She laughs. "Yeah, so if all goes well, we'll be evicting you."

I laugh and kiss her again. "Nice. Thanks for the warning."

"Something tells me you'll manage to find a place." She giggles.

"Yeah, but a place where the neighbor sleeps with me?" I quip, and she laughs again. "That might be hard."

I lean in and kiss her again, and I'm on the verge of kicking the door closed and missing my flight when Sebastian calls up from the bottom of the stairs. "Avery, get the hell off my sister and out of my house."

I groan and let Stephanie pull me down the stairs.

Epilogue

Avery

I lean on the porch rail and watch the movers carrying the last of my boxes into the truck out front. I'd be lying if I said I wasn't sad to be leaving this place. It was single-handedly the most dilapidated place I had ever willingly lived, but if I had my way I would never leave. Well, as long as Stephanie was living beside me. Only she wasn't anymore.

Maddie moved in with Ty last week and Steph moved into a two-bedroom condo in the same building. Sebastian was paying for it. He said he needed it for when he came to check on the renovations this summer, but I'm guessing he just wanted to make sure she had a nice place to live. I purchased the penthouse in the same building and I am hoping that by summer's end when their first renovation job is complete and I am living back here full-time, I can convince her to move in with me. Even if I can't, she will only be six floors away, and I can live with that.

She steps out onto the porch now, wearing overalls and a tank top, her hair piled up in a haphazard bun. Her eyes narrow as she jots something down on the clipboard she's holding. My father steps out after her. "I really hope you're right about the shiplap," she says to him, and he smiles.

"Trust me, in a house this old, the walls will be full of it," he says with a smile. Before my career became his career, my dad was a construction worker. He was in town to finalize the new deal for my clothing line and I thought this renovation project might be a good way for them to meet. Judging by the easy conversation they're having, I think I was right.

My phone beeps in my pocket. It's an alert from a sports news site. I open the article and read the headline aloud. "Beau Echolls has been placed on waivers by the San Diego Saints."

My dad nods. Stephanie looks conflicted. "That should read 'Beau Echolls was placed on waivers by Avery Westwood.'"

"Yeah," my father answers before I can. "Or it could read 'Beau Echolls made his own bed by starting personal attacks against his captain's girlfriend.'"

"That's way too long for a headline," I quip, and my father laughs.

"I should get going," Don says, and looks at his watch. "I have to be in Los Angeles by four."

"It was nice meeting you, Stephanie." He smiles, and it's genuine and quite frankly mind-blowing. "Let me know if I was right about the shiplap."

She nods and then he stuns both of us by reaching down and hugging her, and then me, before he heads to his rental at the curb and drives off. I look up at her. "Wow. He is really nice. Not at all what I was expecting.

"Me neither," I admit, and laugh.

She glances back at the now-empty cottage. "It's going to be a shame to tear out that bathroom you renovated…I'm trying to find a way to keep it in the plans."

They've decided to turn the cottages into a single-family home; apparently that will get them more bang for their buck. I push off the railing and reach for her, grabbing on to the strap of her overalls and tugging her toward me. Our bodies meet with a thump and she laughs. "Admit it," I whisper as I nuzzle her neck. "You want to keep that shower because of all the fond memories I gave you in there."

"No," she replies flatly, and nips my earlobe. "Because I expect you to make even better memories in my new place."

"So bossy," I whisper before I kiss her. She breaks the kiss well before I want her to and moves her lips to my jaw.

"You've built an image as an orgasm-producing sex machine," she tells me, her lips against my ear. "Now you've got a reputation to uphold."

I smile and cup her ass, lifting her up off the ground as she giggles. "You know how important image is to me…now let's go say goodbye to that shower one more time."

She laughs all the way up the stairs and I realize that, for the first time in a long time, I like everything about my life—including who I am. And I owe it all to her.

About the Author

Victoria Denault loves long walks on the beach, cinnamon dolce lattes and writing angst-filled romance. She lives in L.A. but grew up in Montreal, which is why she is fluent in English, French and hockey.

Learn more at:

VictoriaDenault.com

Facebook.com/AuthorVictoriaDenault

Twitter: @BooksbyVictoria

www.ingramcontent.com/pod-product-compliance
Ingram Content Group UK Ltd.
Pitfield, Milton Keynes, MK11 3LW, UK
UKHW022259280225
455674UK00001B/93